MIDNIGHT MAGIC

"Come here," he said, his voice a deep growl in his throat.

She walked toward him, her hands clasped behind her back. She stopped a hairbreadth away from him. "Do you want something, Garrett?"

Didn't she know she was playing with fire? His eyes burned as her scent singed his nostrils. His body pulsed with the sort of need he hadn't experienced since the first time she'd made love to him. But even then he'd felt in control of his own libido. In the past few days she'd heated him up, pushed him away, taunted him with her nearness, and nearly crossed his eyes when she'd made that "confession" down at the clearing. He'd had about all he could stand from her. Like a shotgun with a hair trigger, it wouldn't take much for him to go off. "You know what I want."

"Do I?" She closed the gap between them by sliding her arms around his neck and pressing her body to his. "Maybe you'd better show me."

Books by Deirdre Savoy

SPELLBOUND
ALWAYS
ONCE AND AGAIN

Published by BET/Arabesque Books

Midnight Magic

Deirdre Savoy

BET Publications, LLC
www.bet.com

For the women of the "Purville root," my own Caribbean connection:

Ethelind Farr Reid, my grandmother and the most gentle soul I have ever known.

Aunt Letty, who always reminded us of our heritage, and her daughter Valerie, who took up the torch.

Joan Allen, my aunt, whose generosity knows no limit, and her daughters—Sharon MacMillian, whom I admire more than she knows, and Lynn Allen, whose pursuit of her own creative dreams made mine seem more attainable.

For my sisters, Elyse and Shari-Ann, who did their best to torment my childhood (yes, I finally figured out who the "ghost" in our bedroom was), but have proved to be two of my best friends.

For my daughter, Francesca, who possesses her grandmother's kind spirit, her great aunt's generosity, and her mother's big mouth. That mother's curse really does work.

And most of all, to my mother, Dolores Reid Savoy, my family matriarch, guidepost, chief cheerleader, and friend. I hate to tell you this, but you are Diana Windsor, Camille Thorne, and just a little bit of Eleanor Scanlon—the good stuff, anyway. Hopefully there's a little of your good stuff in me, too.

ACKNOWLEDGMENTS

Thanks to Dr. Dennis Brown, my children's first pediatrician, who put up with my new-mother's neuroses without once threatening to strangle me (though he probably wanted to).

Thanks to my principal, Mrs. Evelyn Fulton, and the members of the P.S. 178 family, who have supported, encouraged, and teased the heck out of me for writing romance.

Thanks to my agent, James Finn, and my editors, Karen Thomas and Chandra Sparks Taylor, for the continued faith in me.

Thanks to Cal Hunter of the Co-op City Barnes and Noble, my home bookstore, for making me feel like queen of the house, and to the members of the Writer's Co-op, who teach me as much as I teach them.

Special thanks to Ms. Emma Rogers, owner of the Black Images Bookstore in Dallas, Texas, for her support of African-American romance writers. Receiving the Emma award from her was truly the highlight of the Slam Jam and a terrific honor.

And a special thank-you to Gwendolyn Osborne. For all you do, this epilogue's for you.

One

Elise Taylor woke as she usually did: jolted by the buzzer of the alarm clock that sat on the cherry wood nightstand beside her bed. A familiar weight pressed against her back as her husband, Garrett, leaned over her to whack the alarm into silence.

"Morning," he growled in her ear. He drew his hand beneath the covers again to slip under her nightgown, which had bunched around her waist during the night. She pressed her lips together as his hand moved lazily over her stomach and upward. A familiar quickening started in her belly, heightened by the slow, thorough exploration of her breasts by Garrett's hand.

Her breasts were small, even after bearing and nursing two children, but Garrett had never complained. He'd always seemed to like her body the way it was, stretch marks and all. As he'd told her once in a semidrunken and completely chauvinistic state, they were his stretch marks, or rather they'd been earned carrying his children, so she should feel honored to have them. In response, she'd stood on a chair and smacked him in the head.

She didn't want to smack him now. Her breath hissed out on a sigh as Garrett's hand delved between her thighs. "Do you know what today is?" he asked.

He wanted to play twenty questions now, when she could barely think beyond the pleasure he gave her? "Friday?" she croaked out.

He laughed, a husky rumble that reverberated through her, too. "It's your birthday. Happy birthday, sweetheart."

She should have known. Garrett always woke her in the same way on her birthday, rousing her simultaneously from sleep and to passion. And later, their children, Alyssa and Andrew, would come in with breakfast in bed for her. She'd forgotten, because she wanted to forget. She didn't want to mark another year passing. She would have been content to let December nineteenth come and go without comment.

December nineteenth. Elise would have sat bolt upright were it not for Garrett's weight holding her in place. How could she have forgotten that, too? Her period, which appeared with the regularity of the full moon, had been due two days ago. Her period had been late only twice in her life, and the reasons for those occurrences were downstairs at that moment scrambling eggs and making a mess of her kitchen.

"Oh, God," Elise whispered, her mind zooming in on a possibility she didn't want to consider. They had agreed after Andrew was born that there would be no more children. She'd gone on the pill then, rather than relying on less effective means of birth control. Truthfully, she didn't want any more children. With the baby in preschool now, she was just starting to have a life again.

Now that she'd turned thirty-eight, her chances of even having a healthy child were lower than she'd like to consider. That thought terrified her most of all. Andrew had been born blue, due to the umbilical cord being wrapped around his neck during the delivery. The doctors had considered it a miracle he'd suffered no brain damage from the lack of oxygen. She never wanted to go through that again—the waiting, the agonizing, the blame she'd heaped upon herself for her body's malfunction. She would not, could not be pregnant.

He nuzzled her ear with his lips. "What's the matter, sweetheart?"

"Nothing." She shook her head. "Nothing." She couldn't tell him now, not when all she had to go on was a late period. Why ruin everybody's day when she had no proof?

She felt him enter her from behind, but her libido had gone cold the moment thoughts of another child had begun to swim in her brain. Garrett didn't seem to notice, though. His hand on her body, his lips grazing the sensitive juncture between her neck and shoulder, the slow, sensual rhythm of his body moving within hers, would normally have had her moaning her head off. But she couldn't seem to feel anything besides a pervasive feeling of dread.

Garrett's breath, coming in short, hot gasps, fanned her cheek. She knew, on this morning in particular, he wouldn't take his pleasure without making sure he'd given her hers first. She arched her back and moaned his name in what she hoped was a convincing manner. In response, Garrett groaned against her ear, quickening his pace, thrusting into her more deeply. She felt the tension coil in his big body, and moments later the shudder of his release.

She lay there, enduring the weight of Garrett's arm resting across her body, the sweep of his breath over her skin, and wanted to weep. For the first time in her life, she'd faked it with her husband. And he hadn't even noticed.

She felt him turning her in his arms to face him. She went to him and buried her face against his chest. He hugged her to him and lowered his head to kiss her cheek. "I'm sorry, sweetheart. Not exactly a five-star performance, huh?"

Elise pressed her lips together. He had nothing to be sorry for. They had a good sex life. He was a gentle, sensitive lover. It wasn't his fault she'd decided to pull a Sarah Bernhardt routine rather than tell him what she was feeling. "That's not it."

With a hand under her chin, he tilted her face up to his. "Then what's the matter, baby?"

Elise studied her husband's handsome, concerned face. In all the years she'd known him, that face hadn't changed much. The beginnings of laugh lines fanned around his eyes now and his dark brown hair had begun to gray at his temples. She touched her fingertips to the small scar that crossed his left eyebrow, a reward from his days playing football in college. She let her hand trail down his cheek to settle on his chest. His body hadn't changed much, either. He'd maintained his athlete's physique with regular games of racquetball and mornings spent swimming laps with her brother, Michael.

She knew this man, had known him for most of her life. Maybe she should tell him. She didn't doubt Garrett would understand, and she knew he wouldn't blame her, as some other husbands might. In the end, she was saved from answering by a knock on the bedroom door.

"Are you people decent in there?"

The voice belonged to her sixteen-year-old daughter, Alyssa. No doubt she had her little brother in tow and a breakfast tray in her arms.

"Just a minute," Garrett called. He placed a soft, moist kiss on Elise's cheek, then rose from the bed to don a T-shirt and a pair of sweatpants. Barefoot, he padded to the bedroom door. "Ready?" he asked.

She smoothed her nightgown into place, adjusted the covers around her, and nodded.

Immediately, three-year-old Andrew bounded through the door and leaped onto the bed beside her. He held a single white rose, which he extended toward her. "Happy birthday, Momma."

Elise hugged her baby to her bosom. "Thank you, sweetheart." Elise took the flower from him and lifted it to her nose. "It smells wonderful."

"Watch out, squirt," Alyssa said, coming toward her mother with the breakfast tray. Andrew scooted out of the way a second before Alyssa set down the tray over her mother's lap. Alyssa sat on the bed beside her. "Happy birthday, Mom. And unlike some people, I actually got you a gift." Alyssa extended a long, rectangular box toward her.

Elise took the box and glanced up at Garrett. He shrugged, indicating he had no idea what Alyssa had gotten her. Elise looked at her daughter. "What is it?"

"Open it already." Alyssa gestured with her hands. "I hope you like it."

Elise smiled, realizing Alyssa must have spent her own money on the gift—a first. "I'm sure I will." She separated the tape on one side from the silver foil wrapping paper and slid the box out. Inside lay a gold charm bracelet with several charms already attached. Elise lifted it from the box, laying the ornate bracelet across her palm. The piece wasn't anything she would have bought for herself. She preferred simple, unadorned quality jewelry. But knowing her daughter had selected it herself made all the difference in the world.

"So, what do you think?"

Elise beamed at her daughter. "It's beautiful, sweetheart. Thank you." She hugged Alyssa, then sat back as she detailed what each of the charms stood for.

Alyssa pointed to a tiny football. "This one is for Dad when you met him. He was a quarterback or something, wasn't he?"

"Yeah, or something," Garrett muttered, obviously disgruntled at having his glory days referred to in such an offhand manner. Elise stuck her tongue out at him. In those days he'd been pretty full of himself. She'd seen it as a personal mission to bring him down a peg.

"And this one . . ." Elise tuned out, noticing the two tiny cherub charms that adorned the bracelet; she supposed they stood for Alyssa and Andrew. Would she need to add a third charm before another year was through?

"Mom?"

Elise blinked and focused on her daughter, hearing the hurt and disappointment in her young voice. "I'm sorry, sweetheart. I was just thinking about all the work I have to get done today. And on top of that, they're doing a spread of the Lincoln house for *Architectural Digest* this afternoon. I want to be there to make sure they shoot it right. I love the bracelet, Alyssa, really I do." Elise extended her wrist. "Would you put it on me?"

Alyssa brightened. "Sure."

While the others had been preoccupied, Andrew had eaten all of her bacon and most of her eggs. "You little glutton," Alyssa exclaimed. "I already fed you breakfast."

A devilish grin lit Andrew's face. "I was still hungry."

Elise turned her head so Andrew wouldn't see her laughing. Thankfully, Garrett herded the children out of the room, threatening both with bodily harm if they weren't ready for school in twenty minutes.

After closing the door behind the children, Garrett settled an assessing gaze on her. He was waiting for her to respond to his unanswered question about what was bothering her, but she was no more prepared to tell him than she'd been a few minutes ago. Instead she changed the subject.

"You'd better get ready yourself or the kids will never let you hear the end of it."

"I know. But we talk tonight."

Elise nodded. "Maybe we can go to dinner, just the two of us?"

"Maybe." Garrett walked toward the master bathroom in the corner of their room.

Once he disappeared inside, she picked at the remnants of her breakfast. She would buy a pregnancy test on the way to work and find some quiet moment in her day to take it. Then when she saw Garrett tonight, she'd have something to tell him. As much as she dreaded the test being positive, the other alternative didn't thrill her either. If she weren't pregnant, there could be any number of reasons why her period was late, most of which she didn't want to contemplate.

Elise speared the last bit of egg with her fork. "Happy birthday to me," she said in a mocking voice, then popped the morsel of food into her mouth.

After dropping Alyssa and Adam at their respective schools, she headed for the local Dunkin' Donuts for a refill of her unspillable cup, picked up a copy of the *Times* at the newsstand on the corner and drove into the parking lot of the Metro-North station in New Rochelle. The ride into Manhattan was just long enough for her to look over her schedule, browse the paper, and gird her loins for the stress of the day. Most people, her husband included, thought all she did was pore over fabric swatches all day.

She'd made a reputation for herself as a perfectionist, the consummate professional who always came in on time and under budget. Sometimes that meant taking a cut in her own commission or working late hours to get everything the way she wanted it, but she wouldn't have gotten nearly as far as she had if she'd gone another route. She knew her employees referred to her as the Wicked Witch of West 57th Street, but frankly she didn't care.

Dressed in her Nancy Reagan suit, so named because it was rich, red, and designed by Oscar de la Renta, she stepped into her showroom office. Dena, the receptionist-secretary-bookkeeper, sat at the black art nouveau desk Elise had scoured half of Manhattan to find. Dena had been with her from the beginning, when she'd had the tiny office down on Houston Street, and had stayed with her when they'd made the move uptown three years ago. Dena was the only one she knew didn't whisper nasty comments behind her back. Dena much preferred to ambush you face-to-face.

"Morning, boss," Dena announced. "Vic Stamos called three times before eight-thirty."

Elise accepted the stack of messages Dena extended toward her. "Didn't I tell you that the minute that man made up his mind, he'd be relentless in getting the job done?"

"That you did," Dena agreed.

Elise sighed. "Anything else pressing?"

"Only one thing. Happy birthday." Dena opened the center drawer of the desk and pulled out a small, rectangular box. "I know you said you wanted to forget this birthday existed, but I couldn't resist."

Elise smiled broadly as she accepted the gold foil-wrapped package. She'd known Dena would ignore her edict as surely as she knew what was inside the box. Every year they indulged each other in their own personal passions. Each year, Elise got a new pen, Dena Charles Jourdan shoes.

After shedding the paper, Elise opened the box and gasped. Inside lay a special edition Waterman pen she'd admired in the latest edition of the Fountain Pen Hospital catalog. The price had been more than Elise had been willing to spend. Dena, on her much smaller salary, certainly couldn't afford such luxury.

Shaking her head, Elise looked down at her employee. "Dena, you shouldn't have."

"I know. Just consider it your birthday and Christmas present for the next two years."

"Either that or I'm going to have to buy you fourteen pairs of shoes."

"Now, there's an alternative worth considering."

Elise laughed and hugged Dena. There was no point in telling the other woman that she'd been too extravagant. Dena would never take the pen back. And truthfully, Dena's generosity touched her. "Thank you."

Before Dena could answer, the phone rang. "How much do you want to bet it's the illustrious Mr. Stamos?" Dena asked, reaching for the phone.

"Two cents. That's all I can afford to lose."

"Taylor Design Associates. Can I help you?" A second later she covered the mouthpiece of the phone and whispered, "It's him."

"I'll take it in my office." Elise plucked two pennies from her change purse, placed them on Dena's desk, then headed down the hall.

Once inside her office, she deposited her coat, purse, and briefcase in the chair opposite her desk, then rounded it to pick up the phone. Punching the button to switch her to the correct line, she tugged off her left earring and put the receiver to her ear. "Vic, what can I do for you?"

"I've decided to go with you. How soon can we get started?"

The man had spent three months jerking her around, having her come up with design after design, change after change, all under the threat of hiring another design firm to handle the renovation of his duplex apartment. She'd put up with it only because Vic Stamos was one of the style setters of the up-and-coming Manhattan crowd. Where he went, others would follow. This one job could lead to many other lucrative contracts.

"That's great, Vic," she said, keeping her tone even. Nothing ruined a deal with a New Yorker faster than showing a little enthusiasm. "We need to meet first and finalize the plans." She flipped open her date book. She didn't have a spare moment before Tuesday. "How about next Wednesday at two?"

"I can't wait that long. Can't you squeeze me in today?"

"Not if you were as skinny as Calista Flockhart. I might be able to do something Monday night."

"No can do. I'll be out of town all next week, and I need to get started as soon as possible." There was a long pause before he added, "I'd hoped you would be more accommodating of my schedule."

Elise rolled her eyes, but said nothing. She recognized Vic's words for the threat they were. If she wouldn't work around him, he'd find someone else who would. She was almost tempted to let him. "All right, can we meet at your place tonight, around seven?" The

Lincoln shoot should be over by then. "But I can't spend more than an hour." Not if she wanted to get home in time for some semblance of dinner with her family.

"Sounds perfect."

"See you then."

Elise hung up, clicked on her computer, and checked her E-mail. There were four messages from Vic, which she deleted; one from her sister, Daphne, which contained a birthday wish and a ribald joke; and three from suppliers, letting her know her orders had come in. Elise sighed. At least some things were going right in her little world.

She brought up the plans for the McDonald kitchen she was set to make a bid on tomorrow afternoon. She doubted Judith McDonald had ever set foot in a kitchen, except to instruct the cook on what to prepare, but for the second time in four years she wanted the kitchen redone. Not that Elise minded. With Judith, money was never an object. Judith seemed to revel in spending as much of her elderly husband's fortune as quickly as possible. But Judith was a perfectionist, perhaps even more so than Elise herself. If one tile skewed a millimeter from its mark, Judith would notice it and demand that it be fixed.

But Elise had no doubt the plans would meet with Judith's approval. From the gold fixtures to the onyx refrigerator, Judith had picked out almost everything herself. Elise's only rub: Judith would expect Elise to oversee the work herself instead of using her usual project manager, a prospect that never thrilled. Elise sighed and clicked the mouse in the appropriate place to print out the designs. Such was the life of the high-powered designer—the life she'd always dreamed of. Just sometimes, like now, it was a pain in the neck.

* * *

Garrett sat in the black leather chair in his office, perusing the screen of the computer monitor that sat on his desk. He'd been staring at the same spreadsheet that detailed the past month's income and expenses for the last fifteen minutes, taking in nothing. Thoughts of Elise intruded every time he tried to concentrate on his work.

An image of her formed in his mind, a picture of her face in rapture. Her neck would arch and her incredible amber eyes would drift closed. And more often than not, she'd call his name in that throaty voice of hers.

She hadn't looked or sounded like that this morning. She'd been a million miles away. He'd known that, and tried to rouse her to the same level of passion he'd felt. But when she'd arched against him, he'd lost it. He wasn't ashamed to admit his petite wife turned him on as much now as she had when he was twenty, but he would've liked to think the years had granted him a modicum of control.

She'd promised him they'd talk tonight, but he doubted they would have the chance for that discussion later tonight. He picked up the phone to call her. As usual, dialing her personal number produced a busy signal. He'd started to dial the general office number when he heard footsteps outside his office.

"Why do we even bother?"

Garrett glanced up to see his best friend and partner, Robert Delaney, standing in the doorway to his office. He and Robert had known each other from their days playing football for Stockton College in upstate New York. When they'd both been sidelined by injuries, they'd focused on getting through med school, Robert as a plastic surgeon, himself as a pediatrician.

"Why do we bother to do what?"

"Practice medicine at all. Have you seen the new reimbursement schedule from American Healthcare?" Robert came into the room, holding the paper aloft. He sat in one of the two chairs that faced Garrett's desk. "Two dollars for a prophylactic shot. Two dollars? Between the vaccine and the damn lollipop, we spend more than that per kid."

"What are you complaining about? Most of your patients pay cash, and besides, with all your volunteer work, you're giving your services away."

"I know, but I hate what it does to this practice."

Garrett sighed. Beneath his words ran a familiar undercurrent: that Garrett's end of the practice was actually losing money while Robert's kept them afloat. Robert didn't blame him for that. With the advent of HMOs, many doctors, particularly pediatricians, made less and less per patient, and were forced to work longer hours in hopes of making up the slack. Garrett himself had fallen victim to the same syndrome, spending more time away from home than he liked. He knew Elise resented it, and he was no longer as close with either of his children as he would have liked.

He hadn't intended to tell Robert about his plans. He hadn't intended to tell anyone until it was a done deal, but he didn't see that he had much choice in the matter.

"I'm looking into something that might turn things around."

Robert's thick eyebrows shot up. "Don't tell me you've started playing the lottery."

"Not likely. I'm thinking of putting my expertise to better use. You know Jeanie Wilkins. Her youngest is about a year old now."

"Yeah," Robert said, humor evident in his voice. "The build of a linebacker topped off with the face of a shar-pei. Yet she and her husband continue to crank one out every year and a half. What about her?"

"Her younger sister is a staff writer for *Treatment* magazine. She seems to think there's a need for a definitive book on African-American baby and child care, and her publisher thinks so, too. She wants to coauthor one with me."

"Make sure your face is the only one on the jacket if you want to sell any books."

Garret snorted. Ever since Robert had met and married the irrepressible Dr. Lindsay Carpenter, he'd developed a sense of wit Garrett would never have expected of him.

"I don't know if anything will come of it. I promised I'd meet with her. She should be here any minute." Garrett glanced at his watch. "In fact, she's late. Maybe she won't show up at all."

He almost hoped she wouldn't. The whole idea was probably crazy, but for a few moments when he'd talked to her on the phone, working on a book had seemed like the perfect solution to his problems.

His hopes were immediately dashed by the sound of the phone intercom buzzing. He stabbed the button to put Sandy, the receptionist, on speakerphone. "Yes."

"Jasmine Halliday is here to see you."

"Jasmine, huh?" Robert asked, standing. "Every Jasmine I ever met was trouble."

Garrett shot him a droll look and stood. "Behave yourself or you'll have to leave."

"I have no intention of staying. I have a consult in five minutes. I just want to get a look at her. I-I-I—" Robert stammered, as a tall, slender woman appeared in the doorway.

She glanced at Robert, but Garrett noted she headed

straight toward him, extending her hand. "Dr. Taylor, I'm so glad to meet you."

Momentarily bemused, he surveyed the young woman. She wore a navy blue dress, which ended at midthigh. Her long, shapely legs were encased in flesh-colored stockings and dark blue high-heeled pumps. He drew his gaze to her face. High cheekbones and deep-set eyes were accentuated by pouty lips and a flawless ebony complexion. Her black hair was swept up into a French twist. Although she strove to give off an aura of maturity, Garrett doubted she was any older than twenty-two. All in all, she was one of the loveliest young women he had ever seen. How on earth had Jeanie ended up with a sister like this?

Garrett shook her hand. "Likewise." He gestured toward Robert. "This is my partner, Robert Delaney."

"Pleased to meet you," she said, extending her hand toward Robert.

"Same here." Robert shook her hand, then stepped back. "If you'll excuse me, I have to see to a patient." Robert walked toward the door, but paused under the archway, facing Garrett. Raising his eyebrows comically, he pantomimed a curvaceous figure before heading to his own office.

Garrett pressed his lips together to suppress a grin and turned to the woman standing across from him. He gestured toward the chair Robert had vacated. "Won't you sit down?"

"Thank you."

She sat, setting her briefcase and purse at her feet. "What can I do for you?" he asked.

"As I told you over the phone, my publisher is branching into books as well as magazines. They want to develop a line of definitive health guides covering everything from pediatrics to geriatrics. My editor asked me which book I'd like to work on, and I immediately knew which one I wanted. Baby care books are a booming business. The same for anything African-American. It was a natural choice. These types of books sell better when at least one of the authors is in the medical profession."

True. People wanted the assurance of a medical degree to back up medical advice. "But why me?"

"I don't have any children of my own, but Jeanie raves about you. She's gone through several pediatricians, but she says none of them were as thorough, as caring, or as knowledgeable as you are. You may not be aware of this, but when this year's list of the best doctors in the city comes out from *New York* magazine, your name is going to be on it."

"I had heard something about that." In fact, a reporter from the magazine had hounded Garrett into giving an interview and letting him tag along on his rounds at the hospital. But if he were so darn good, how come he was so darn broke?

"I read the paper you had published last February in the *New England Journal of Medicine* on controlling ADHD through diet. You have a concise, open writing style. I wouldn't consider doing the book with anyone but you."

Uncomfortable with the overflow of praise and the fervor in the young woman's voice, Garrett slid his gaze to the blotter on his desk.

"What would the project entail? I mean, what would I have to do on my end?"

She leaned down and pulled a sheaf of papers from her briefcase. "Here's the proposal that I gave to my editor. Of course, if there's anything you'd want to add or change, you'd be welcome to do that."

Garrett skimmed through the pages—a detailed outline of the book. She'd planned chapters on everything from bringing the baby home from the hospital, to the first-year checkup. In between, there were chapters planned on vaccinations, breast-feeding, childhood illnesses, developmental stages, and a variety of other topics. At first glance, he couldn't think of anything pertinent she'd left out.

Stacking the papers neatly, he placed them on his desk and sat back in his chair. "I see you've done your homework."

"I'm always very thorough, Dr. Taylor."

Garrett blinked. Was that a hint of suggestiveness he detected in her words or in the smile she sent him? Probably not. She'd been nothing but professional in every other way. Still, something about this young woman disconcerted him.

"Please think it over, Dr. Taylor," she continued. "Paul, my editor, will be giving you a call on Monday."

"Monday? Why the rush?"

"Due to certain fiscal realities, they're trying to get the contracts signed and the checks issued before the new year." She stood and extended her hand toward him. "I don't suppose I have to tell you how much I'm looking forward to working with you."

Garrett stood also and shook her hand. But there was that smile again, not exactly seductive, but certainly more effusive than the situation warranted. "Thank you, but I can't guarantee I'll have an answer for you so soon."

"That's for you and Paul to work out. I appreciate you taking the time to meet with me."

Garrett dropped his hand to his side. "I'll walk you out."

He led her down the corridor that had been painted white and decorated with oversize Pokémon characters.

He helped her on with her coat and issued her out the front door. When he turned around, Robert was standing right in front of him, his arms crossed over his chest and a questioning tilt to his eyebrows.

"So? What did Miss Va-va-va-voom offer you?"

"As I said, she's working on a book and is looking for a coauthor with medical credential."

"And she just happened to pick you?"

"That's what she says. I haven't agreed to anything, though."

"But you will?"

"I'm thinking about it," Garrett said. But he knew he would if the offer proved lucrative enough.

Robert laughed. "Yeah, right. I wonder what Elise will have to say about this, given the shapeliness of your coauthor, I mean."

Garrett shrugged, but he'd wondered the same thing himself. "Good question," Garrett said, then strolled the short distance to his office and shut the door.

Returning to her office after lunch with a client, Elise sneaked off into her private bathroom in her office, locked the door, and got the pregnancy test from her pocketbook. Elise pursed her lips together. She wasn't sure she wanted to know what the results of the test would be. Right now, all she wanted to do was slink home and have a nice hot bath.

She huffed out a breath, opened the package, and pulled out the foil-wrapped stick inside. She didn't bother with the instructions. She knew what she had to do: pee on the stick and wait for the little window to turn pink. But several minutes later, absolutely nothing had happened. Now, what on earth did that mean?

Hearing a loud knock on the bathroom door, Elise

jumped, dropping the stick to the floor. "Boss, are you in there? You've got to leave for the shoot in fifteen minutes."

Elise dragged a long breath into her lungs and let it out slowly. "I'll be right out." She bent, picked up the stick, and tossed it into the toilet. She flushed it away and washed her hands. As she reached for a towel, she caught her own reflection in the mirror above the sink.

"Good Lord," she whispered, running her fingers through her short, light brown hair to straighten it. Her honey brown complexion appeared sallow in the glow of the fluorescent lights that ringed her mirror. Her eye makeup had smudged and her lipstick was nonexistent. She quickly repaired the damage, then stepped back from the mirror to gauge her total appearance. Her gaze fell on the wrapper for the pregnancy test in the garbage pail under the sink. If she weren't pregnant, then something else had to be wrong. But what?

Dena called to her again. Elise sighed. She'd have to worry about her own problems later. On the way across town, she'd give her gynecologist a call and see if Dr. Burton could fit her in some time next week.

It was almost nine-thirty when Elise walked up the stone pathway leading to her front door. The Lincoln shoot had taken forever, and Vic had spent an hour trying to get her into his bed before getting down to business. Elise wasn't particularly surprised that the house was already dark. Garrett had probably taken the kids out to eat when she hadn't shown up at the expected hour. But usually the foyer light was kept on for anyone coming home late. Even that light was out now.

She stuck her key in the lock and turned it. She knew her own house well enough to find her way around in the dark. But suddenly the room flooded with light and a sea of faces appeared before her.

"Surprise!" they shouted in unison.

Elise, stunned, stood stock-still, surveying the crowd in front of her. Her gaze settled on Garrett. A pointed party hat sat askew on his head and a sleepy Andrew rested in his arms. "Happy birthday, sweetheart," he mouthed.

In front of all assembled, Elise Monroe Thorne Taylor burst into tears.

Two

Garrett handed his son to his brother-in-law, Michael, and went to his wife. Wrapping his arms around her, he drew her closer, shielding her from the view of the others. Even with her wearing three-inch heels, the top of her head barely came up to the middle of his chest. He scrubbed his hands up and down her back. "Baby, what's the matter?"

Sniffling, she pulled away from him. She looked up at him, offering him a tremulous smile. "You scared the daylights out of me."

Garrett chuckled. "I guess I don't have to ask you if you were surprised."

"No." She swiped at her eyes with the sides of her fingers. "I had no idea. Whatever possessed you to do this?"

Garrett knew Elise hated surprises. She liked life orderly and neat with no unplanned bumps in the road. According to her, her business was chaotic enough; at home she wanted normalcy, as much normalcy as one could have with a teenager and a preschooler about.

"Blame it on your oldest child. She seemed to think a party was just what you needed."

"She would." Elise shook her head. "Remind me to rescind her allowance later. For now, we have company."

Elise stepped away from him, going first to her father and kissing him on the cheek. Judging by the graciousness with which she greeted her guests, no one would guess how uncomfortable it made her to find twenty-five unexpected visitors in her home.

After a few moments, Garrett went to her, wrapped his arm around her waist.

"How does it feel to be thirty-eight?" he heard someone ask.

"Who knows? I'm still numb from that greeting you guys gave me."

"She still feels pretty good," Garrett offered, giving her waist a squeeze. "But when she turns forty I'm trading her in for two twenties."

Elise craned her neck to slant a glance back at him. Chuckling, Garrett said, "Excuse us, please. I'm sure my wife has a few words to say to me best spoken in private."

He led her over to the stairs and leaned against the wall, pulling her against him. "Feeling better?"

"Yes. Thank you, Garrett."

He squeezed the back of her neck, and, as usual, she let out a little purr of contentment. He knew she referred to both his rescue and his letting Alyssa have her way. "You do realize she's probably buttering you up for something."

"As long as it's not a coed ski trip like last year. I had too much fun saying no to that one."

Garrett chuckled again. "Why don't you go up and change?"

"Good idea. I feel like I've been in this suit forever." She pulled away from him and turned to walk up the stairs.

"Don't take too long." He swatted her backside for emphasis.

She spun around, ready to protest, but he folded his arms in front of him, daring her to say anything. She might protest, but she liked the occasional Neanderthal move on his part.

Laughing, she tilted her head to one side. "I will get you for that later."

"I'm counting on it."

Rolling her eyes, Elise turned and continued up the stairs. Garrett leaned his back against the wall and watched her assent. The sexy sway of her hips served both as a promise and a threat. Tonight, when he made love to her, she wouldn't be a million miles away, she'd be right there with him. And she'd expect him to make it up to her for the fiasco this morning. He couldn't wait to try.

But more than that, he wanted to know what bothered her. Normally, a surprise party wasn't enough to make her cry. Something was going on with her, something she hadn't as yet decided to share with him. And if he were honest with himself, the two of them had grown more distant in the past couple of years. He spent little time at home, and when he was there, she wasn't. He couldn't remember the last time the two of them had done something as mundane as see a movie together. In some ways, he couldn't blame her for keeping her troubles to herself. But what to do about their current situation? He honestly didn't know.

Garrett turned and loped the rest of the way down the stairs.

After changing into a royal-blue silk lounging outfit, she touched up her makeup yet again and descended the stairs. Rather than join the party in the living room, she slipped around the stairway to the back of the house to enter the kitchen. She stopped short, finding her sister, Daphne, seated at one of the kitchen chairs, a plate of food in front of her. Both Daphne and Michael's wife, Jenny, were expecting—Daphne any day now, Jenny sometime next month.

Elise stepped into the kitchen, striding toward the cabinet that held the casual wineglasses. "What are you doing in here?" she asked her sister.

"Stuffing my face and hiding from my husband."

Elise poured herself a glass of merlot from the bottle on the counter and took a sip. "Why?"

At one time, Daphne's husband had not been a subject the two women could have talked about calmly. In the time Nathan and Daphne had been married, Elise had made her peace with Nathan, and the two had actually become friends.

Daphne smiled mysteriously and popped an hors d'oeuvre in her mouth. "Don't tell anyone, but I've been in labor for the past four hours."

"What?" Elise set her wineglass on the counter. "Are you kidding me? Why aren't you at the hospital?"

"All they'll do is poke me and probe me and make me miserable. My midwife told me to stay away from the hospital as long as possible, so that's what I'm doing. I promise you, I'm fine."

"So help me, Daphne Ward, if your water breaks over my new carpet, I'll kill you."

"The name is Thorne, Daphne Thorne, a fact you keep seeming to forget. Nathan's okay with the fact that I didn't change my name. Why aren't you?"

Elise grinned. "Because then I'd have nothing to pick on you about." Elise sighed. "So this is it, huh? I'm finally going to be an aunt. I really don't appreciate you having this baby on my birthday."

"Only for another hour or so." Daphne winked at her sister. "I'll try to hold out."

Elise shook her head. She'd been a wreck when she'd gone into labor with Alyssa, and here Daphne radiated a calm Elise doubted she'd ever felt in her life. Elise hugged her sister. "I'm so happy for you, Dee."

"You and Garrett will come with us to the hospital?"

"Of course." Garrett already served as pediatrician for Nathan's daughter, Emily, and would for the new baby, too.

"Then you'd better get back to your party while you can."

Elise rolled her eyes. "For now. Later on, I'm definitely going to kill Garrett."

"If I had a dime for every time you said that, I'd be a wealthy woman. Come on, Elise, you know it's a sweet gesture. He really loves you, you lucky devil."

Elise smiled. "I know. I just had one bear of a day today. That's why I was late." She considered telling her sister about the pregnancy test, but the decision was taken from her when Daphne's face contorted with pain. Elise squeezed her sister's hand. "Are you okay?"

Daphne shuddered. "That was the worst one yet. Maybe you'd better get Nathan."

"I'll be right back." Elise hurried around the front way, through the dining room and foyer, to reach the living room. Nathan was sitting on the sofa talking with Garrett, while eighteen-month-old Emily bounced on his lap. Both men looked up as she approached.

"I was beginning to wonder what happened to you, birthday girl," Garrett teased. He extended his arm around her waist, drawing her to sit on the arm of the sofa beside him. "I thought we'd have to cut the cake without you."

"It seems we may have another birthday very soon."

Garrett's brow furrowed. "Why do you say that?"

"Daphne's in labor." Elise's gaze shifted from her husband's face to Nathan's. "Your presence is requested in the kitchen, Nathan."

Elise pursed her lips to keep from laughing as all the color drained from Nathan's face. "Why didn't she tell me herself? How is she?"

Garrett lifted Emily from Nathan's grasp and settled her on his lap. "Why don't you go in the kitchen and ask her?"

Nathan rose from the sofa and headed for the kitchen. After he'd gone, Garrett squeezed Elise's waist, drawing her attention. "How is she?" he asked.

"Remarkably composed about the whole thing. She wants us to go to the hospital with them."

"Not a problem. I'd already promised Nathan I would meet them at the hospital when the time came."

"I think the time is now." Elise stood and took Garrett's hand. She probably worried for nothing, but, remembering Andrew's difficult birth, Elise wouldn't feel comfortable until Daphne was in the hospital under medical care.

Elise walked toward the kitchen with Garrett following her. She stopped short in the archway. Nathan had his arms around Daphne, rubbing her back in a gentle motion. Her cheek lay against his chest; his lips grazed her temple as he whispered words of comfort to her. The tender sight brought the mist of tears to her eyes. She blinked them back and stepped onto the blue-and-white tiled floor.

"Enough of that, you two. I think we'd better get Daphne to the hospital."

Daphne lifted her head and looked at her sister. "On one condition—I don't want Jenny to come."

"Why not?"

"In case I scream my head off, I don't want to scare her. She'll be going through this herself next month."

Elise shook her head. She'd gotten her mother's looks, except for the streak of white hair that adorned her mother's temple, but Daphne had gotten her altruistic spirit, an uncommon empathy for others' feelings. "I'll ask her to watch the children," Elise offered. "Emily and Andrew will love it, though Alyssa thinks she's old enough to fend for herself."

"She is."

"Don't start," Elise warned. "You wait until Emily is sixteen. Then come back and talk to me."

Daphne opened her mouth to respond when another pain overtook her. "I'd better get changed so we can go," Elise volunteered. Nobody protested.

Fifteen minutes later, after announcing the reason for their departure to the others, the four of them climbed into Garrett's Navigator for the trip into Manhattan. Daphne's midwife met them at the hospital, but it was hours before little Arianna Camille made her entrance into the world. Nathan and Daphne named her after their own mothers, neither of whom were alive to see their granddaughter being born.

While Daphne was made comfortable in a bed on the maternity ward upstairs, Garrett volunteered to bring the baby to the room. Elise looked over at Garrett, appreciating the incongruity of such a big man holding such a tiny baby.

He turned to her, smiling. "She's perfect, Lesi," he said.

Those were the same words he'd spoken to her when Alyssa had been born, using a nickname she hadn't heard from his lips in years. Her mind drifted to when Andrew had been born. She remembered the room being full of people, doctors, nurses, pediatricians waiting to whisk Andrew to neonatal ICU. She'd expected Garrett to follow them to ensure Andrew's care. But he'd stayed with her, holding her hand while they stitched her up, and she cried out of fear for her baby's health.

I love you, Garrett. The words popped into her mind, but never quite made it out of her mouth. Garrett didn't notice anyway, as his attention centered on the baby.

"I'm going to take her upstairs for a minute," he said. "I'd like to check her out more thoroughly. Do you want to come?"

Elise shook her head. "I think I'll stay with Daphne and Nathan for a while. Come and get me when you're done."

"Okay. I won't be too long."

After Garrett left, Elise surveyed the small room to make sure Daphne hadn't left anything behind. She hadn't. Elise picked up her own coat and Garrett's and exited the room.

Daphne was just settling into bed when Elise got to her room. Elise deposited the coats in one of the chairs and went over to Daphne's bed.

Daphne looked radiant, but sleepy. Nathan, who sat in a chair beside the bed, looked about ready to pass out.

"How do you feel?" Elise asked.

"Like someone pulled me backward through a bush." Daphne shifted in bed. "I don't think I've ever been so tired in my life. How come nobody told me about this part?"

"For the same reason you didn't want Jenny to come to the hospital. Nobody wants to scare off the uninitiated. If you'd known what you were getting yourself into, would you have done it?"

"I didn't exactly do it on purpose this time." Daphne closed her eyes. "Nathan, you're having the next one. Remember that."

Nathan grinned. "I'll see what I can do."

They lapsed into silence, and a few moments later Elise noticed that Daphne had fallen asleep.

"I'd better go," Elise said. "You should try to get some sleep, too. It may be your last opportunity for the next five years."

Nathan leaned forward in his chair, rubbing his eyes. "It already feels like I haven't slept in five years." He rose from his chair and walked to where she stood. "I really appreciate your coming to the hospital with us. I know it meant a lot to Daphne. And to me, too."

Elise rose on tiptoe to accept his embrace.

"Ward, if you must maul someone's wife, please maul your own."

Elise pulled away from Nathan and turned to see Garrett wheeling a clear plastic baby bassinet into the room. Inside it lay the baby, swaddled in a pink and blue receiving blanket. A tiny pink cap adorned her head. She sucked on two of her little fingers, just as Emily had as an infant. The three conscious adults gathered around the sleeping baby.

"She's beautiful, Nathan," Elise said.

"Did you expect otherwise?"

"Actually, no," Garrett answered, "since she gets her looks from Daphne."

Nathan put his hand on his heart and sighed affectedly. "You wound me, friend."

"The truth hurts."

Elise rolled her eyes. In the past year, Garrett, Nathan, and her brother, Michael, had formed an alliance of sorts. When they were together, it was all the women could do to keep the three of them in check.

"We'd better go. You've got an early day tomorrow, and I'm ready to drop."

After saying their good-byes, Elise and Garrett

headed down to the tiny hospital parking lot to their car. Elise settled in beside Garrett, opening her coat and fastening her seat belt. Once they pulled out onto Amsterdam Avenue, Garrett cupped his hand over Elise's thigh. "How are you doing?"

"Holding up, I guess. How about you?"

"Wake me up when we get home."

Chuckling, Elise looked out the window. The city, even this far north, was adorned with lights and other decorations for the holiday season. Only seven shopping days left until Christmas, or technically six, as midnight had come and gone hours ago. As usual, Elise had started her shopping in August and hadn't set foot in a store since Halloween.

She turned her head and studied Garrett's profile. He gazed out at the road before them, his total concentration on the trip home. It reminded her of this commercial she'd seen on television that showed a mother and child driving in a car, both of them silent. The caption underneath the picture read ANOTHER MISSED OPPORTUNITY FOR TALKING WITH YOUR CHILD. She'd never have a better opportunity to discuss things with Garrett than she did now that they were alone together. But somehow she couldn't bring herself to say anything.

Her gaze settled on Garrett's hand still resting on her thigh. She didn't know why, but seeing it there unaccountably depressed her. Elise turned back to the window, scanning the view from their position on the Major Deegan Expressway, and sighed.

Monday morning Garrett had barely returned the phone receiver to the cradle when Robert's head peeked in the doorway of Garrett's office. "So, what's happening?"

Chuckling, Garrett shook his head. "What are you? Part bloodhound?"

"Whatever do you mean?"

"I'm sure you know I just hung up the phone with the editor from that magazine. Don't play dumb. We jocks get enough of that as it is."

"Former jocks, that is."

"Yeah, that, too. I'm sure you're dying to know what they offered, so I won't keep you in suspense. Without getting into numbers, they offered me a nice chunk of change for basically serving as a consultant for the author."

"Which you could do in your sleep."

Garrett shrugged. "I told them I'd like to look over the contract before I said yes to anything."

"But you are going to do it?"

Garrett folded his arms across his chest, an amused smile on his face. "And how much are they paying you to push me along?"

"Not a cent. I just think it's a great idea. These days, you can't spit in a room full of doctors without hitting some quack who's written a book about something—and making good money at it, besides. Why shouldn't you take advantage of the gravy train while it's still running?"

Garrett leaned back in his chair. Why not, indeed? A picture of Jasmine Halliday formed in his mind. There was one reason right there.

"You can sit up now."

The five most welcome words in any woman's vocabulary. Elise slid her feet out of the stirrups and swung herself into a sitting position. "So, what's the verdict?"

Dr. Burton paused to shed her examination gloves before answering. "Everything looks fine, and you are definitely not pregnant. Why don't you get dressed and we'll talk in my office."

Elise did so, fastening the buttons of her black Liz Claiborne dress with unsteady fingers. The office was across from the examining room. Elise went to the other room and sat facing Dr. Burton. Delores Burton was only a few years older than Elise, but with her rounded figure and compassionate brown eyes, she exuded a maternal essence Elise found comforting.

"What do you think it is?"

"There can be any number of reasons for a missed period. How have you been otherwise? Anything unusual going on in your life?"

"Just the usual madness. My family threw me a surprise birthday party and nearly scared me into a heart attack. Other than that, nothing."

"You're thirty-eight now, correct?"

"Yes."

"Hmmm." Dr. Burton tilted her head to one side. "Have you had any hot flashes, heart palpitations, any other menstrual irregularities?"

"Not that I can think of." But as she said it, she remembered feeling flushed a couple of times lately, episodes that she'd attributed to the stress of her job.

"How old was your mother when she went through menopause?"

"I don't know if she ever did. She died when she was forty-two. Are you suggesting that's what's happening to me? Menopause? I'm too young for that."

"Not really. Your menses didn't start until you were fourteen. That's pretty late. And women who start late tend to finish early. And we're talking perimenopause here, the time that leads up to the cessation of menstruation, which can last for years."

"Oh, joy," Elise said drolly. She sighed and sat back in her chair. The construction of chrome and leather was poorly made and uncomfortable. "So, what can I expect?"

"Let's not jump the gun here. A simple blood test will tell us, but without any real symptoms, there could be a million other reasons for a missed period, the most likely of which is stress. In the meantime, I'll give you some pamphlets to look over and there's more than enough information on the Internet. Look some of that over and we'll talk next week about some of your options."

Elise nodded. She'd definitely taken up more than the fifteen minutes Dr. Burton had promised her. "I'll schedule an appointment before I leave."

Dr. Burton stood and rounded the desk. She cupped Elise's shoulder with her palm. "It's not the end of the world, you know. Millions of women go through it every day." The doctor gave her arm one last pat before heading out the door.

Elise sighed. Millions of *old* women went through it every day. She wasn't even forty yet, the official age of old-ladyhood. She'd often joked to herself that she couldn't wait for menopause—no more periods, no more cramps, no more excuse to claim PMS. But she honestly hadn't expected it to come so soon.

Aside from the obvious symptoms everyone knew about, she really had no idea what to expect. Garrett would know, but she wouldn't ask him. She wouldn't tell him about it until the tests came back and she knew for certain. Not until she'd figured out how she felt about it herself.

Elise gathered her things, went to the nurses' station, and made an appointment for the following week. She tucked the pamphlets Dr. Burton had left for her in her briefcase. When she got back to her office, a vase of two dozen roses awaited her on her desk. The attached card read, CONGRATULATIONS, AUNTIE. LOVE, G. But when she called his office to thank him, he wasn't there, and nobody knew where he'd gone.

By the time Garrett made it back to his office in the shadow of Columbia University from his foray into midtown, it had started to snow. Although Elise bought most of the holiday gifts, he usually got the kids an extra something, shopped for his own friends, and, of course, picked out Elise's gift. He'd been on his way to pick up an antique clock Elise wanted for the living-room fireplace when he'd seen a negligee in the window of Victoria's Secret, one that reminded him of the outfit she'd worn their first night together. He picked that up, too, but he wouldn't put it under the tree. He would save that for when they were alone.

He stamped his feet on the welcome mat, dislodging snow and ice from his boots and coat.

"Jasmine Halliday is waiting for you in your office."

Garrett's eyebrows lifted and his body went on alert. What was she doing there? He took off his coat and hung it in the closet by the door. He strode the short distance to his office and paused in the doorway.

Still wearing her coat, Jasmine Halliday sat in the same seat she'd occupied before. "Ms. Halliday? What can I do for you?"

She stood and stepped toward him, extending a manila envelope. "Paul told me he was sending the contract over to you, and since I was in the neighborhood,

I thought I'd save him the messenger fee and bring it myself."

"Thank you." Garrett accepted the envelope, opened the flap, and slid out the sheaf of papers.

"I suggest you have someone look those over before you sign them. Or I can give you the number of a good agent."

Obviously she considered it a foregone conclusion that he would sign. "I'll have my lawyer look them over."

"Just remember we've got a December 28th deadline on this. I hope Paul will hear from you before then."

"He will."

She tightened the sash on her coat. "I guess I'd better be going."

He took the hand she extended toward him, expecting her to shake it. Instead she leaned up on tiptoe and attempted to kiss his cheek. But even at her height and in heels, she didn't quite reach. "Enjoy your holiday."

Garrett swiped at the spot of moisture on his neck as she walked away from him toward the outer door. He'd fax a copy over to his attorney. But no matter how lucrative the contract, he wondered what exactly he'd be getting himself into if he signed it.

Elise sat back in the leather chair in her home office. Both of the children were in bed, and for the second night in a row, Garrett had secreted himself in his study. She had no idea what he was doing in there, but not a sound came through the common wall shared by both rooms.

Time to give up the ghost, Elise decided. She hadn't gotten one ounce of work done. She'd been in her office only a few minutes when Dr. Burton had called, confirming her diagnosis of earlier that day. Elise had spent the time since then fiddling with her computer keys and obsessing about what changes to her life the start of menopause would bring. She'd read the pamphlets the nurse had given her, as Dr. Burton suggested. If anything, they made her feel worse instead of better. Until then, she'd thought the occasional hot flash was the most she'd have to worry about.

Elise glanced at the digital clock that winked at her from beside her laptop. Nearly midnight. She switched off the computer, stretched the kinks out of her back, and went to find Garrett.

He answered her knock immediately, seeming to welcome her when she came into the room. Yet he placed the papers in his hand facedown on his desk when she approached.

She pretended not to notice. She sat on Garrett's lap, wrapping her arms around his neck. She hadn't done that in ages, but somehow it seemed appropriate. He leaned back, settling her against him. "What are you still doing up?"

"I came to say good night." She made a point of glancing around the room, from the papers on his desk to the conveniently blank computer screen to the books open on his desk. "What are you up to?"

"A little research. A difficult case at work."

She didn't believe him, but she didn't have a chance to question him further. His mouth claimed hers, gentle, nibbling, but undemanding. She shut her eyes tightly, as anxiety zinged through her stomach, sensing that he hadn't touched her out of desire, but with the aim of silencing her questions.

He pulled away from her and touched his fingertip to her cheek. "I'll be up in a minute."

She wanted more from him, both on a physical level and an emotional one. They hadn't made love the night of her birthday or the night after that. Saturday night, they'd both fallen into bed exhausted; Sunday night, she'd spent with her sister, helping Daphne settle the new baby at home.

At this rate, they wouldn't be making love tonight either. Garrett's preoccupation stung her, especially since what she wanted most was his reassurance that her concerns were neither petty nor silly, as she feared. As Dr. Burton said, millions of women went through menopause every day. She didn't know why it made such a big deal to her, but it did.

But he seemed eager to have her go, so she slid off his lap and stood. "Don't take too long," she said, then reluctantly left the room.

After passing through the living room and foyer, she ascended the sloping staircase to the upper floor. She checked on each of the children. Andrew was out, dead to the world. Alyssa pretended to snore. She probably had her cordless phone under the blanket with her. Too tired to take up the too-familiar fight over phone usage, she closed her daughter's door and headed next door to her own room.

Finding Garrett's clothes from earlier that day strewn across the bed didn't surprise her. She put up with his need for disorder the same way he tolerated her need for absolute neatness. But as she picked up his shirt, her eyes widened, finding a smudge of berry-colored lipstick darkening the collar.

Elise sank down on the bed, eyeing that stain. Who did Garrett know who wore that distinctive shade of lipstick? Elise shut her eyes and reminded herself that many of the mothers of Garrett's patients considered him a friend and would think nothing of kissing his cheek in gratitude.

That's what she told herself. But that information didn't help at all. Not one little bit.

Three

Garrett hung up the phone after completing a call to
his attorney and sat back in his chair, crossing his arms
in front of him. The contract, it appeared, was a gen-
erous one, allotting him a good advance and standard
royalties, and containing no noxious clauses that would
stand in the way of him signing it. The contract lay on
his desk, open to the page designated for his signature,
but he didn't sign it. He didn't know if he would.

For one thing, he hadn't talked with Elise about it
yet, and considering last night, he doubted she'd be in
the mood to discuss publishing contracts or anything
else with him.

She'd come into his study and sat on his lap. She
hadn't done that in forever. The way she'd snuggled up
against him promised a night of passion. He'd sent her
up to bed, straightened his study and followed her. But
by the time he'd gotten upstairs, Elise had turned out
the light and had already gone to sleep.

He'd slid into bed beside her, and pulled her against
him. She'd offered just enough resistance for him to
know that she wasn't really asleep.

"What's the matter, baby?" he'd whispered against
her ear.

"Nothing." She'd pulled away from him, scrunching

as far over to the other side of their king-size bed as she dared without risking falling on the floor.

Garrett had gritted his teeth. That was the problem with Elise. That was the problem with her whole family. The minute you did anything to displease any of them, they withdrew into themselves, like turtles seeking the protection of their shells. But for the life of him, he couldn't figure out what could have triggered such a response in her in the five minutes intervening between his study and their bedroom.

Garrett had shifted onto his side, away from her, determined to let her stew in whatever juices she'd decided to take him to task for. Then he'd thought he heard her sniffle. He'd lifted his head to look back at her. She hadn't moved and not another sound had come from her side of the bed. Huffing out a long breath, Garrett had laid his head on his pillow, but only much later had he actually fallen asleep.

This morning, he'd risen when she had, though he didn't have to be into his office until later. But he needn't have bothered. She'd barely spoken two words to him, and nothing that didn't have to do with getting the children up and ready for school.

As usual, she'd sent Alyssa and Andrew out to the car first, while she collected her purse and briefcase. He'd cornered her by the front door and wrapped his arms around her.

"Sweetheart, say something to me."

"I'm going to be late for work."

Completely frustrated, he'd let her go, stepping back and shoving his hands into the pockets of his sweatpants. She'd darted a glance at him. For a moment he'd thought she'd tell him something.

"I'll be home late tonight. Dinner is in the fridge."

With that she'd pulled open the door and gone out

into the cold December morning, leaving him chilled as well.

"Busy?"

Robert's voice jolted Garrett out of his musings. Garrett cleared his throat. "Not at all. What's up?"

"I'm leaving for the hospital in a few moments." Robert glanced at the papers on Garrett's desk. "Still haven't decided what you're going to do about the book?"

"Not yet."

"Why not? Afraid your prospective coauthor has the hots for your bod?"

Garrett crossed his arms and glared at Robert.

"Don't look at me like that. I saw how she looked at you when she came to the office. If you'd been a piece of steak, that she-wolf would have gobbled you up on the spot. But, hey, there are worse things in the world than having some young, nubile temptress interested in you."

Robert obviously thought this a topic of great humor, but Garrett did not. "Don't you have somewhere to be?"

"All right, I'll be serious." Robert sat in one of Garrett's chairs. "So she's attractive. Or is that the problem? You're interested in her, too."

Despite Robert's casual tone, Garrett suspected Robert would leap on him and try to beat the crap out of him if he got anything but the desired answer. Robert was one of the few people who knew all Elise had done for him, not to mention providing him with the only real family he'd ever known. "No, I'm not interested."

"Then what's the problem?"

"A wise man doesn't put himself in a cage full of lions and expect not to get bitten."

"I see your point." Robert adjusted his coat collar

and put on his gloves. "Let me know how things turn out."

"As soon as I know, you'll know."

"I'd better."

"What are you doing here?"

Elise had been down on 28th Street shopping for the perfect faux ficus to plant in the corner of a client's living room when she'd decided to stop by Nathan and Daphne's town house on East 83rd Street to see how she was doing. She hoped the enthusiastic and entirely fake smile she'd plastered on her face didn't crack as she advanced toward her sister's bed. "Some greeting, after I rearranged my whole schedule to come and see you. Not to mention the ride on the crosstown bus."

Daphne held the baby in her arms. Elise placed a kiss on each of their cheeks. "Where's Nathan? I had to let myself in with my key."

"He took Emily to the store to pick up some things at the supermarket."

Elise gave a mock shudder. "The infamous Nathan Ward food shopping. That image boggles the mind."

"Tell me about it. He's actually learning to cook. He made me spaghetti once and it didn't kill me, so now he thinks he's a chef."

Daphne tried unsuccessfully to shift her position in bed while still holding the baby. "How would you like to hold your niece for a moment?"

"I'd love it." Elise shed her coat and gloves and laid them at the foot of Daphne's bed. She went to the adjoining bathroom and quickly washed and dried her hands before scooping the baby from Daphne's arms. Little Arianna wore a pink stretchie with a white collar edged in lace. Gone was the little pink cap the baby had worn in the hospital. She ran her hand over the baby's hair, curly like Nathan's but jet-black in color, like Daphne's. Elise sat on the edge of her sister's bed. "She's so beautiful, Dee."

Elise stared down at the baby. Although she was only a few days old, her hazel eyes were bright and alert. Elise touched her fingernail to one of the baby's palms. The baby immediately grabbed it. Elise knew from Garrett that was a test of a baby's neurological development. The baby wouldn't let go of her finger, though. The baby brought it to her mouth and began to suck on it.

"I think someone's hungry," Elise said in the universal singsongy voice adults reserve for babies. Elise extracted her finger from the baby's grasp and used it to tickle her tummy. The baby rewarded her with a toothless openmouthed expression of glee. "You are hungry, aren't you?"

"That's nothing new. Someone is always hungry." Daphne leaned forward for Elise to place the baby in her arms. "But I've never heard you resort to baby talk before, not even with your own kids."

Elise shrugged. "I guess it's different being an aunt."

"You're different. What's going on with you? I didn't say anything at the time, but when you burst into tears the night of your party, I nearly gave birth right then from the shock. You never cry."

"If you'd had the day I'd had, you would have cried, too."

"Really." Daphne merely stared at her sister with her head cocked to one side. Elise looked away, unable to meet her sister's assessing gaze. She couldn't look at the baby, either, who lay in her mother's arms nursing happily. The image only served to remind Elise that while Daphne's reproductive life was just beginning, her own was coming to an end.

Elise got up from the bed and did something she never did. She paced along the side of Daphne's bed. "I just have a lot on my mind right now."

"Like what?"

"Well." Elise hedged. She wanted to tell her sister. She wanted to tell someone who would understand her mixed emotions and sympathize. Yet she also worried that to tell Daphne would be a betrayal of Garrett. But in the end, her need for commiseration won out.

Elise sat on the edge of Daphne's bed. "I think my marriage is falling apart."

Daphne stared back at her in wide-eyed amazement. "You're kidding me, right?"

Elise shook her head. It was no secret that Daphne adored Garrett. Everyone adored Garrett. She couldn't think of anyone who wouldn't automatically assume that if trouble had come to paradise, it had to be her fault. Perhaps childishly, she felt the need to vindicate herself.

"Last night, Garrett came home with lipstick stains on his collar."

Daphne blinked and shook her head. "Do you think he's having an affair?" Her voice held such an incredulous note that Elise almost laughed. Until a few days ago, the thought would have been inconceivable to her, too. And though she honestly doubted that Garrett would ever cheat on her, something was going on with him, something that he hadn't shared with her. It stung to know that he hadn't confided in her.

Elise sat on Daphne's bed. "I don't know, Daphne. I don't know. Things haven't been the same between us lately. He's been distant the last few days and I . . ."

Elise trailed off, not wanting to tell her sister about her trip to the gynecologist's office. Daphne didn't need to know that if she followed her sister's example she might only have a few years left to bear her husband's children.

"You what?"

"I haven't exactly been forthcoming with him either. I guess it's more than just recently. Our relationship hasn't been the same since Andrew was born. Garrett's worked longer hours and my business has expanded tremendously. We've had less time together and when we do see each other . . ."

"You're too busy groping each other's bodies to talk?"

Color rose in Elise's cheeks. "What a delicate way you have with words. But yes."

Garrett was a very physical man. He enjoyed touching and being touched, and not just in sexual ways. He'd think nothing of hugging her or the kids spontaneously. She was probably the only woman in America who didn't complain about the lack of cuddling from her husband. And since the caliber of their physical relationship hadn't changed, she'd had an easy time of convincing herself that everything else remained the same between them.

But even that had changed now. Between the episode the morning of her birthday and her pulling away from him last night, she'd distanced herself from Garrett physically as well.

"What do you intend to do about it?"

Elise pressed her lips together and shrugged. "I don't know. Probably nothing until after the holidays."

Daphne bit her lip. "I don't think that's wise. Weren't you the one who told me how you spent the New Year was how you would end up?"

"No, I said *who* you spent the New Year with was

who you'd end up with at the end. Besides, you know I don't believe in that superstition."

"Well, I did spend last New Year's with Nathan, and we are married and have a new baby, so you were right about that. And isn't how you spend the New Year as important as who you spend it with? How would you feel ending the next year in as much torment as you feel now?"

"Obviously, that wouldn't be pleasant."

"Then talk to Garrett. Now. Don't put it off. Things that get put off have a way of never getting said at all."

"Maybe," Elise answered, but she knew she wouldn't. Not unless she had some inkling as to what he might say. What if he surprised her and told her he was having an affair? She had never before understood wives who sat by silently while their husbands philandered, but once you acknowledged that a problem existed, you had to do something about it. She'd have to admit her marriage was over, because she couldn't live with a man who wouldn't be faithful, no matter how much she loved him.

With the holidays upon them, it wouldn't be fair to her children to disrupt their lives and forever taint the Christmas season for them. No, Elise would bide her time and wait until after the New Year. Which meant they'd mark their seventeenth wedding anniversary on January first, if only by default.

Elise sighed and stood. "I've got to get back to work."

Christmas at the Thorne family home was always a festive occasion. Christmas had been Camille Thorne's favorite holiday, and her widower and her children carried on the tradition in her absence. The grounds, the windows, and the roof were decorated so elaborately that passersby stopped to admire the scene.

Usually the festive atmosphere filled Garrett with contentment. Born the only child of two free spirits that eschewed traditions of any kind, he'd never known much in the way of holiday celebrations. And when they'd died in a plane crash on the way to some adventure, he'd been raised by his mother's spinster sister, who'd been more sanctimonious than pious, more censorious than righteous. Anything not connected with the religious aspects of the holiday had been anathema in her house.

But today, content didn't describe his mood. Both he and Elise had put on happy faces for the kids this morning while they opened presents. Then, like two prize fighters after the bell has sounded, each of them went to separate corners of the house—he to his study and Elise to the kitchen to bake the ham they planned to take to her father's house.

And now, the two of them sat across from each other at the dinner table, sharing polite conversation with the rest of the Thorne family. Garrett glanced over at her. She spoke with her father, Jasper, who sat between them at the head of the table. He let his gaze wander over her, knowing her attention centered elsewhere. She really was one of the most beautiful women he'd ever seen, with her cap of light brown hair, flawless, honey brown complexion, and delicate brows arching over large, expressive eyes. But for all its beauty, her face held strength also, in her square jaw, high cheekbones, and the small, off-center cleft in her chin.

And unlike her sister, Daphne, who was tough as nails on the outside and a marshmallow beneath, Elise was aesthetics and grace on the surface, but inside possessed a core of steel that nothing could penetrate.

There was a part of her that no one touched, not even him. He didn't fault her for her ironclad determination and resilience, as they had saved him more than once. But sometimes, like now, he wished he knew how to reach her.

As if she sensed his gaze on her, she turned to look at him. Their eyes met across the table, and for a moment, she didn't look away. Despite the faint smile on her lips, the sadness in her eyes tore at his heart. Without saying a word to him, she turned away, responding to something her brother said.

How had this chasm opened up between them in a few short days? Not for the first time, he wanted to drag her off to another room and shake her until she told him what was bothering her. But if he did that, she'd probably think he'd lost his mind. She might not be far off.

As the meal wound down, he glanced at his daughter, Alyssa, who sat at the foot of the table across from her grandfather. She'd inherited her mother's beauty, his height, and a bundle of raw energy, from where he didn't know. She fastened her gaze on him, her face lit by a thousand-kilowatt smile. She glanced at Elise, then back at him, a hint of devilment in her eyes. What was she up to now?

"I have one more holiday surprise," Alyssa announced, rising to her feet. All eyes turned to her; even the little ones focused their attention in her direction.

"I entered this contest on the radio. You had to be the one-hundred-third caller to win a pair of tickets to see the Traction concert at Madison Square Garden."

"And . . ." Elise interjected.

"And, I won. Along with the tickets, they put your name in a drawing for a dream holiday vacation on Milagro Island."

"Absolutely not. Don't even think your father and I would allow you to go."

Alyssa rolled her eyes. "Duh, Mom. I know that. Besides, you have to be eighteen to go. I wanted to give my trip to you and Dad . . . as long as you let me go to the concert."

"Young lady, that is blackmail," Elise said in a frosty voice.

Garrett eyed his wife through half-closed lids. Elise was definitely not amused. "Actually, it's closer to extortion. You haven't been spending time with Grandpa Rusty again, have you?"

Ever since Jenny and Michael had married two years ago, Jenny's father had treated Alyssa and Andrew as if they were his own grandchildren, a reality that left Garrett with mixed feelings.

"Da-ad," Alyssa complained in the universal whine of teenagers.

The kitchen buzzer sounded. Elise tossed her napkin on her plate. "I'd better check on dessert."

Garrett watched her push back her chair and make a hasty exit from the room. Since it was Jenny's dessert that had finished baking, Elise had no reason to check on anything. But in typical Elise fashion, she escaped from a conflict rather than jumping into the fray, at least at first. Whenever her emotions ran high, she went off somewhere to cool down before addressing the issue.

He turned back to Alyssa. "Tell me about this concert."

Later, when Elise didn't return to the table, Garrett went to look for her. He found her upstairs in the room she'd once shared with her sister, Daphne. She stood by the window, facing away from him, looking out at the night sky. She clutched an ancient pink teddy bear in her arms.

"Baby, what are you doing in here?" he asked.

She whirled around to face him, obviously surprised. "I didn't hear you come in."

Garrett stepped into the room and closed the door behind him. No matter what might be going on between them, Elise placed her children's welfare above anything else.

"I suppose you've come to plead Alyssa's case."

She didn't add the words *as usual,* but from her tone she might as well have. "Come on, Elise, she wants to go to a concert, not a brothel. What's the big deal?"

"Don't be naive, Garrett. How do you think all those kids up in the nosebleed section entertain themselves? Even I know they're doing drugs and drinking alcohol, and there's not a soul up there to monitor them."

"But these are front-row tickets, right there on the floor. And they have backstage passes for after the show."

"Way to convince me to let her go. Like I want her meeting those people."

Elise sighed and turned away from him. For a long time, she said nothing, her head downcast. "Honestly, I don't care about the concert. As long as we know who she's going with and she takes a cab home, I don't have a problem with it. But the manipulation I do mind. I get enough head games from the people I work with. I don't need any more from my family."

Garrett went to her and wrapped his arms around her from behind. "Is that really what's bothering you?"

"She didn't trust us—trust me—to be fair."

Garrett huffed out a heavy breath. Elise blamed herself for Alyssa's attempt at deception, but in truth, they were both to blame. When it came to the children, he was completely indulgent, giving them whatever they asked for. He saw them so infrequently that guilt motivated him to give them things since he couldn't give them time. If it weren't for Elise reining him in, the children would be spoiled rotten and uncontrollable. He did her a disservice by always making her the bad guy who ruined everyone's fun. But he also knew she misread the situation.

"Sweetheart, she's sixteen. And she has far less freedom than most girls her age. I'm not complaining about how you handle things with her. But the truth is, we say no a lot more often than we say yes. And she really wants to go."

"As I said, I don't mind if she goes. At least it's not the Meadowlands."

Smiling, he rested his chin on the top of her head, remembering a Prince concert they'd gone to back while they were in college. Garrett's car had broken down on the way to New Jersey. A van had pulled up, and several questionable-looking characters had poured out of it. At first, Garrett had been sure they were about to be mugged, or worse. He'd made Elise stay in the car with the doors locked while he confronted the group. He didn't relax until one of the guys pulled out a toolbox and offered to try to fix the car. When it became clear the car was dead, the group had asked them if they wanted a ride to the concert.

Elise had shocked him by not waiting for a response from him, climbing into the back of the van and sitting cross-legged on the ratty old carpet that covered the floor. He'd stood there for a moment, simply staring at her. No one at school would believe the high-and-mighty Elise Thorne would ride in such a vehicle, let alone set her pristine behind on a van floor.

She'd smiled up at him, obviously guessing his thoughts, and asked him if he intended to join them or if she should go on alone. Other than drag her out of the van, he'd had no choice but to climb aboard.

Later, when he'd asked her why she'd done such a crazy thing, she'd answered, "We had seventy-five-dollar seats. I wasn't about to let them go to waste."

"No, it's not the Meadowlands." He squeezed Elise's waist. "So that leaves us with the question of what to do about this dream vacation of hers."

"Like either of us could just pick up and go on vacation. You have your patients and I've got Judith McDonald and Vic Stamos to worry about."

When was the last time the two of them had done something spontaneous, unplanned? Probably that van ride to the Meadowlands.

"Why can't we? I've got a light week coming up. It wouldn't take much trouble to cancel a few appointments. Robert and Matt Peterson could handle any emergencies that come up."

She narrowed her eyes and scrutinized his face. "You're not serious."

The incredulousness in her voice solidified his desire to go. "Do you have anything pressing you can't get out of?"

Elise shrugged. "I guess not. Most people are too busy celebrating to worry about decorating."

"Then why not?"

"Because it would be crazy, that's why." She tilted her head to one side. "You're not really considering this, are you?"

"Let me see: me, my beautiful wife, alone in a tropical paradise. What a nightmare!"

She smacked his shoulder with the flat of her hand. "You bum."

He caught her hand, brought it to his lips, and kissed

her palm. "We haven't had a vacation alone since Andrew was born."

"We've both been too busy."

He shook his head. Neither of them had taken the time to plan one. "It's free. That should appeal to your sense of frugality."

"Flattery isn't going to get you anywhere."

He slipped his hand under her sweater and cupped her breast. He pushed aside the lace decoration of her bra and brushed his thumb across her nipple. He felt a surge of satisfaction when her breathing hitched and her delicate throat arched.

"Stop it, Garrett," she protested, her voice breathy. "I can't think when you do that."

Good. If he gave her too much time to think about it, she'd say no. She was right, it was madness to pick up and go. But it was equally mad to stay, to feel the life slowly draining out of their marriage and do nothing.

"Come with me, Elise."

She raised her head so that she looked at him levelly. "Are you sure you want to go with *me?*"

He frowned, wondering why she'd placed such emphasis on the word *me*. "Of course."

She sighed, lowering her chin to her chest. He held his breath, waiting for her answer. When she lifted her head, a hint of a smile turned up her lips.

"All right, Garrett. Let's go."

Four

Garrett settled back into the first-class airline seat and fastened his seat belt. In a few moments, their plane would take off for Puerto Rico. Another short plane ride later they would reach their ultimate destination of Milagro Island.

As the plane began to taxi down the runway, he felt Elise take his hand. She didn't mind flying, but the take-off and landing got to her. He turned to her and squeezed her hand. "It'll be over soon."

She offered him a weak smile. "You say that every time."

"And I'm right every time, aren't I?"

"Be that as it may, I'll feel better when we're in the air."

Garrett leaned back, took Elise's hand, and wrapped it around his bicep. He closed his eyes. "Then do what I do. Go to sleep. The flight isn't that long."

"You could sleep through an atom bomb," she scoffed, but he felt her relax beside him.

Her fingers dug into his arm as the plane took off, but once they were in the air, her grip eased. Several minutes passed in which neither of them said anything.

"Elise?" He opened his eyes and gazed at her. Despite herself, she'd fallen asleep. He studied her face.

Aside from her shorter hairstyle, her appearance hadn't changed much since the first time he'd seen her.

His mind drifted back nearly twenty years to the time when he and Elise attended Stockton College in the tiny town of the same name in upstate New York. He'd been a junior, studying biology on a football scholarship, when she'd walked into his life.

But if it hadn't been for one of his teammates, he probably wouldn't have ever noticed her. . . .

He was sitting in the bleachers after a practice, waiting for a friend of his to show up, when Randy Fletcher took a seat beside him, leaning his elbows on the row behind them. At first Randy didn't say anything, which suited Garrett just fine. Then Randy spoiled it by making a savoring sound in his throat.

"Look at that backfield in motion."

Garrett focused his attention in the direction Randy looked. Immediately, his gaze settled on a girl walking across the grass in front of them. She was a tiny thing with long, light brown hair held back from her face by a thick headband. She wore the short pleated uniform skirt of the girl's field hockey team, ankle socks, and a pair of black-and-white cleats. Garrett leaned back, resting his elbows against the bleachers behind him. "So?"

"Don't you know who that is? Elise Thorne, freshman, Miss Untouchable 1981."

Garrett shrugged. The whole team joked that *Randy* wasn't just a name, but a character description for the starting quarterback. He always had some girl that he was either sleeping with, wanted to sleep with, or had dumped because she wouldn't put out.

Garrett didn't even like Randy, but the other man was oblivious to censure from anybody. If anyone showed dislike toward Randy, he swore they were simply jealous of him and ignored them. "And I should care, why?"

"I plan on touching her."

Something about the way Randy spoke made Garrett focus his attention on the girl again. She faced him now, having joined some of her teammates who knocked the hard dimpled hockey ball back and forth among them, probably waiting for the coach to show up. Someone hit the ball to her. With an athlete's reflexes, she positioned her stick and whacked the ball. It sailed past the girl she hit it to. A slow smile of satisfaction spread across her face, one that revealed a seriousness and determination that he found surprising. "Not one of your usual airheads."

"So says the man who's dating the luscious Tanya."

"I know what Tanya is and what she isn't." And Tanya was not an airhead. She modeled to pay her tuition, so people assumed she hadn't a brain in her head. At nearly six feet tall and stunningly gorgeous, wherever she went men got stupid in her presence, not the other way around. Absolutely no one believed she majored in physics with plans for getting a Ph.D. He hadn't believed it himself, until he'd sat beside her in organic chemistry. She'd breezed through an A, while he'd struggled to get a B+.

Tanya also wasn't his girlfriend, not anymore. They'd remained friends, though the physical part of their relationship had fizzled out over a year ago. Nobody believed that either.

"I'm sure you do," Randy drawled. "And don't think I don't envy you that knowledge. But something tells me that little one out there wouldn't mind showing me a thing or two."

Something told Garrett otherwise, but he didn't bother to try to convince Randy of that. Randy only saw what he wanted to see. But when Randy moved to get up, Garrett grasped his arm without thinking. "Why don't you leave her alone?"

Randy shrugged off Garrett's grasp. "Why should I?" A smug grin spread across Randy's face. "Don't tell me you want her for yourself."

Garrett didn't miss Randy's insinuation that in a competition between the two of them Randy would without question emerge the victor. "She's not my type. But I do know one thing." He nodded toward the girl on the field. "She's a lady. She'll shoot you down in two seconds flat."

"Now, we'll just have to see about that, won't we?"

Randy hopped down from the bleachers and strode across the track lanes and onto the field. The group of women parted as Randy approached, allowing him to pass. The object of Randy's interest seemed to be the only one oblivious to him, until the girl next to her elbowed her and gestured in Randy's direction. She turned and folded her arms in front of her.

Garrett couldn't hear what they were saying, but he waited for the moment the girl would tell Randy to get lost. Disappointment flooded through him when she accepted a pen from him and wrote something on his hand, probably her phone number. After that, Randy strutted away like a peacock out on a stroll.

Garrett frowned, watching as the girl's teammates surrounded her, laughter and congratulations on their faces. He didn't suppose many of the girls on campus were immune to Randy's looks or his stature on the team or his family's wealth. But for some reason, it had mattered to him that she was different.

"Earth to Garrett, come in, Garrett."

Garrett focused on the hand waving in front of his face. He hadn't noticed Tanya approaching, but she stood beside him now, an amused smile on her face. "Hey. I didn't see you there."

"Obviously. Are you ready to go or are you still watching the show?"

"No, I'm ready." He gave one last look at the girl, shook his head and followed Tanya off the field.

Shivering from the frigid November air, Elise pulled her jacket more tightly around her. She'd allowed her roommate Michelle to talk her into coming to this ridiculous football game, only because Michelle claimed to have fallen madly in love with Brian Purcell, one of the players. He, on the other hand, didn't know she existed.

Michelle had told her she intended to declare her affection the minute the game ended. What Michelle hadn't told her but Elise had figured out for herself was that Michelle had invited her to the game hoping to capitalize on Randy's interest in Elise, since Randy and Brian were best friends. Michelle planned to use her as bait to attract Randy's—and therefore Brian's—attention.

In the meantime, Elise's toes grew numb inside her fur-lined boots. She rubbed her gloved hands together, surveying the field before her. What was it about this game that held such fascination? A bunch of sweaty, grunting, hulking men chasing one another around the field or butting heads like rams at a rutting contest. Definitely not her idea of a good time.

At least field hockey required some skill, some finesse. She never would have joined the team in the first place, if the coach, a close friend of her father's, hadn't asked her. Of course, the only reason the coach had asked her was his friendship with her father.

She consoled herself with the fact that the game would end soon. The two-minute warning had been announced ten minutes ago. The players were lining up for another play at the far end of the field. The visiting team had advanced the ball nearly to their own goal line. The quarterback threw the ball for what should have been a short pass. But he missed the mark and a player from the home team caught it instead. Immediately he began to run toward the opposite end of the field. And ran and ran. The other team tried to stop him, but with the help of his teammates, he evaded them all.

The crowd rose to its feet. Caught up in the moment, Elise stood, too, craning her neck to see over the others. Lord, he was beautiful. He ran with an economy of movement and grace she never would have expected in such a large man. He didn't stop until he'd passed the goal line. But he didn't spike the ball or do one of those ridiculous dances she hated. He dropped the ball to the ground, slipped off his helmet, and leaned over with his hands on his knees, breathing hard.

Even with her limited knowledge of the game, she recognized that what he had done was remarkable. The crowd erupted in cheers and suddenly his teammates surrounded him, whooping and hollering and hugging one another.

Confused, Elise turned to Michelle. "What's going on?"

"That touchdown won them the game. There are only ten seconds on the clock. Unless the Hornets make some miracle play, we won." Michelle grabbed her arm. "If we want any chance of getting out of here anytime soon, we'd better go now."

Michelle's plan had been to meet up with Randy and Brian after the game when they emerged from the locker room. Elise and Michelle claimed seats on one of the benches outside the sports center to wait. While Michelle fidgeted and paced, Elise pulled her sketch pad from her purse and drew.

After a few minutes, Michelle asked, "What are you doing?"

Elise turned her pad and showed Michelle the sketch she'd drawn of number forty-four dodging a tackler.

Michelle took the pad from her, studying it for several seconds. Finally she fastened a sly gaze on Elise. "I think you like him."

Elise snatched the pad away from her friend. Heat stole into her cheeks. "I like the way he moves." Seeing the broadening smile stretch across Michelle's face, she added, "I mean, on the football field."

"Mm-hmm." Michelle turned away from her to stare at the door. "What on earth takes those guys so long in there? And they talk about us women."

Elise let out an exasperated sigh, but said nothing. She wouldn't mind if they stayed in there until the next millennium. She loathed the idea of seeing Randy, even if it were only to make a hasty introduction. He'd interpret it as interest on her part, which couldn't be further from the truth. Honestly, men like Randy made her flesh crawl. Until now, she'd been successful at avoiding him. She hoped Michelle appreciated the sacrifice she made, but she doubted it.

At last the door swung open, but Randy didn't step into the cool afternoon sunshine. Two other men, ones she didn't recognize, walked toward them. The one on the left immediately drew her attention. She gauged him to be about six and a half feet tall, though her calculation could be off. She only stood five feet, four inches herself.

Brown-skinned, muscular, with a straight, Roman

nose, square jaw, and dark brown eyes, he was one of the most attractive men she'd ever seen. Unconsciously, Elise's lips parted and her breath hissed in on a gasp.

Michelle leaned closer to her and whispered, "It's him."

"Him who?"

"Garrett Taylor. Number forty-four. Your bronze Adonis running back."

"Get out!"

The men had to pass them to get to their car. For the first time in her life, Elise waited for a man to notice her. As they walked by, he offered Michelle a benign smile, but when his gaze fastened on Elise, his eyes went cold and the smile on his face receded. The two men climbed into a red BMW and drove away.

Elise sat back, her shoulders drooping. She hadn't imagined the censure she'd seen in his expression. He didn't know her from Eve, so what was that all about?

She glanced at Michelle, who eyed her suspiciously. "Are you sure you don't know him? Homeboy there sure seems to know you."

And he doesn't like what he sees. Elise had never had that reaction from a man before. Men usually made fools of themselves around her, which annoyed her more than played to her sense of vanity. Frankly, all the attention bothered her, especially because it came from something she had no control over—her looks. But never had a man actually snubbed her before. Shaking her head, she contemplated Garrett Taylor's response to her.

The door swung open again and several players strode out. Among them were Randy Fletcher and the object of Michelle's affection, Brian Purcell. Elise didn't have to worry about being ignored now. The men flocked around the two women. Randy took the seat next to

Elise, draping his arm across the back of the bench behind her.

"What are you two ladies doing out here all alone?"

Before Elise could answer, Michelle, who smiled directly at Brian, said, "Waiting for you, of course."

Brian put one foot on the bench beside Michelle and leaned toward her with his elbows on his knees. "Then I hope we were worth the wait."

Elise would have rolled her eyes in disgust if she could have gotten away with it. But since Michelle had made her own introduction, Elise considered herself off the hook.

Elise stood, gazing down at Michelle. "I'd better be going."

Randy rose to his feet in a second. "Don't tell me you're deserting us. We're heading over to Tony's for a victory celebration."

Great! Elise eyed the group of men around her, high on endorphins, testosterone, and their own senses of self-importance. Add a few beers, some high-calorie carbs and salty meat, and they would probably turn pretty ugly. She glanced at Michelle, who looked back at her imploringly. She couldn't care less about deserting the team, but she did feel guilty about abandoning her friend to this group of Neanderthals.

Michelle rose to her feet and grabbed her arm. "She's coming." Michelle stood four inches taller than Elise, outweighed her by thirty pounds, and seemed to have no intention of loosening her grip.

Elise sighed. "Just for a little while."

The four of them piled into Randy's sports car, Elise in front with Randy, Michelle in back with Brian. Elise had tried to sit in the back with Michelle, but none of the other three had accommodated her seating plan. Ignoring the others, she stared out the window, trying to figure out some way to extricate herself from this ridiculous double date.

Tony's Italian restaurant was a hangout for jocks of all kinds, just off the campus grounds. Well, a hangout for male jocks, anyway, with the typical red-and-white checkered tablecloths, paneled walls, and a photo gallery of the "stars" who'd come to visit the restaurant. A picture of Frank Sinatra occupied the center spot. Elise assumed his signature had been forged. The Chairman of the Board had more sense than to set foot in this place.

Elise glanced across the table at Michelle. Both women sat on inside booth seats, Elise next to Randy, Michelle next to Brian. For all her supposed worldliness, Michelle seemed absolutely smitten by Brian, her cool facade peeled back to expose an insecure, obsequious girl Elise neither liked nor recognized.

As for Randy and Brian, they greeted everyone who came in from their booth at the front of the restaurant like the king and heir apparent welcoming visitors to court. Not surprisingly, most of their fellow players moved on to sit at the back of the restaurant.

The door swung open again, and *he* walked in. Tanya Robinson strode in beside him, her arm linked with his. Tall, voluptuous, outgoing, Tanya possessed everything Elise did not. Randy greeted the new arrivals as he had all the others, but Elise sensed a tension between the two men. And this time Garrett didn't look at her at all. After speaking to Randy and Brian, he led Tanya to the back of the restaurant and sat with the others.

"Now, there's a friendly guy," Michelle remarked, looking right at Elise.

Elise's expression soured. She got Michelle's hint,

though she didn't want it. She had no more intention of taking advantage of Randy's friendliness than she had of chasing after Garrett Taylor or any other man. But Garrett's behavior intrigued her and his obvious snub made her furious. Who was he to treat her like that? He probably had to beg his professors to give him passing grades so that he would be allowed to play ball. If her grades held up, she'd have a 4.0 average at the end of the semester.

Randy's arm slipped around her shoulders, drawing her attention to him. He sat far too close to her and the motions of his hand on her arm were too familiar for her comfort. She needed to figure out a way to get herself and her roommate out of there, though Michelle didn't seem too eager to go anywhere.

For the moment, Elise pretended to be interested in the conversation. Yet she felt as if someone was staring at her. But when she turned her head to check, neither Garrett Taylor nor anyone else stared back.

Garrett hadn't come to the library to spy on Elise Thorne, but once he'd spotted her across the room, he couldn't take his eyes off her. As usual, she'd left her light brown hair loose around her shoulders. She tucked a strand of it behind her ear, cocked her head to one side, and continued writing on the pad in front of her.

He'd thought she was pretty the first time he'd seen her. But that had been from a distance. When he'd seen her up close two days ago after the Hornets game, her beauty had nearly knocked him on his butt. Then he'd reminded himself that if she was waiting outside the locker room, she was probably waiting for Randy. That thought had kicked the wind out of his libido. And when he'd walked into Tony's and seen her with Randy draped all over her, he couldn't even look at her.

Despite himself, he still felt drawn to her. She continued writing, oblivious to him watching her. Or maybe not quite oblivious. Her head lifted and she looked directly at him. Immediately, she looked away, scribbling furiously on her pad.

Garrett swallowed. If he wasn't mistaken, he'd seen a look of embarrassment on her face in that instant before she looked away. Was she ashamed that he'd caught her looking at him?

A dark shape crossed his field of vision, settling beside Elise. Randy sat on the desk beside Elise's chair. Until now, Garrett wouldn't have believed Randy knew where the library was. He couldn't hear what they said, but he got the impression she wasn't as taken with Randy as he'd first assumed. Or maybe she hadn't made up her mind about him yet. But when Randy walked away, she stared after him for a long moment.

He didn't know what made him do it, but he quickly gathered his books and walked over to her table. He had no idea what he would say to her, but he cringed inwardly when he heard the words that came out of his mouth.

"Is that the kind of guy you go for?"

She sat back in her chair and crossed her arms, turning glacial amber eyes to him. "When that becomes any of your business, I'll let you know."

"It's just that you struck me as being a little more intelligent than the bimbos he usually dates."

"With friends like you, Randy doesn't need any enemies, does he?"

"He's my teammate, not my friend. Guys like Randy give the rest of us a bad name."

One corner of her mouth lifted in a mocking smile.

"Seems to me the rest of you don't do so bad earning that name on your own."

Whether loyalty to Randy or a general dislike of him prompted her words, Garrett didn't know. Either way, she didn't seem interested in a word he said. "If I were you, I'd be careful."

He left before she had a chance to respond or he had a chance to say anything dumber than he already had. He never should have said anything. What she did *was* none of his business.

Though he'd like to think he wanted to save her from making a mistake, in truth, nothing more noble than jealousy motivated his actions. He didn't want Randy to have her. He didn't want anyone else to have her, either. He'd probably have warned her away from Gandhi if he'd been in the picture.

Randy had been right about one thing: Garrett did want her. And he was right about something else. In a competition between the two of them, Garrett would probably come out the loser. He didn't possess Randy's looks or popularity or family connections, all the things that seemed important to the girls on campus. For the first time since Garrett had known Randy, he wished he did.

Thursday nights, the little coffeehouse on Warring Street bristled with college students hanging out and relaxing since classes were over for the week. Elise settled into the overstuffed chair next to Michelle, setting her cappuccino on the table before her.

"Hi, stranger," Elise said. Ever since the football game less than a week ago, Elise hadn't seen much of her roommate. She'd agreed to meet Michelle here to make sure her she still counted among the living.

"Hi yourself." Michelle took a sip from her cup. "Brian's meeting me here in a few minutes."

Elise groaned. Michelle hadn't the finesse to disguise the fact that this meeting was a setup. No doubt, Randy would be joining them as well. The man was tenacious, she'd give him that. Ordinarily she admired that quality in a person, but for the life of her she couldn't figure out why he'd bother. He could have his pick of most of the girls on campus.

Her gaze slid to where Garrett Taylor sat. She'd noticed him, surrounded by a group of guys in the corner, when she'd come in. Two weeks ago, she hadn't known he existed, but suddenly every time she turned around he was there.

Their gazes met and he raised his cup to her in salute. She looked away, not knowing what to make of him. More often than not, he looked at her with this censorious scowl on his face, as if he disapproved of her. Yet he'd warned her about Randy . . . not that she needed him to tell her anything about Randy. She'd heard stories about how Fletcher the Lecher had earned his reputation.

So, why had he warned her? She couldn't believe jealousy motivated him, not when he had Tanya to keep him company. But then, why would he care who she dated?

Randy and Brian chose that moment to make an entrance. Brian settled in the chair next to Michelle, greeting her with a brief kiss on the mouth. Randy grabbed a wooden chair from another table, turned it around and sat. He leaned close to her, a slow, appraising smile spreading across his face. "Long time, no see, pretty lady."

Not long enough. Elise pushed back her chair. She

glanced at Michelle, catching the other woman's attention. "I'm going to put some money in the jukebox."

The volume of conversation of the kids in the coffeeshop usually made turning on the jukebox an exercise in wasting money. Elise didn't care—anything to get up from the table. And if Michelle had a brain in her head, which Elise seriously doubted, she'd have caught the hint to join Elise in the corner of the room.

She scanned the song titles listed in the jukebox window, pretending to look for a song she wanted to hear. A few seconds later, she felt someone come up behind her. At first, she assumed it was Michelle, until Randy's breath brushed her cheek as he leaned forward to rest his hands on the glass on either side of her. "Play G7," he whispered in her ear.

She knew what Randy was about. He'd chosen this public forum to stake his claim to her. She had no idea what song G7 was, but to be perverse, she slipped her coins into the slot and pressed two buttons without looking. The sound of Michael Jackson's "Beat It" filled the speakers.

"That's not what I asked you to play."

"No, it's not." She stooped and slipped under Randy's arm and went back to her seat. Tugging on her coat and slinging her bag over her shoulder, she glanced at Michelle. "I'm out of here. I'll see you back at the dorm." That is, if Michelle bothered to show up. Right now, Elise couldn't care less what Michelle did.

Elise swung around, right into Randy's chest. "Where do you think you're going?"

"Home."

Randy leered at her as if she'd issued him an invitation to her bed with that curt monosyllabic answer. "Well then, let me get my coat."

Elise held up a hand against his chest to forestall

him. "Let me say this slowly so that maybe it will sink in. I am not interested in dating you. So why don't you do yourself a favor and find someone who is and leave me alone."

Elise skirted around him and headed for the door. She'd barely made it outside when Randy overtook her, standing in her path.

"Nobody walks away from me like that."

"Then I must not be nobody." She glanced down at his hands gripping her forearms, then back to his face. "Let go of me."

Immediately he adopted a conciliatory attitude that Elise recognized as being entirely fake. "Come on, baby, you know I didn't mean that the way it sounded."

Elise glared back at him, her anger mounting. "Let go of me," she repeated.

Instead he backed her against the gratings of the closed store next door and brought his mouth down on hers. Revulsion roiled in her belly as Randy's tongue slid into her mouth. Suddenly his hands were everywhere, and his hips ground into hers.

Elise didn't think; she acted. One minute Randy was towering over her. The next he was on the ground, flat on his back. Not a perfect throw, but she wouldn't complain about it. Especially since she'd heard Randy's head crack on the sidewalk when he landed. He wasn't moving, but she assumed that he lay there more out of shock that she'd done something to him than from actual injury.

Randy touched his hand to the back of his head, then brought it to his face, obviously checking for blood. "What the hell is wrong with you, you crazy broad? All I did was kiss you."

Elise wiped her mouth with the back of her hand. All he did? He'd actually expected her to submit to him or he would never have tried such a stunt in a public place. God only knew what he did in private, but in public he had a reputation to protect.

She leaned down to shout in Randy's face, "The next time a woman tells you to leave her alone, I hope you'll remember this moment and think twice."

She straightened, fixing her coat and adjusting her pocketbook on her arm. As she turned to leave, she caught sight of the coffee-shop window in the periphery of her vision. Several stunned faces pressed up against the glass, staring back at her. Mortified, Elise squeezed her eyes shut. Everyone inside must have witnessed what had transpired between her and Randy. And one face stood out among the others. Garrett Taylor, standing, looking at her with an expression she didn't understand.

Hearing Randy groan, Elise looked down. He'd started to get up, and she didn't want to know what he'd do when he got to his feet. Elise whirled and ran in the opposite direction.

By the time Garrett made it outside the coffee shop, Randy had gotten to his feet. He dusted off his clothes, glancing in the direction Elise had gone. "That bitch!"

Garrett leaned his shoulder against the window, his arms crossed over his chest, his hands formed into fists. His blood boiled and his eyes burned. Obviously Randy intended to go after her, which Garrett would not allow.

"I wouldn't if I were you."

Randy glared over his shoulder at Garrett, then turned to face him. "Is that some sort of threat?"

Garrett shook his head. "Just an observation. She threw you flat on your back the first time. Next time she might not go so easy on you."

"Go to hell, Taylor."

"And besides, when this gets back to Coach Thompson, and I can promise you it will, you'll be lucky if you're not benched for the next game, so why don't you quit while you're ahead?"

For a long moment, Randy glared back at him. "Don't get on your high horse with me. I may have struck out tonight, but you'll never have her, either." Randy turned and stalked off in the opposite direction.

Garrett watched Randy for a moment, willing his anger to recede. He didn't have to tax his brain to imagine what Randy had done to cause such a reaction in Elise. He wanted to make sure she was all right.

He found her sitting on one of the benches that lined the park on Oliver Street. As he approached, her head came up. Even in the dim light of a streetlamp he could see the wariness that immediately came into her eyes. That look slowly gave way to one of annoyance. "What do *you* want?"

Garrett fought to contain a smile. He didn't mind her being angry with him, as long as she wasn't afraid of him. "I wanted to make sure you were all right."

"I'm fine. I always enjoy making an idiot out of myself on a Thursday night."

"If you ask my opinion, Randy's the idiot. Where did you learn to throw people like that?"

"I've studied karate since I was five. My mother believed that girls should know how to protect themselves."

"Smart woman."

She nodded, but said nothing, looking up at the stars for a long moment. "Don't you have something better to do than interrogate me?"

"Not at the moment. Come on, let me walk you home."

She considered the hand he extended toward her, but she didn't take it. Shrugging, she rose to her feet. "Why not, since there's absolutely no chance of you trying to ravish me?" She started walking in the direction of the dorms.

He shoved both hands in his jacket pockets and followed her. "There's not?"

"Of course not. You don't even like me."

"What gave you that idea?"

"You did. You're always glowering at me. The first time I met you, you looked at me as if I were a bug on the dining-room table."

"That's because I thought you were interested in Randy. I was on the field the day you wrote your phone number on his hand."

She laughed, a vibrant, tinkling sound he'd never heard before. "Do you have a pen?"

He pulled one from his jacket pocket and handed it to her.

She stopped walking and turned to face him. "Give me your hand."

He did so and she used the pen to mark something on his hand.

"That's the number I gave Randy."

They'd reached the campus buildings. In the dim light, it took him a moment to figure out what she'd written, but when he did, he burst out laughing. The "number" she'd written was I81-U812.

"It took him two days to figure out I'd given him a phony number."

She started walking again, heading east toward her dorm building. They reached it within five minutes. She paused at the outer doors, obviously not wanting him to come any farther. He accepted that, but he couldn't let her go without setting her straight about a few things.

"There's something I think we ought to clear up."

She eyed him with her head cocked to one side. "What's that?"

A smile formed at the corners of his mouth. "I never said I didn't like you. And if I weren't absolutely sure you'd slap my face or worse, a little ravishment would definitely not be out of the question."

She averted her gaze, but he'd already seen the smile on her face. "I doubt I could reach your face."

He took her hand and touched her fingertips to the side of his face. "That wasn't so hard, was it?"

She surprised him by cupping his face in her palm, leaning up and kissing his cheek. "Thank you," she whispered.

"For what?"

"For walking me home."

She dropped her hand and stepped back. She might not fear him, but she didn't entirely trust him, either. "Does this mean we're friends now?"

Her smile turned to a frown. "Like you and Tanya are friends? I don't think so."

"There is nothing going on between Tanya and me."

"Really?"

He didn't miss the sarcasm in her voice. With a finger under her chin, he tilted her face up to his. "Really."

She focused her large, amber eyes on him, looking into his eyes as if to assess the truth of his words. He sensed a softening in her, as her gaze drifted lower to his mouth. Her lips parted slightly, and he wondered if she expected him to kiss her.

God, he wanted to. Her lips looked soft and moist and inviting, but he didn't dare. Unlike Randy, he didn't make a habit of taking advantage of vulnerable women. Despite her bravado, he suspected the night's events had shaken her.

Garrett cleared his throat and straightened. "I'd better go. Are you going to be okay?"

She nodded. "I'll be fine. I'm going to go up and take a nice hot bath and go to bed."

An image of her nude and covered in bubbles formed in his mind. He had to shake his head to clear it away. "If you need me, call me." He took the pen out of his pocket and wrote his phone number on her palm. "I'm serious. It doesn't matter how late."

"All right."

Feeling uneasy, he watched her walk into the building and get in the elevator. Randy had walked away earlier, but Garrett doubted that Randy would let tonight be the end of it. Randy had been furious at Elise for humiliating him in front of the coffee-shop crowd, and further incensed by Garrett coming to her defense. Randy would want retribution, but Garrett had no idea what form that retribution might take.

Five

Now Elise had two men to avoid: Randy, for obvious reasons, and Garrett, for wholly unexpected ones. If anyone had told her a month ago she would find herself daydreaming about some jock, she'd have told them they were insane. Yet, when she reviewed the sketches she'd done in the last few days, not one of them had anything to do with art class or interior design. *He* dominated every one. Most were drawn from memory of him blazing across the football field, but the one of him she'd done in the library by far outstripped the others. She'd nearly died of embarrassment when he'd looked up and caught her watching him.

She hadn't seen either man since that fateful night two weeks ago when Garrett had walked her home. Randy appeared to have given up on pursuing her, though she doubted she'd heard the last from him. For the time being, she'd let some other woman worry about him.

As for Garrett, just as their paths had unaccountably crossed, they seemed to have mysteriously uncrossed. That suited her fine, too. That night he'd walked her home, she'd thought he was going to kiss her. If she were honest with herself, she'd wanted him to kiss her, if only out of curiosity. The last time she'd allowed anyone that close to her, she'd still worn pigtails and braces.

She'd believed him when he told her that he and Tanya had ceased to be a couple a long time ago. Something told her that if Garrett Taylor ever got serious about a woman, he'd stay that way. She had no time to be serious about anything aside from her schoolwork. She knew too many women who allowed some man to distract them from their studies or who quit entirely for marriage and babies. She refused to fall into that trap, to wake up one day and find she'd done nothing with her life.

Elise packed up her drawings and locked them in her desk drawer. She still shared the same room with Michelle, whom she no longer trusted. And now that Brian had dumped her, Michelle returned to the room each night. She discovered painfully that the only reason Brian had dated her was that Brian and Randy had made a bet as to which one would get "his" roommate into bed first. Once Brian won, he had no further use for Michelle.

How ironic that Michelle, who had sought to use Elise to gain her own ends, got played herself by someone with more expertise in the matter. Elise supposed that fell under the category of being careful what you wished for.

And another reason for Randy to despise her. He hadn't won with her on any front.

The residents of Stockton joked that the town only had two temperatures: July 15th and blizzard. Outside her dorm, the weather raged in full wintry force. Elise donned coat, scarf, hat, and mittens and headed for the door. Despite the brevity of the walk, she froze on the way to the church, anyway. She'd volunteered to help serve holiday dinner to church members and indigent residents of the town in the basement of the little church just off campus. Church members paid five dollars for the privilege; poor folks got in free.

By the time she reached the church, her nose had reddened and her eyes watered. After a few minutes of helping set up the steam trays from which the food would be served, her insides warmed and her skin glowed. And then *he* walked in.

She knew the minute he arrived. Each time someone opened the door a chilly blast rushed in with them. It took him fifteen minutes to make it from the door to where she stood. In a town where everything revolved around the resident college and the college revolved around the football team, the players were feted wherever they went.

While she worked, she stole glances at him, knowing he devoted his attention elsewhere. Unlike Randy, who browbeat others with his status, Garrett seemed to attract people with his humor and warmth. Such warmth, like the glow of a fire, could be intoxicating. Elise tamped down on her emotions, straightened her spine, and forced the smile from her face.

And then he was standing in front of her, smiling, his hands in the pockets of his leather bomber jacket. She scanned his face, noticing for the first time that a small scar cut across his left eyebrow. She wondered how he'd gotten it, until she reminded herself that she didn't want anything to do with him.

"You didn't call me."

"You said to call you if I needed you. I didn't need you."

"Ouch. You do know how to hurt a guy, don't you? Both literally and figuratively."

Despite his words, she sensed the amusement in him, and it annoyed her. "What are you doing here?"

"What do you mean?"

"This food is for the poor. And if I'm not mistaken, you're not exactly starving."

His brows knitted together and the line of his jaw hardened. "I help out here every year, which you might have noticed if you'd looked at the volunteer roster."

He walked past her to claim an apron. He tied it around his waist and took a position a few servers down, relieving the woman who carved the turkey.

Elise let her shoulders droop. That had gone rather well, she thought sarcastically. Though she didn't want to date him, she didn't want him to think badly of her, either. Sighing, she concentrated on doling out mashed potatoes and a gooey brown liquid that served as gravy.

Hours later, the volunteers had served nearly one hundred turkey dinners. Exhausted after the cleanup, Elise sat on one of the vacated chairs, trying to gather enough energy to walk home. Garrett strolled out of the kitchen then, his apron gone. He wore a pair of jeans and a cream-colored cable-knit sweater, both of which clung to his muscular body in ways that didn't leave much to the imagination. He stopped short, finding her seated in his path.

"What are you still doing here?" he asked. "I thought you'd gone to Tony's with the others."

"I have to catch a bus home first thing in the morning. Besides, I'm exhausted."

"I'm not surprised. You did more than your share of the work today."

Elise chewed the inside of her lip. Most of the other helpers had volunteered only for a couple of hours, and when their time was over they'd left. But Elise had made a commitment to help and she'd been intent on staying until the last person left. So she'd had to take up the slack for those who left. But she hadn't thought Garrett had noticed.

"Is that why every muscle in my body is calling me names right now?"

"That bad?"

"Worse. But don't let me keep you from joining your friends."

Garrett smiled. "You're not. I'm not going to Tony's, either."

"Why not?"

"Too crowded, too much noise. I'm not in the mood." He extended a hand toward her. "Come on, let me take you home."

This time she did take his hand. She would never get out of the chair if she didn't. When he pulled her to her feet, she looked up at him. "Thank you."

He ignored her gratitude. "Where's your coat?"

She pointed across the room to where a few remaining coats hung. "Mine's the brown shearling."

Not only did he get her coat, he helped her into it and tied her scarf around her neck. He pulled on his own jacket and took her arm. "Let's go."

She knew he intended to walk her all the way home, and she didn't argue. All things considered, she appreciated his chivalry. If she dropped in the street somewhere from exhaustion, he was big enough to carry her home.

They left the church and walked toward the campus in silence. After a while, she looked up at him, sensing a question in him. His answering stare only confirmed her opinion. "What?" she asked.

"Just curious. What were you doing there tonight?"

Elise slanted a glance up at him. "Fulfilling my

mother's expectations of me. How about you? You said you volunteer every year. Why?"

He sighed, looking straight ahead, but other than that, he remained silent.

"I told you mine. Aren't you going to tell me yours?"

He looked down at her, a sexy grin on his face. "That only works with showing."

She couldn't help the smile that lifted the corners of her mouth. "Well, I'm not showing you anything. Especially since you won't answer my question."

"It's a long story."

Wasn't it always? Whenever someone didn't want to tell you something, their story expanded by geometric proportions. She continued walking, her eyes on the path ahead of them. "You don't have to tell me. I shouldn't have pried."

Hearing Garrett exhale a heavy breath, she glanced up at him. "You want to know what I do for the holidays? Nothing, usually. I haven't got any family, and I'm not comfortable imposing myself on someone else's. I usually stay here."

"Alone?"

"Most of the time."

She didn't know what to say to that. Spending any holiday alone was so alien to her that she couldn't imagine how he must feel about that. She said the only words that popped into her mind. "You could spend Thanksgiving with me. With my family."

He glanced down at her, a sardonic smile on his face. "Don't joke like that. I might take you up on your offer."

"I'm not joking. You're welcome to spend Thanksgiving with my family, if you like."

He looked at her a long moment, not saying anything.

"I'm not a charity case, you know. Don't try living up to your mother's expectations through me."

"I'm not." Her mother would never forgive her if she found out she knew someone spending the holidays alone and didn't invite them over. Her mother had invited complete strangers to dine with them. "I really want you to come. Though I have to warn you, you'll have to share a room with my brother, Michael."

Garrett's eyebrows lifted. "What's wrong with him?"

"He just turned fourteen, and thinks he knows everything."

Garrett laughed. "Sounds like me when I was his age." He shoved his hands in his jacket pockets. "I'll think about it."

She assumed that meant no. "If you change your mind, I'm catching the eight-thirty bus to Manhattan."

"I said I'll think about it."

Elise didn't say anything. He was trying to be polite and not out-and-out refuse her offer. She couldn't blame him. He had no idea what her family was like. When they reached her dorm, she barely said good night to him, feeling oddly deflated that she couldn't possibly see him again until Sunday night, when she would return to campus.

So, the next morning when Garrett showed up in a blue Datsun and loaded her bag in the trunk of the car, she stood by mutely, too surprised to say much of anything.

Garrett looked over at Elise for perhaps the millionth time since they'd started driving an hour ago. She sat beside him, her legs drawn up under her, a sketch pad on her lap. She'd hardly said two words to him since they'd started out. He wondered if she regretted her hasty offer of dinner with her folks. He wondered if he'd been crazy to accept, but the promise of spending a single holiday with a remotely normal family had proved too tempting for him to pass up.

"What are you drawing?"

She picked up her pad and showed him—a grove of trees in full autumn colors. Though she'd drawn in pencil, he could "see" the hues of red and gold, brown and yellow. He wondered how she'd managed such an accurate representation bouncing around in the car. The old Datsun didn't offer a terribly smooth ride.

"You're very talented. Is that what you're in school for, art?"

"Interior design, actually. I've always drawn, though. I find it relaxing."

"Interior design, huh? I would have pegged you more for a business type."

"Why?"

He stole a look at her. "I don't know. You have that polished look, never a hair out of place. Even after working for hours at the church, your makeup was still intact." Everything except for her lipstick. That had worn off, leaving her lips with a rosy glow. "You're not exactly the bohemian type."

He glanced at her to gauge her reaction to his assessment. She looked back at him with her head cocked to one side. "What are you doing?" he asked.

"Trying to guess what you're studying."

"I'll make it easy for you. I'm premed."

"Really?"

He smiled, hearing the incredulousness in her voice. "Not all jocks have hockey pucks for brains."

"I never said that. I thought you'd want to play football professionally. According to Michelle, you and

Randy are probably the only ones on the team who have any hope of that."

"I've had an offer, from a scout that was in the stands for the Hornets game, but I haven't made up my mind."

"Why not?"

"Because a lifetime of having people try to bash my head in isn't my idea of fun. Not to mention a very short career, which could be made shorter by injury." He shook his head. "For now, football pays my tuition and gives me enough to live on. I'm not interested in the long haul."

"So, why don't you tell them no?"

"Because I'm not crazy. We're talking about a lot of money. And I don't know if I'd make it into med school. My grades are good, but nothing to write home about. I'd probably jump at it if they didn't want me to start next year instead of finishing my degree."

"Sounds like you have a lot to think about."

"Mmm," he answered. Then he changed the subject to the one that interested him. "So, what's your family like?"

Elise shrugged. "My dad's a biology professor at Columbia, my mom's a music teacher. I told you about my brother, Michael. My sister, Daphne, is into some militant feminist 'all men are beasts' phase. She turned sixteen at the beginning of the month. Your typical family, I guess."

Not so typical in his estimation. "You sure your mom isn't going to freak out finding she has another mouth to feed?"

"Probably. But only because she doesn't know you're coming. Then she'll be mad at me, not you." She closed her sketch pad. "Do you mind if we make a pit stop soon? I need to freshen up."

He pulled into the next rest stop, opting to wait in

the car until she returned. As she got out, her pad tipped off the seat and landed on the floor of the car.

He leaned over to pick it up, and one of the pages caught his eye. A drawing of a player charging down the field. The number *44* emblazoned on the player's chest put to rest any doubts he'd had about whom she'd drawn. Other pictures of him followed: him on the field, one of him in the library that day he'd seen her, a sketch of his profile that she could only have done during this trip. Now what on earth should he make of that?

He glanced up to see her walking toward the car. He quickly arranged her book the way she'd left it, not wanting her to find him snooping.

"Ready to go?" he asked, once she'd seated herself and fastened her seat belt.

"Ready."

Garrett steered back onto I-95 with a smile on his face.

Camille Thorne was a tall woman who bore the same facial features she'd passed on to her daughter. Her hair was jet-black, though, except for a streak of gray at her left temple. Garrett's first thought when she opened the door to them was that if Elise looked like that in twenty years, it wouldn't be a bad thing at all.

She paid him no attention at first, embracing her much shorter daughter. "Welcome home, darling," she said, holding Elise's shoulders and gazing at her. "Looks like college is agreeing with you."

"Thanks, Mom. It's good to be home." She gestured in his direction. "This is Garrett Taylor. He's going to be staying with us for the weekend."

Camille looked up at him, her amber eyes boring into

him. "Is he now?" She extended her hand, which he shook. "Welcome, Garrett."

"Thank you for having me."

Camille led them into the hallway. "Everyone else is in the living room."

Elise and her mother walked ahead, leaving him to bring up the rear. Before they reached the living room Camille bent toward her daughter and whispered, "You will meet me in the kitchen in five minutes."

When Elise introduced him to her father, brother, and sister, they each stared at him as if he were an alien species brought in for experimental purposes.

Her father recovered first. He stood and offered Garrett his hand. "Glad to have you, son."

"Thank you, sir."

"Forgive us for being so antisocial, but the Jets game is on." He motioned for Garrett to sit. "Are you a football fan?"

Garrett sat on the sofa next to Elise's brother. Michael grunted a greeting and turned back to the game. He glanced at Elise's sister. She sat sideways in her chair, her face buried in a book.

"Daddy," Elise said, "Garrett plays for the Wolverines."

"Get out," Michael said, suddenly interested in him. "What position?"

"Oh, great!" Daphne exclaimed before Garrett had a chance to answer. "Just what we need around here—another caveman."

Garrett looked to the spot in the hallway where Elise stood. When their eyes met, she shrugged as if to say, *I told you.* She turned to follow her mother into the kitchen.

* * *

Elise pushed through the swinging door to the kitchen and stepped inside. Her mother stood at the counter chopping onions. Elise hoisted herself onto the counter next to her mother. "You wanted to see me, Mom?"

Her mother's hand stilled in midair. "Have you lost your mind?" Elise's spirits dropped and the smile fell away from her face—assuming her mother objected to her bringing Garrett home. "I don't have enough food to feed that man. Just look at him. He must eat a ton. Why didn't you call me and let me know he was coming?"

"I didn't know myself until he picked me up this morning." Even though she realized her mother wasn't angry with her, she felt the need to explain herself. "He's all alone, Mom. I knew you wouldn't mind."

"And he doesn't exactly hurt the eyes, does he?"

Elise turned away, heat rising in her cheeks. "No, he doesn't."

Her mother said nothing for a while, focusing on preparing dinner. "I won't have any foolishness going on in my house. I don't know what you do up at school, but he'll stay in Michael's room and you'll stay away from him."

Elise snapped her mouth closed as her mother fixed her with a penetrating stare. For all her mother's lady-like demeanor, she could sometimes be more blunt than Elise cared for. "It isn't like that. He's just a friend."

"Yes, and I was born yesterday and believe everything people tell me."

"It's true. He hasn't so much as kissed my hand."

"But given the chance he'd do more than that, and you'd let him, so let's not kid each other. I can't dictate what you do away from home, but while the two of you are in this house, you will behave yourselves."

Seeing no point in arguing the issue, she said, "Yes, Mom."

"Good. Now go check the refrigerator and see if we have anything defrosted that I can feed this man."

"His name is Garrett."

"Yes, then go find Garrett something to eat."

Elise slid from her perch on the counter and headed for the refrigerator.

Hours later, Garrett sat at the kitchen table polishing off a glass of milk and a thick slice of the cake that had been served earlier as dessert. Not a sound broke the silence of the night, except for a faint humming noise coming from the refrigerator. He leaned back in his chair and crossed his arms in front of him.

Dinner had gone better than he'd thought it would. He'd half expected them to treat him as his aunt would have handled an unexpected guest: make the person as uncomfortable as possible until they left. Consequently, he'd never brought anyone home. Growing up, he'd ended up isolated, since hanging out at someone else's house invariably led to them wanting to visit his. He supposed that's why he and Tanya found it so easy to remain friends. Her family was as kooked as his; they both had avoided them as much as possible.

But Elise's family was different. A bond of warmth, of mutual admiration and respect, existed among them all. Their conversations were full of laughter and intelligence. For the first time Garrett found a place he wanted to belong.

But most of that had to do with Elise. He saw a side of her now that he'd never seen at school: warm, funny, more relaxed than he'd ever imagined she could be. He wanted to see more of that Elise, and not just here.

Hell, he wanted her period, and it drove him crazy. Especially now, when he had no hope whatsoever of doing anything about it.

Hearing a noise in the outer room, he sat up and listened. A second later, the kitchen door swung open and Elise appeared in the doorway. "Michael, are you . . ."

She stopped short, realizing that he, not her brother, occupied the kitchen. She wrapped her robe around herself and tied the sash, but not before he'd gotten a good glimpse of the long, bare legs that her short nightgown revealed. Her hair floated around her shoulders, loose and sleep-tousled. For the first time ever, he saw her sans makeup. If anything, she was prettier without it.

"I couldn't sleep. I didn't think anyone would mind if I raided the refrigerator."

"And here my mother was afraid she wouldn't have enough food to feed you."

He got up from the table and put his dishes in the sink. "You make me sound like a glutton."

"No, just . . ."

With a hint of a cocky grin on his face, he suggested, "Big?"

She gave him a droll look. "I'd better get back to bed. I suggest you do the same." She turned to leave.

"Elise, wait."

She stopped, but she didn't turn to face him. "Yes?"

He walked toward her until he stood right behind her. "Thank you."

She did turn to face him then. "For what?"

He shrugged. "Inviting me here. The way your family welcomed me. I didn't know what to expect."

"I told you your coming wouldn't be a problem."

"I guess I don't have much experience with families like yours."

She said nothing for a long moment. Then she looked up at him with such a soft expression in her eyes that his breathing hitched in anticipation of what she would say. "What happened—to your family, I mean?"

Usually, when someone asked him about his background, he evaded the issue, but he wanted her to know. "My parents died when I was six. I don't remember them, except from a few pictures. My aunt raised me. She died my freshman year."

She lowered her head. "I'm sorry."

He tipped her chin up with his index finger. "Don't be. I told you, I'm not a charity case. I only told you because I wanted to be honest with you."

"Thank you."

A tiny quiver in her lower lip drew his attention to her mouth. Her tongue darted out to lick her lower lip. He burned to do the same thing. Slowly, he lowered his head to touch his mouth to hers. He was so much taller than she that she had plenty of time to get out of harm's way, if she wanted to. But the moment their lips touched, she sighed and her lips parted as if in invitation for more. He ran his tongue along her lower lip and she opened more for him. He didn't need to be invited a third time. He touched his tongue to hers, initiating a slow, thorough exploration of her mouth.

God, she tasted sweet, which didn't surprise him. But the passion with which she kissed him back did. Her arms wound around him, and her delicate hands touched down on him. Her fingers made a whisper-soft study of his back, driving him crazy, making him groan into her mouth.

Immediately, she pulled away, looking up at him with wide, panic-stricken eyes. "I—we, we can't, Garrett."

She looked so horrified that he almost laughed. Did she really think he'd try to seduce her on her parents' kitchen floor? He straightened away from her, his humor getting the better of him. "Was the kiss that bad?"

Deadpan, she lifted one shoulder and let it drop. "I'd give it a C-minus."

Liar, he wanted to say. As first kisses went, that one had been an A+. "I'll try to do better next time."

She tilted her head to one side. "Who says you'll get a next time?"

"I will." He leaned toward her, his gaze centered on her mouth. Her eyes drifted shut, and her lips parted, but he didn't kiss her. At the last minute he turned his head and whispered in her ear, "Go back to bed, Elise, before I do something I shouldn't."

He backed up, giving her enough room to leave. Her eyelashes lifted, and if he weren't mistaken, he saw disappointment in her amber eyes. He hoped the expression on his face didn't mirror the self-satisfaction he felt at the moment. He knew his hopes were for nothing when she straightened and folded her arms across her chest, giving him an arch look.

"You, Mr. Taylor, are much too sure of yourself."

"Only about some things."

She speared him with a look that said he shouldn't be so sure about what he thought he knew. "Good night, Garrett." She turned and sauntered through the kitchen door.

Garrett rubbed the back of his neck, watching the kitchen door swing back and forth in the wake of her departure. Either she was going to have to grow some more, or he was going to end up with a permanent crick in his neck.

He went back to the sink, washed his dishes, and put

them in the drainboard. Then he followed Elise's advice and headed back to bed.

Elise went back to her room, closed the door behind her, and leaned her back against it. Her body still tingled and when she ran her tongue along her bottom lip, it was him she tasted. So much for her promise to her mother to stay away from him.

She honestly hadn't intended to meet him in the kitchen. Her brother, Michael, was the family night owl and she a light sleeper. Often the two of them met up in the kitchen for a late-night snack. She would have stayed in her own bed had she known that Garrett, not Michael, had gone downstairs in search of food.

Elise sighed. It didn't help to know that her mother had been right, as usual, both about Garrett's intentions and her reaction to him. When she'd found him sitting there in a T-shirt and a pair of sweatpants, her breath had caught in her throat. She'd never seen him that bare before; only imagined the muscles that bulged in his arms or the breadth of his chest delineated by the tight clothing.

The way he looked at her, his gaze hot and probing, had stirred an answering warmth in her belly. She'd known at that moment that if she wanted to keep her word to her mother, she'd better make a hasty retreat to her room. But she hadn't. She'd stayed, daring him to follow through on the promise she'd seen in his eyes.

She'd claimed she was going to bed to see what he would do. It hadn't surprised her that he'd kissed her, but her own reaction *had* shocked her. She knew what people called her behind her back: the Ice Woman, Miss Untouchable, Frosty the Snowwoman. It had never bothered her before, because she'd believed those things about herself, that inside she was cold and unmovable.

No one had ever made her feel like Garrett had in that one brief kiss: hot, flushed, excited, and incomplete. Hearing him groan, she'd pulled away from him, fearing that if he'd wanted more, she would have gladly given it to him. Frosty the Snowwoman would have melted right there on her mother's kitchen floor. Thankfully, he'd joked with her and let her salvage a little bit of her pride.

Suddenly the light beside Daphne's bed flickered on. When her eyes adjusted, Elise saw Daphne in bed, leaning up on her elbows. "How quaint. Moonlit trysts in Mom's kitchen. She'll love that."

"She'll never know anything about it, unless you tell her."

"She won't hear it from me. I just wanted to tell you, as guys go, Garrett's okay."

Daphne clicked off the light and Elise heard the rustle of covers as Daphne settled down in bed.

Elise closed her eyes and leaned her head back against the door. She didn't bother to suppress the laughter that bubbled up inside her. Daphne actually liked a man? What on earth could happen next?

Six

All in all, the weekend hadn't gone too badly, Garrett mused as he stowed his bag and Elise's in the trunk of the car Sunday morning. Thanksgiving dinner had been a treat, full of good conversation, great food, and a pervasive feeling of family that had warmed him more than the hot apple crisp that had been served for dessert.

But never, not for one moment, had he been left alone with Elise again. He'd bet the entire household knew about the kiss they had shared that first night. While he sensed they didn't disapprove of him, they weren't going to let him make any time with her, either.

And in their own way, each of them had warned him about the consequences should he do anything to hurt Elise. The most creative had been Daphne's concerning certain bodily parts no longer being part of his body. A chilling prospect, since among all of the Thornes, she alone seemed bloodthirsty enough to carry out the threat. He leaned against the hood of his car, watching Elise and her mother embrace at the curb.

"Thanks for everything, Mom." Elise stepped back and both women turned to face him.

Elise said, "I guess we better go."

He straightened and opened the car door for her. She slid inside and fastened her seat belt.

He turned to Elise's mother, intending to thank her for her hospitality. No matter that her husband earned the family bread, Camille Thorne was its heart. They all deferred to her, even Elise's father, Jasper. He couldn't imagine this family functioning without her.

She surprised him by embracing him warmly. "You take care of yourself," she said, stepping away. She looked up at him in a way that said, *And my daughter, too.*

"I will. Thanks again for having me." He got into the car beside Elise and revved the engine. "Ready?" he asked.

"Ready."

Garrett pulled away from the curb.

Two hours later, Garrett looked over at Elise. She hadn't said much after they'd left New York. She held her sketch pad on her lap, but she hadn't opened it. She stared out the passenger-side window as if fascinated, but frankly the scenery wasn't that interesting.

"Did I do something to upset you?"

She turned and looked at him as if she'd just realized he sat next to her in the car. "No, of course not." She lowered her head. "I was just thinking."

"What about?"

"My family."

"Didn't we see them a couple of hours ago?"

"Yes." A self-deprecating smile curved her lips. "It's funny, I love the freedom I have at school, and half the time I'm home, I can't wait to get back. But then I miss being able to go to my mother's room to talk, or share late-night snacks with my brother, Michael. As much of a pain in the neck as Daphne's been lately, I'm going to miss her, too." She looked away from him. "I guess it's the same old story. The grass being greener on the other side."

He nodded, but he had no idea how she felt. When he'd left home to go to college, he hadn't looked back. The only time he'd returned to his aunt's house had been for her funeral. He'd been absolutely amazed to find that the old bat had somehow squirreled away sixty thousand dollars, considering the spartan way she lived.

That money could have paid his tuition at a decent four-year college without him having to rely on an athletic scholarship. But she'd left every cent of it, as well as the deed to her house, to her church. The insurance money barely covered her burial and the cab ride back from the cemetery.

He reached over and took her hand, lacing his fingers with hers. He acknowledged the contact was more for his sake than for hers. He acknowledged his need for connectedness, especially with her. He stroked her palm with his thumb.

She glanced up at him, her eyebrows arched. "What are you doing?"

"Holding your hand."

"You're supposed to be driving."

He grinned. "I can do both. I'm a man of many talents."

She pulled her hand from his. "Don't worry. I'm not going to fall apart or anything stupid like that." She fished a pencil out of her handbag, then opened her sketchbook. She began to draw, effectively shutting him out again.

* * *

Elise closed her sketchbook as Garrett pulled up in front of her dorm. She'd spent the last half hour drawing his hands, big hands that had made her tremble when he'd held hers. She'd also spent the last half hour thinking about him and what each of them wanted, and she'd come to a decision.

Although after that first night, they hadn't spent a moment alone together, she'd been with him almost every minute. She'd watched him and seen the ease with which he fit into her family. Both her mother and Daphne had voiced approval of him, and once her father found out he majored in biology, he'd invited Garrett into his study to see all the icky things the rest of the family avoided like the bubonic plague. Even Michael, the self-appointed defender of his sisters' virtue, had informed her that Garrett was okay.

And sometimes, when Garrett looked at her, she wished that they were back in the family kitchen and she'd waited to find out what forbidden thing he would have done. If she didn't watch herself, she'd do more than melt, she'd fall for him, and falling in love with anyone definitely did not fit into her plans.

She released her seat belt. "Thanks for the ride, Garrett. I guess I'd better head up."

He unlatched his own seat belt. "I'll walk you."

She'd come to a decision, but she didn't want to share it with him yet. "There's no need."

She got out of the car, going around to the trunk. He followed her, opened the trunk, and pulled out her bag, but he didn't hand it to her. "I'll walk you up," he repeated.

She should have known she wouldn't get rid of him that easily. She shrugged and walked ahead of him toward the building. They got on the elevator and rode to the fourth floor in silence. When they got to her door, she reached for her bag, but Garrett held it away from her.

"Aren't you going to invite me in?"

She shook her head. "I don't want to give you the wrong impression."

"What impression is that?"

"That anything could develop between us."

"Then why did you let me kiss you?"

"I shouldn't have let you do that." She reached for her bag again, but he pulled it back out of her reach.

"But you did. Why?"

"I was curious."

"About what?"

Glancing up at him, she pressed her lips together. He couldn't let her off the hook, could he? Not before she told him everything. Well, she supposed he did deserve an answer from her. "I wanted to know if I'd feel anything if you kissed me."

"And did you?"

Heat stole into her cheeks, and an answering warmth flooded her belly. His expression turned smug, and she knew that even if she lied and said no he'd never believe her. "Yes."

"Then what's the problem?"

"I'm not looking for a serious relationship."

"What makes you think I am? Maybe all I want is a little of the aforementioned ravishment?"

He was teasing her. Either that or he had not one ounce of self-awareness. If all he wanted was sex, there were a hundred other girls on campus who'd be willing to oblige him. He wouldn't need to try to win her over. If that's all he wanted, he wouldn't have stopped at one kiss in her parents' kitchen. He would have tried to see how much he could get away with before she shut him down. He couldn't even break up with a woman properly. Any other man would have told Tanya so long and moved on after their physical relationship had soured. He cared enough about her to remain her friend.

"Whether or not you want to admit it, Garrett, you are the commitment type, and I don't want to be tied down."

His jaw tightened and his hand flexed at his side. "I see." He set her bag down at her feet. "Thanks for Thanksgiving dinner. See you around, Elise."

He turned away from her, heading toward the stairs rather than the elevator. Part of her wanted to call to him, to tell him to come back. She'd made him angry, though she hadn't intended to. But she'd been sending him mixed signals since they'd met, and the time had come for her to stop.

She got out her key and inserted it into the lock, but the door swung open when she tried to turn it. The sight that greeted her made her mouth drop open and her throat clog. Finally she got out one word. *"Garrett!"*

Annoyed with himself, Garrett pushed through the stairway door and drew up short. Could he possibly have handled things worse with Elise? He shouldn't have snapped at her. He couldn't fault her for seeing into him more clearly than he would have liked. He did want more from her than just a friendly roll in the hay. He didn't know exactly what that more was, but it didn't matter. He would never try to force the issue with her. At least she hadn't told him she wanted them to be friends.

He started down the stairs, but he hadn't taken more than three steps before he heard Elise scream his name. He raced up the stairs and into her open apartment. He almost bumped into her, as she stood just inside the door, her hands covering her open mouth. All around her was chaos. The entire room had been trashed. Clothing, toiletries, books littered the floor. Elise's pillows had been slashed and their contents strewn all over the room.

"Elise?"

She turned wide, horror-filled eyes to him. "Who would do such a thing?"

One word formed in his mind: *Randy*. Randy, who wanted to pay Elise back for spurning him. Of course, Randy wouldn't have bothered to do it himself. He'd probably paid someone else to do his dirty work. Garrett kept his opinions to himself, not wanting to scare her.

"Probably somebody looking for money or something to sell." He hoped his words didn't sound as hollow as they felt. Even if someone had tried to rob her, they didn't need to do so much damage. "Don't touch anything. We ought to call campus security and the police."

She nodded and followed him into the hallway.

Both the police and campus security were nonchalant about the incident. More than twenty dorm rooms had been broken into, so they weren't going to break their necks trying to find out who'd been in this particular one. The police left, asking Elise to compile a list of missing items for them to investigate.

Once they were alone again, Elise stood in the center of the room, surveying the damage. "I don't even know where to start."

"I'll help you."

She turned to face him. "You don't have to do that."

He smiled, as her words lacked any conviction whatsoever. "Yes, I do." He bent and picked up what turned out to be one of her nightgowns. "This could prove interesting. What the rest of the world doesn't know about Elise Thorne."

She snatched the gown away from him. "Don't get any ideas, if I let you stay."

That bit of advice came too late. He'd already imagined her in that short black nightie, and the picture didn't appear to want to fade anytime soon. "I'll help you clean up; then I'll go."

For a moment she looked like she would protest, but she also looked absolutely spent, and in the end she let him stay.

Three hours later, the room was presentable, if not actually clean. They'd discovered that nothing had been taken, except for every article that Michelle owned. Apparently she'd taken the holiday weekend to move out. But neither Garrett nor Elise believed Michelle had made such a mess of the room. Elise hadn't voiced the suspicion, but he wondered if it had occurred to her that Randy might be responsible.

Reluctantly, Garrett reached for his jacket. "I guess I'd better go."

Elise stood by the door, her lips pressed together, her eyes large and uncertain. She folded her arms in front of her. "I guess so."

He didn't want to leave her, but he didn't want to press his luck, either. "I could stay if you wanted me to."

"Would you?"

He couldn't have resisted the plea in her liquid amber eyes if he'd wanted to. "Tell you what, I'm starving. Call Tony's and order us a pizza. I'll pick it up and come back with my bag. Will you be all right while I'm gone?"

She nodded. "You don't mind?"

He touched his fingertips to her cheek. "I'll be right back."

He left, admonishing her to lock the door and not open it for anyone but him. He stopped by his apartment before he went back to her room, grabbed the pillows off his bed and a couple of blankets.

By the time he got back to her room, she'd changed into a pair of sweatpants and an oversize T-shirt and had pulled her hair back into a ponytail. She didn't look more than sixteen years old.

She took the pizza from him, and he set his bags on the floor. They ate sitting on the freshly vacuumed carpet using her bed as a backrest. Or rather, Garrett ate and Elise picked the cheese off her slice. She looked so tired, she threatened to keel over into the pizza box any second.

"It's time we got you into bed, young lady. It's nearly midnight and we both have to go to class tomorrow morning."

Thankfully, she didn't argue with him. He helped her to her feet, pulled back the covers on her bed, and waited until she'd lain down to cover her.

"Good night, sweetheart." He leaned down to place a soft kiss on her forehead. When he started to pull away, she grabbed his arm. He sat on the bed beside her.

She gazed up at him with heavy-lidded eyes. "Why are you being so nice to me?"

"Just my warped personality, I guess."

She lifted her hand and cupped his cheek. "It's not warped, it's sweet."

He took her hand and laid it on top of her covers. "And you're so tired you don't know what you're talking about."

"Yup."

"Elise Thorne says, 'Yup.' " He moved his hand as if he were demonstrating a headline. "Story on page six."

"I am not that, um . . . uptight, am I?"

"You, never." He ran a finger along her cheekbone. "Now go to sleep."

"Garrett?"

He looked down into her troubled eyes. "Yes, sweetheart?"

"I'm scared."

"Don't be. Whoever did this is probably harmless."

"I mean, of you. You're the only man who's ever really liked me, ever really been nice to me."

He brushed a stray hair away from her face. "And that scares you?"

She nodded. "I don't want to fall in love with you."

"Is that a possibility?"

She didn't say anything for a long time, and he held his breath wondering what she would say. Finally she opened her eyes and looked directly at him. "Yes."

He didn't know what to say to that bit of honesty, especially since she'd probably given him that answer only because she lacked the energy to lie. He supposed he should feel guilty for questioning her at such a vulnerable time. Instead, relief washed through him, realizing that she pushed him away not from disinterest, as he feared, but the opposite emotion. It would have to do for now.

"Go to sleep, Elise. We'll talk in the morning."

She turned away from him and rested her head on her folded hands. He sat there a few minutes, until her breathing evened out and he was sure she slept. Then he got up and changed into a pair of sweatpants, arranged his blankets on the floor beside her bed, and settled down. He'd just closed his eyes when she called his name.

"Garrett?"

"Yes?"

"Thank you."

He snorted. "You're welcome." He turned on his side and instantly fell asleep.

The next morning, when Elise awoke, Garrett had already gone. She couldn't blame him. After all she'd put him through last night, she wouldn't be surprised if he never spoke to her again. She squeezed her eyes shut, remembering how she'd confessed to him her fear of falling in love with him. Well, considering his hasty departure, she didn't suppose she ought to worry about that too much. Right about now, he probably thought she was a kook anyway.

Elise got out of bed and padded over to the mini-refrigerator in the corner. It contained nothing but some old milk she wasn't brave enough to drink. They'd thrown out whatever food she'd hoarded in the room, since they couldn't be sure it hadn't been tampered with. If she wanted breakfast, she'd have to go out for it.

She shed her sweatpants on the way to the bathroom and reached for the hem of her top to yank it over her head when she heard a key turn in her lock. Automatically she got into a stance to protect herself. A second later, Garrett pushed the door open.

"Whoa! It's only me."

Instantly, her body relaxed, but her mind went on alert. Garrett had come back? Why? Then she noticed the white paper bag he held in his hands.

"I got us some breakfast." He deposited the bag and

her keys on her desk. "All things considered, you might want to put on some clothes before you eat it."

She looked down at herself and the top that barely covered her panties and exposed her legs. "I'll be right back.

She showered quickly and dressed in a pair of black slacks and a white Oxford shirt, then put on her usual makeup before leaving the bathroom. When she came out, Garrett was sitting on her bed, reading the local paper, a cup of coffee in his hand.

She crossed to the desk and picked up her coffee. "Don't you have a class this morning?" she asked.

He lowered the paper. "Are you trying to get rid of me already? I haven't finished my coffee."

He seemed more amused than offended. "Not at all. I just don't want you to miss a class because of me." She brought the cup to her lips. The coffee was sweet and still warm, just the way she liked it. "Anything interesting in the paper?"

"There's an article on the break-ins. As usual, campus security has no idea who was behind them." Garrett tossed aside the paper and stood. "If you're ready, I'll walk you to class."

Her first class was in the Tisch Building on the far end of campus. Garrett decided against driving there, as what little parking surrounded the building was reserved for faculty. Garrett left the car parked in front of Elise's dorm and the two of them set out on foot.

Several faux marble steps led up to the glass-and-steel building. Although a crowd of students milled around the front of the building, Garrett noticed Randy right away, leaning against the wall by the entrance. There was no doubt in his mind that he waited there for Elise. What the hell did he want? Surely not to confess his part in having Elise's room trashed.

Garrett took Elise's arm, grateful he'd followed his instinct to go with her to class. He hadn't told her that the paper had reported that in all cases but hers, several valuable items had been stolen. He was more sure now than ever that Randy had been behind the break-in.

As they moved toward the door, Randy stepped in their path. Garrett narrowed his eyes, glaring at his teammate. "What do you want, Fletcher?"

Randy ignored him, focusing on Elise. "I heard you were one of the people who got robbed over vacation. I wanted to make sure you were all right."

"You didn't have to do that. I'm fine."

Randy looked up at him, grinning, though his eyes were cold as glass. "If I'd known you had Taylor here looking out for you, I wouldn't have bothered."

Elise opened her mouth to speak, but Garrett squeezed her elbow before she got anything out. "Why don't you go on up? I'll see you later."

She looked like she might protest, but she slid past Randy and went inside the building. When he was sure she was gone, he turned to Randy. "You shouldn't have bothered trashing her room, either."

Randy held up his hands as if in surrender. "I had nothing to do with that. I was up in Connecticut with my folks."

"I'm sure you were. I'm sure you had someone else dirty their hands for you."

"You'll never prove that."

Garrett noted Randy didn't deny his involvement this time, only claimed Garrett wouldn't be able to prove it. Garrett didn't need proof, as he didn't intend to involve campus authorities anyway. Randy he could handle on his own.

"I'm only going to say this once. Stay away from her."

Randy's expression grew smug. "And what if I don't? What are you going to do about it?"

Garrett stood three inches taller than Randy and out-weighed him by fifty pounds. He leaned closer to Randy and whispered in a deadly voice, "Believe me, you don't want to find out."

He pushed past Randy and went inside the building to find Elise.

Three days later, Elise opened her door to find Garrett on the other side, waiting for her. He'd waited for her every morning since the break-in, walked her to class, and picked her up when it finished. Those times he couldn't be with her, he sent some other behemoth to follow her around. Two days ago, she'd noticed a giant of a man following her. She'd waited until she was inside the crowded student union to turn around and confront him. After some coercion, he'd confessed that Garrett had sent him to watch over her.

Now Garrett stood in front of her, a grin on his face. "Ready?" he asked.

She leaned on one hip and glared at him. "This has got to stop."

Suddenly, his eyes held a stubborn intensity that told her he would not back down. "I told you, I don't want you to be alone."

He hadn't said so in words, but she knew he thought Randy was responsible for the break-in. Even if that were true, he couldn't follow her around forever. "I can take care of myself."

"I know you can, but you shouldn't have to."

She couldn't argue with him on that, so she said noth-ing. She locked her door and, ignoring him, headed toward the elevators. He followed her, crowding her into the corner of the tiny elevator car.

Didn't he realize he made things worse for her instead of better? Despite her complaints, his diligent protection of her softened something inside her she wanted to remain hard and unyielding. He terrified her more than anything Randy might do.

"You don't need to bother bringing me home tonight."

"Why not?"

"I have a date." She glanced up at him to gauge his reaction.

He continued to stare up at the light panel. "Really? With whom?"

He probably wondered how she'd managed to arrange a date with anyone with his constant surveillance of her. But hearing the strain in his voice, the urge to tell him she didn't have a date at all welled up inside her. She was meeting a classmate for coffee to discuss a group project for class.

"A friend," she answered, finally.

"Have a good time." He stepped off the elevator and waited for her to do the same, but he didn't look at her. Feeling unaccountably saddened, she started off for class with Garrett silent beside her.

As usual for a Thursday night, the coffee shop was crowded and noisy.

"You want to get out of here?" Steve, Elise's companion, asked. "Where do you want to go?"

He was the lone man in her art history class whom everyone swore had to be gay. Elise wasn't taking any chances. "Someplace public."

"We could go over to the student union. There's some

sort of party going on there. If we get bored with this stuff"—he pointed to their books—"we can go dance."

Elise shrugged, seeing no harm in that. On a party night, the crowd at the union rivaled the one at the coffee shop. Besides, the union had a guard on duty twenty-four hours.

But when they got to the building, it appeared deserted, except for the guard sitting at the front desk. Looking sheepish, Steve said, "I guess the party must be tomorrow night."

"Must be."

Steve sighed heavily. "Part of the reason I wanted to come here is that I left a book of mine in the chess room earlier today. I tell you what. You wait here and I'll go get it. Then we'll figure out where to go." He started walking toward the elevators that would take him to the club rooms on the third floor.

Elise sighed, letting her shoulders droop. What was she being so cautious about? Steve stood only a few inches taller than she did and made a stick look like a redwood tree trunk. And anyone who belonged to the chess club had to be a nerd. "Steve, wait," she called. "I'll go with you."

The chess club occupied the last room on the north corridor of the building. Something about the silence of the building and the darkened corridors made the hair on the back of Elise's neck bristle. She'd forgotten that the rooms up here were soundproofed, as some of the clubs held parties the other clubs didn't want to hear. Anything could go on up there and no one would be the wiser.

Elise stopped, intending to turn back. She glanced over her shoulder. The elevator doors still stood open, and she intended to get back on it. Without looking at him, she said, "Steve, I ch—"

"Don't tell me you're leaving so soon."

Elise froze, hearing Randy's voice. She turned to find him standing just inside the chess-room door. She looked over at Steve, who refused to return her gaze. Contempt for him combined with fear for herself clogged her chest, making it difficult to breathe. "How could you?" she asked.

"Get out of here," Randy commanded. With one apologetic glance at Elise, Steve slunk toward the nearby staircase and disappeared through the door.

Now completely alone with Randy, she drew herself to her full height. With more bravado than she felt, she faced him and asked, "What do you want, Randy?"

"I've been waiting to get you alone without that guard dog of yours trailing behind you."

"I don't need a guard. How's your head doing?"

Automatically, his hand went to the spot he'd hit on the pavement. When he realized what he'd done, he straightened. "You won't need to practice your self-defense techniques on me. I just want to talk."

She believed that like she believed in the Tooth Fairy. "So talk."

"Couldn't we do that sitting down? I promise, I'll sit across the room."

She let her gaze rove over Randy, while she assessed her options. She'd heard the elevator doors close behind her, and as slow as that thing moved, he'd definitely catch up to her before it returned. The stairs offered no better option. If he overtook her there, it would be as bad as being alone with him here. But every room in the building had a silent alarm that fed into the security desk downstairs. If she could trip it, she'd be all right.

"You'll sit across the room?" she asked, pretending to acquiesce.

He crossed his heart. "I promise."

On shaky legs she walked toward him. He moved aside and let her pass.

"Sit over here." He indicated a black leather sofa against the wall.

She sat on the edge of the sofa, searching the room for the alarm button, while Randy closed the door and took a seat across the room on a rolling chair. He leaned back, and she noticed the button on the wall—right over his left shoulder.

Elise bit her lip. She'd have to give him credit for being more clever than she'd thought. Well, she was no slouch in that area herself. She pasted a smile on her face. "So what did you want to talk to me about?"

One corner of his mouth lifted in an evil grin. "How long did it take you and loverboy to clean up your room?"

"You are the one who had my room destroyed, aren't you?" In answer, he shrugged, but he didn't deny it. On an instinctive level, she'd always known that Randy had been responsible. She'd never expected him to admit it, though.

"I was angry. I saw you get into Taylor's car Wednesday morning. I really cared about you, but you threw me over for him. He's nothing."

"He's more man than you'll ever hope to be." Elise pressed her lips together, wishing she'd kept her mouth shut. Randy's eyes narrowed and he slowly rose from his seat.

"Maybe it's time we found out."

Seven

Garrett sat at the back of the coffee shop, drowning his misery in a cup of cold coffee that he could no longer taste. Someone was talking to him, droning on, but he paid no attention.

When Elise told him she had a date tonight, he knew she'd come here. During the week, there were only two places to go: Tony's or the coffee shop. Knowing her, he knew she'd pick here.

So he'd come here after his last class and watched her walk in with Steve. Instantly, he'd known this was no date—not one ounce of chemistry crackled between those two. She'd lied to him to make him angry or get rid of him. She'd accomplished both. When she'd left with Steve, he hadn't bothered to follow.

But two seconds ago, Steve had come back in—alone. He seemed nervous, and when he went to pay for his coffee, he dropped his change on the floor. He hadn't been gone long enough to make it to her dorm, let alone make it back. If Steve was here, where the hell was Elise?

Ignoring the curious looks of those around him when he suddenly rose to his feet, Garrett walked toward the front of the store. Steve still stood at the condiment stand, adding milk to his coffee.

Without preamble, Garrett asked, "Where's Elise?"

Steve looked up at him, and Garrett saw fear in the other man's eyes. "She wanted to leave."

"Where to?"

"She—I—"

Wherever she'd disappeared to, Elise was in trouble, that much he knew. "Where is she?" When he didn't answer, Garrett grabbed him by the throat. "Tell me, or they'll need a vacuum cleaner to pick you up off the floor."

"Randy asked me to bring her to the student union."

Garrett released him, shoving him back against the wall. "And you did it?"

"He's my cousin. I didn't know why he wanted me to bring her there."

But Garrett supposed he'd figured it out by now. Steve wouldn't look him in the face, but he said in a quiet voice, "If I were you, I'd get over there now. They're in the chess-club room."

"Do something right. Call campus security and let them know where she is."

Garrett sprinted the two blocks to the student union. Thoughts of Randy touching Elise, hurting her, haunted him. He should have followed her when she'd left the coffee shop. Randy had just about promised he would try something. But he'd let his guard down because she'd hurt him. He hoped Elise didn't pay too dear a price for his lapse in vigilance.

Arriving at the student union, Garrett headed directly for the stairs to the right of the deserted security desk. He took the stairs two at a time. When he reached the third floor, his lungs burned and his muscles ached, but he didn't care. He burst through the door, then stopped short.

Randy lay on the floor, his hands between his legs,

cupping his groin. Elise stood over him, breathing heavily, but apparently unhurt. He must have missed Randy's emasculation by a few seconds. He should have known Elise wouldn't have let Randy do anything to her without a fight.

"Garrett," Elise said, and she ran to him, jumped into his waiting arms, and tightened her arms around his neck.

He hugged her to him, stroking his hands over her back, feeling her tremble. With one hand, he tilted her face up so that he could look at her. "Are you all right?"

She nodded. "I'm fine. What are you doing here?"

"I came to find you. Steve told me where you were."

She buried her face in the side of his neck. "I was so stupid to trust him."

From the corner of his eye, he saw Randy rise to a sitting position. As long as Elise was okay, he had another matter to attend to.

He set her on her feet. "Go downstairs and find the security guard."

Her eyes scanned his face. "Why? What are you going to do?"

His eyes on Randy, he pushed her behind him. "Just go."

"I didn't touch her, man." Randy got to his feet, his gaze focused on Elise. "Tell him, I didn't touch you."

"Only because I didn't give you the chance."

"Damn it, Elise," Garrett said. "Do what I told you."

"You want me to leave so that you can bash his head in."

He nodded. "That was the plan."

"Well, I won't do it. As much as I'd like to see his face rearranged, he's not worth it, Garrett. You know the college will never tolerate you going after him, no matter the reason. You'll lose your scholarship, you'll lose everything. Please, Garrett, he's not worth it."

Garrett sighed. She was right and he knew it. The coach as well as the school had a very strict antiviolence policy. He'd have to console himself with the fact that if any justice existed in the world, Randy would be expelled and that would solve the problem right there.

He cupped Elise's cheek in his palm. "All right, you win."

"Thank you." She smiled, and then her eyes widened.

He turned to find an elevator full of police and security guards descending on them, and in the midst of them was Steve. Elise immediately stepped in front of him. Garrett grabbed her around the waist and held onto her. "If I can't get expelled, then neither can you."

She relaxed against him, nodding. "You can let me go."

Undaunted, Steve came over to her. "I'm sorry about tricking you. I didn't realize what Randy was up to. I hope he didn't hurt you."

"No. And thanks for bringing the cavalry."

They all looked over at Randy, who'd already been handcuffed. One of the police officers informed her that she would have to come down to the station if she wanted to press charges.

An hour later, after Elise had recounted her story to the police's satisfaction, Garrett walked her home.

"What do you think will happen?" she asked him.

"Who knows? As Officer Simpson said, he didn't actually do anything to you. I don't think they'll make a criminal charge stick, but he'll probably be expelled, unless Daddy's money buys him out of this one, too."

She nodded and fell silent. He couldn't stand it anymore, this ability she had to completely lock him out.

He grabbed her hand and led her to a nearby bench. He sat and pulled her down beside him.

"Why do you keep shutting me out?"

She lifted her head and looked at him. "I beg your pardon."

"I need to know. Why do you keep shutting me out? One minute you run to me for protection, the next you won't even look at me. What are you afraid I'm going to do to you?"

"It's not you. It's me. I don't want to end up like my mother."

"Your mother? She seems completely content to me."

"Now, maybe. But a lifetime ago, she was a promising pianist."

"And what happened? She got married and your father expected her to stay home?"

"No. She still used to tour, and when my dad could he would join her."

"Then what?"

"I came along. When my mother found out she was pregnant with me, she gave up her career."

"Did she ever tell you that she minded making that sacrifice?"

"No, but I would watch her. Sometimes we'd go to concerts and she'd get this wistful look in her eyes, like she wondered what she could have accomplished if she hadn't quit."

"What has that got to do with us?"

"Are you planning to accept the offer to play pro next year?"

"No, I'm not."

He half expected her to tell him he was crazy to give up such a lucrative prospect, but that didn't seem to faze her a bit.

"Then don't you see, Garrett? You'll graduate next

year and go to medical school. If anything, you'll need a wife that works to support you, and I've got three more years of school, at least. Interior design isn't brain surgery, but it has its place in the world, and it's important to me. I wouldn't want to give it up only to wonder later what my life would have been if I'd stuck it out."

He didn't bother to tell her that he would never ask her to make such a sacrifice. Despite the strange logic of her argument, he doubted reason would reach her now.

He cupped her shoulder in his palm. "Sweetheart, you seem to have our whole lives planned, and we haven't had one real date."

She brushed his hand away. "You're making fun of me."

"No, I'm not. But couldn't we start with going to the movies Saturday night and work our way up to a mortgage and two-point-three kids?"

She laughed and hit him on the shoulder. "I guess."

She looked up at him, a hopeful smile on her lips. He ran his thumb along her lower lip. "Would I be completely out of line if I told you I wanted to kiss you now?"

She didn't say anything, but her lips parted and her eyes drifted shut. He lowered his head and touched his lips to hers. That's all he'd wanted, but once he'd tasted her, it wasn't enough. He slid his tongue over her lips to mate with hers. She moaned and kissed him back, rubbing her tongue against his in a way that made his body harden and his resolve weaken.

He pulled away from her while he still had the chance. "I'd better get you home." Together they headed to her dorm.

When Garrett pushed open the door to Elise's room,

they found Michelle waiting on Elise's bed. As soon as she saw them, she rose to her feet and approached them.

"Where have you been? They've been trying to reach you all afternoon."

"It's a long story. Who's been looking for me?"

"There's been an accident at home. Your mother is in the hospital."

Elise took a step back, her hands rising to cover her mouth. "Oh, my God! How bad?"

"I don't know. But your father wants you to come home right away."

Jasper Thorne didn't strike Garrett as an intemperate man. If he called Elise home, the seriousness of her mother's condition warranted it.

After all she'd been through that day, he expected Elise to collapse or, at the very least, fall apart. She did neither. She got her bag from the closet and started packing. She moved with the stiff, brittle movements of an automaton. Garrett hesitated to leave her, if only to get a few of his belongings together.

"I'm going with you. It's too late to get a flight to New York until tomorrow morning. I'll drive you."

"Garrett—" she started to protest, but he refused to listen to any of it. He got Michelle to stay with Elise until he returned. First he went to find Coach Thompson to tell him what had happened and to let him know he'd probably be gone a few days. Then he went to his apartment to pack a few things. When he got back to Elise's dorm, she was pacing the room, ready to go.

The drive to New York was excruciating. Tired and worried, both for Elise and her mother, he wished Elise would sleep. Instead, she stared out the window as silent and still as a stone.

When they got to the hospital, they found out Elise's mother had been struck by a hit-and-run driver earlier that day. She'd suffered massive internal injuries and hadn't been expected to hold on as long as she had.

A few minutes after they arrived, Jasper came out of his wife's room to find Elise. "Your mother wants to see you now."

Elise walked on unsteady legs toward her mother's room. Daphne told her that their mother had been banged up pretty badly, but Elise was unprepared for the sight of her mother bruised and bloodied by the accident. She sat in the chair beside her mother's bed, taking one of her mother's hands in both of hers. After all she'd been through that night, she couldn't hold herself together any longer. She lowered her head as tears began to seep from beneath her lashes.

Her mother squeezed her hand. "I have something to tell you, Elise, and I want you to listen."

Elise wiped her eyes and lifted her head. "Yes, Mom."

"I know you think otherwise, but I've never regretted my decision to stay home with you children. It had always been what I planned. My dream had been to play at Carnegie Hall, and I'd done that. Anything else was gravy. I've always been grateful your father made enough money that we could afford to give our children everything we wanted without too many sacrifices.

"I lived my life exactly the way I wanted. I have no regrets, except that I won't see you children grow up and get married or hold my grandbabies. But life never offered me any guarantees about that anyway."

Elise squeezed her eyes shut. How could her mother be so matter-of-fact about her own death? Despite seeing her mother, Elise couldn't grasp the reality of it.

"How about the Steinway? You always wanted a grand piano."

Her mother smiled. "A pipe dream, that's all. We had more important things to spend money on, like braces and summer camp and college. Where would I have put it, anyway?"

"How about in Dad's study, next to the formalde-hyde-filled jars of God-knows-what."

"Then I would have had an even harder time getting you children to practice."

Camille turned her head to look at her daughter. "Promise me something, Elise."

"Anything."

"Don't be so afraid of life. Grab your opportunities when you can. That's the only way to live your life without second-guessing every choice you make."

"I promise."

"I love you, Elise. Always remember that."

"I know, Mom. I love you, too. I—" Elise broke off as a look of intense pain flashed across her mother's face.

"Please send your father in. I'm feeling very tired."

Garrett watched Elise walk from her mother's room. She stopped by where her father stood. "Mom wants to talk to you."

Then she walked to Garrett and laid her cheek against his chest. "Hold me, Garrett," she whispered.

He wrapped his arms around her, holding her close. "How is she?" he asked.

"Tired."

And a few minutes later, she was gone.

He'd once wondered how this family would cope without their matriarch, and in fact, they couldn't. Jasper was disconsolate in his grief; Michael was so consumed with rage, it was impossible to talk to him. Elise withdrew into silence. Only Daphne seemed capable of exhibiting an outer calm. That, Garrett supposed, might have something to do with the skinny kid who followed her around.

He could only hold onto one of them, and he wasn't going to let Elise go. He drove her back to school in time for finals, but neither of them got a grade above a C. And slowly, in the months that followed, Elise began to come back to herself. For spring break, he dipped into the money he'd saved from summer jobs and took her on vacation, hoping that finally she was ready to be part of life again.

Elise stood on the balcony of her hotel bedroom, staring out at the clear night sky. A warm breeze stirred the air, taunting her already overheated body. She thought taking a cold shower must be a euphemism for some other activity, because she'd bathed in frigid water and all it had done was pucker her skin.

At the other end of the suite, Garrett lay in bed, probably asleep already, oblivious to the fact that she was slowly burning up inside. He'd brought her to this Mexican paradise, claiming she'd have her own room. That's what he'd said, but she hadn't really believed him. She'd thought he'd brought her here as a means of taking her to his bed. If truth be told, she would have gone gladly. She loved him and wanted to be with him. She'd been shocked to discover when they'd arrived that he'd kept his word.

And he'd kept his hands off her the entire time. In the three days they'd been there, they'd swum together, snorkeled together, fished, sunbathed, and fallen asleep cuddling on the sofa together. But aside from a few unsatisfying kisses, he hadn't touched her any more here than he had in the past few months at school.

And she wanted him to want her, to ache the way she ached. She'd tried everything she knew to entice him. She'd flirted with him, complimented him, touched him in ways she never had at school. She'd gone to the gift shop and bought a new bikini that was little more than some dental floss with a couple of modesty panels attached. And still Garrett had been unmoved.

Somewhere in the distance, she heard a clock chime. Twelve bells—midnight. Only seven more hours before they boarded a plane headed for New York. Seven more hours before she went back home as much a virgin as she'd started out.

She remembered her mother's words about living life with no regrets. She would take matters into her own hands. Take a more direct approach. She shrugged off the jacket to the white peignoir set she wore, leaving only the sheer white gown beneath, fluffed out her hair, and strode to Garrett's door. Taking a deep breath for courage, she knocked.

A moment later the door opened. With a hand resting on the doorknob, he leaned against the door. He wore only the bottoms to a pair of black pajamas, leaving his chest bare. She sucked in her breath and focused on his face. His return gaze was hot enough to singe.

A hint of a smile lifted the corners of his mouth. "What can I do for you, Elise?"

She tilted her head to one side. "You know what I want."

"Tell me."

He couldn't make this easy for her, could he? "I want you to make love to me."

With trembling fingers she lifted her hands to her

shoulders and slid the spaghetti straps down her arms. The gown slithered silently to the carpet.

His gaze swept over her, and she gripped her fingers together, waiting for a response from him. Finally, his eyes focused on her face. He whispered one, rough syllable: "Damn."

She took a step toward him and leaned into him. "Kiss me, Garrett."

He did; then all she could think about was the feel of his mouth on hers, the play of his skin against hers. When he bent to lift her into his arms, she clung to him, kissing him with all the passion inside her.

He sat on the bed, positioning her so that she lay half on his pillows, half across his lap. His hand rested on her stomach, his fingers making lazy circles on her belly.

"Do you have any idea how beautiful you are?"

She shook her head, basking in his praise, but wanting to deny it also. Even she knew her body wasn't anything special. Too boyish, with small breasts and no hips to speak of. Or, as Michelle would say: "Dogs like bones; men like meat." And Elise didn't have any anywhere that counted.

"This isn't fair."

"What do you mean?"

"You've seen all of me, but I haven't seen all of you."

He lifted her legs from his lap and rose from the bed. He unsnapped his pajama pants, let them slide to the floor, and stepped out of them. "Is that better?"

Elise swallowed. She wasn't so naive that she didn't know what a naked man looked like. She'd even snuck a peek or two at Michelle's *Playgirl* magazines. She'd seen nearly all of him already in his swim trunks, all sinew and hard muscle. But she'd certainly never seen anyone so well endowed. Logically, she knew their bodies would fit together, but a small irrational part of her feared the unknown, feared he'd hurt her.

He cupped her face in his palms. "It'll be okay, Elise. I promise. Maybe not so much the first time, but after that, it'll get better. Do you trust me?"

"Yes." She did trust him, completely. He'd never hurt her intentionally, that she knew.

He kissed her then, and his hand covered her breast, molding the soft flesh in his palm. She moaned and shifted, trying to get closer to him.

"Take it easy, baby," he whispered against her ear. "We have all the time in the world."

His hand drifted to her other breast, cupping it to give him better access to her nipple. He swirled his tongue over the dark tip. A tempest began to coil in her belly, one that grew with every stroke of his tongue. She gasped as he drew her nipple into his hot, hot mouth and suckled her.

His hand trailed down her abdomen to tangle in the nest of light brown hair at the juncture of her thighs. "Open your legs for me, sweetheart."

She did, just enough for him to slide his hand between them. His fingers found her, circling over her sensitive, slick flesh. Her neck arched and she called his name.

"I'm here, sweetheart."

His hot breath fanned across her neck a moment before his lips touched down on the side of her throat. She inhaled, breathing in the musky, masculine scent of him. She couldn't seem to keep still. Her hips moved against his hand and tiny tremors wracked her legs.

"Garrett," she moaned, her back arching as he slid one finger inside her. He continued to stroke her with his thumb, making her writhe, making her ache.

"Baby, I need to be inside you."

She heard the breathlessness in his voice and smiled. She'd wanted him to want her, and he'd wiped away any doubt that he did. "Yes."

He pushed her legs farther apart and positioned himself over her. In one thrust he was inside her. She felt no pain, just the length and breadth of him filling her completely.

She wrapped her legs around him as he began to move inside her, slowly, deliberately. She opened her eyes and looked up into his smiling face.

"How are you feeling?" he asked.

She heard him laugh when she whispered, "Wonderful."

He leaned to one side and covered her breast with his palm. His hand circled downward, to stroke the core of sensitive flesh between her thighs. She gasped and arched against him as wave after wave of pure pleasure washed over her.

A second later she felt Garrett stiffen above her and groan deep in his chest. Then his whole body shook with the power of his release.

He rolled onto his back, taking her with him. One of his hands stroked her back, the other tangled in her hair.

"I'm sorry, sweetheart."

She lifted her head and stared down into his troubled face. "For what?"

"I hadn't planned to come inside you. I didn't wear a condom because I knew it would hurt you. But I didn't intend to get you pregnant the first time, either."

She leaned down and kissed his mouth. "It's okay, Garrett. It's the wrong time of the month for that."

"Are you sure?"

She poked him in the chest. "Now who's the worry-wart?" When his frown stayed firmly in place, she sobered. "Garrett, I love you. Whatever happens, we'll face it together, okay?"

He shook his head, chuckling. "Okay."

"What's so funny?"

"Do you realize that's the first time you told me you loved me?"

"Yes, I realize that. And I also realize you haven't said it back."

"I've told you that every day for the past four months. You haven't been paying attention."

Yes, he had, just not in words. She'd known all along that only a man who loved her would have stuck by her during all she'd put him through. "I love you, Garrett," she repeated. She had a lot of time to make up for.

Garrett straightened as the huddle broke for what he hoped was the last play of the game. They were down by fourteen, with no hope of recovery. Shading his eyes with his hand, he looked up into the stands to where Elise sat. On occasion, when they played at home, she came to watch him. He wished she'd stayed home this time. They'd stayed up the night before studying, talking, making love—everything but sleeping. If she were an eighth as tired as he was right now, she should have stayed in bed.

He'd never thought he'd miss Randy, but at least the guy could play ball. His replacement couldn't throw a pass worth anything—half the reason they were down by so much. But Randy's father's money hadn't proved sufficient to keep Randy from getting expelled, especially after what he'd done to Elise became public. Several other women stepped forward to say that Randy had tried the same kind of thing with them. Not all of them had been as lucky as Elise had. The Fletcher family fortune had managed to keep it out of the papers that their heir apparent was currently serving one to three in a minimum-security prison.

The center snapped the ball, and predictably, the QB handed the ball off to him. Garrett spied a hole in the line and headed through it. Out of nowhere, a slicing pain ripped through his leg and exploded out through his body. The next thing he knew, he lay flat on his back in the middle of the field. A face hovered over his—the opposition's new linebacker, a kid built like the love child of a Mack truck and a refrigerator.

"Hey, man, are you all right?"

The kid offered him a hand up, but when Garrett tried to put weight on his left leg, his head swam and nausea roiled in his stomach. He rolled back on the ground, squeezed his eyes shut, and tamped it down. It was embarrassing enough to be laid low by a freshman. He refused to add puking his guts up to it. He flexed his right hand, feeling leather beneath his fingertips. At least he'd managed to hold onto the ball.

Somewhere through the haze of pain and over the din of the crowd, Elise's voice, high-pitched and frightened, reached him. *"GARRETT!"*

And then she was beside him, her eyes wide and her hair wild around her face. For once she didn't look like she'd stepped off the pages of *Young Miss* magazine. He let go of the ball, lifted his hand and brushed her hair back from her face. "Sweetheart, you're not supposed to be on the field."

She knocked his hand away. "Shut up, you big idiot. The coach let me through. Are you hurt?"

If nothing on his body was broken, it should have been. His knee felt as if someone had set it on fire and put it out with a sledgehammer. The poking and prodding of the team's doc didn't help any, either. But he didn't want to worry her. "I just need to walk it off."

She hit him on the shoulder. "You aren't going anywhere, except on a stretcher."

Said stretcher arrived a few minutes later. As they began to wheel him off the field, he called to them to stop. He grabbed Elise's hand. "I have something to ask you."

She looked down at him with concerned eyes. "What is it?"

"Marry me, Elise?"

She shook her head and squeezed her eyes shut. "You're proposing to me *now?* You're out of your mind."

Maybe, but he needed to know while his future was uncertain. He needed to know that it was him she wanted, not the promise of either of the career paths that were open to him, or had been until a few minutes ago. He gave her hand a tug. "Answer me."

"Hell, no, I won't marry you." She whirled away from him, and for a moment he feared he'd angered her so much that she'd deserted him. But when they loaded him into the ambulance, he found her already waiting inside. Both of them ignored the ambulance attendant who climbed on behind him.

"I thought you'd left me."

"Of course not. I told you once that whatever happened, we'd face it together, didn't I?"

"Well, then you have the surgery instead of me, okay?"

"Very funny. I heard the doctor say he thinks you tore the ligaments in your leg. Are you in a lot of pain?"

"I passed pain ten minutes ago. I'm already into delirium."

"Oh, Garrett."

He wished he'd kept his mouth closed, seeing the tears well in Elise's eyes. "I'm fine, Lesi, really."

Those were the last words he spoke before the ambulance hit a bump in the road, jostling his leg. As darkness descended, he heard Elise say, "When he gets better, I'm going to kill him."

Night had fallen by the next time Garrett opened his eyes. He lay in a hospital bed, his back propped up, his leg in a cast from hip to toe. At some point someone told him he'd torn the anterior cruciate ligament in his leg, but no one had to tell him that he wouldn't be playing football again. Even with the speediest recovery, the college season would end before his cast came off. With that type of injury, he'd be lucky if he didn't walk with a limp for the rest of his life, never mind play pro. Oddly, having that avenue closed off to him didn't bother him as much as he would have thought.

"You're awake," he heard Elise say. Then he saw her, sitting in a chair across from his bed. She rose and came to sit beside him. "How are you feeling?"

"Did you get the number of the truck that hit me?"

"I believe it's twenty-three, and he's now on *my* hit list."

"I'd better warn him to watch out for his manhood around you." He could kick himself for reminding her of such an unpleasant episode. He took her hand. "I'm sorry, sweetheart. I shouldn't have brought that up."

"It's not that."

She said nothing for a moment, her head downcast. If he didn't know her better, he'd swear the pattern on his hospital gown fascinated her. Then she lifted her head and looked at him, her lips pressed together, her eyes troubled.

"What is it, baby?"

"I wasn't going to tell you this until you made your decision about what you wanted to do, but I spoke to my godfather about you."

"Who's your godfather?"

"The dean of admissions of the College of Physicians and Surgeons at Columbia."

Garrett's breath whistled out through his teeth. "What did you tell him about me?"

"That you would make a brilliant doctor one day and that I was in love with you. He's got a spot on the roster for you next year if you want to go."

"How can I be accepted to a school to which I didn't apply?" He hadn't bothered, knowing his grades weren't good enough to get in.

"Yes, you did. I filled out the papers and sent them in."

He let his head drop down to his chest. She'd done this for him, made sure he had the option to go to medical school, if he wanted it. And he knew that right now she worried he'd be angry with her for intervening on his behalf.

He tugged on a strand of her hair. "What about a scholarship?"

The corners of her mouth tilted upward. "I'm working on it."

He cupped her cheek in his palm. "Thank you." His hand slid around to capture her nape and pull her toward him. He brought her mouth down on his for a gentle kiss. "You'd do all that, but you won't marry me?"

"No. Not yet. We're too young, Garrett. I couldn't even drink champagne at my own wedding."

"That's the only reason?"

She nodded. "Ask me again after graduation. Mine, not yours."

She married him the New Year's Day after she got her diploma. Less than three months later, she'd found out she was pregnant with Alyssa. He would have preferred more time alone with Elise before they had children, but when he looked down at the little life they'd created, he knew it didn't matter. They were living the life they were meant to live.

The years had been wonderful, exasperating, exhausting, and the most fulfilling of his life. In all that time, he'd never doubted that their marriage would last forever. . . .

So how had things gotten to the point that he carried a book contract in his suitcase that he hadn't told her about, and she was so distant that the only smile she offered him was a plastic one designed to trick him into thinking everything was all right?

And how was he going to fix it?

Eight

"At one mile across and three miles wide, Milagro is one of the smallest islands in the Caribbean."

Elise glanced at the pilot-cum-tour guide who sat beside her in the red-and-white Cessna that brought them from Puerto Rico to its tiny southern neighbor. He'd kept up a steady stream of conversation during the twenty minutes they'd been in the air. She knew more about the island than she ever thought she wanted to know. Officially called *Isla de los Milagros,* Island of Miracles, its name had been anglicized over the years to Milagro Island. Milagro boasted lush vegetation and a wide assortment of indigenous fruit. The inhabitants, a mixture of Taino and Arawak Indians and the descendants of almost every island in the Caribbean, lived together harmoniously, exporting fruit and tea and importing tourists.

The island had been privately owned for more than thirty years. The present owner had bought the island a little under a year ago.

As the plane soared over the blue Caribbean waters, the island came into focus. Covered in dense foliage, the land mass gradually rose from sea level to a central mountain peak. Except for its color, it reminded her of a giant scoop of ice cream.

"How much longer until we get there?"

"About five minutes."

Five minutes, Elise mused. Five minutes until she and Garrett were completely alone together. They'd probably both fall into bed for a few hours' sleep. Neither of them had gotten much rest since they'd made the decision to come here. Christmas night, they'd packed what belongings they had handy that were suitable for the trip.

Elise had spent the following day getting Dena and her other employees up to speed on all the projects that were in the works. Alyssa and Garrett had shopped for the few items they needed, including a bathing suit for her. Elise shuddered, wondering what on earth they had picked out for her.

But sooner or later, they would be alone and awake and they would have to face whatever was going on between them. Elise both dreaded and anticipated that moment.

The plane dipped and tilted to one side, making Elise's stomach lurch. They swung around, circling to the far end of the airport and the landing strip below. Elise swallowed and squeezed her eyes shut as the plane bounced to a bumpy landing.

"We're here." The pilot slipped out of his seat and let down the stairs for them to exit. Elise followed him out of the small opening and onto the tarmac. An elderly brown-skinned couple stepped forward as she disembarked. The woman wore a blue-and-white muumuu over her ample figure. The gaunt man beside her wore a camp shirt in the same fabric tucked into a pair of white pants. Elise would guess their ages to fall somewhere between sixty-five and one hundred and seven, but their features were similar enough for her to wonder if they were brother and sister.

"Bienvenido," the woman said, stepping forward. "Welcome to our little island. I am Verity Tremaine, and this old rooster here is my husband, Aristotle. Welcome."

"Thank you. I'm Elise Taylor, and this is my husband Garrett." While the two men shook hands, Elise said to Verity. "Your name means truth, doesn't it?"

"That is correct, miss."

"Please, call me Elise."

Verity looked Elise up and down, from her hair, which had somehow managed to hold up during the trip, to the soles of her Kenneth Cole sandals, with a critical eye. "No, I think *miss* will suit you just fine."

Elise blinked, unsure whether or not she'd just been insulted.

Verity turned to her husband. "Old man, I think there's some luggage you need to be attending to."

"Don't try to peck at me, you old hen. I know what needs doing."

Aristotle started toward the suitcases the pilot unloaded from the plane. Garrett picked up one of Elise's bags. "I'll take care of that."

Aristotle shooed him away with a wave of his hand. "This is my job, and the day I'm too old to do it, I'll take the gas pipe and be done with it."

Aristotle grabbed for the handle of the bag and, faced with the prospect of a tug-of-war with an old man, Garrett let it go. Aristotle gave a nod of triumph and started off. "The van is this way."

Elise glanced at Garrett, who looked back, shrugging.

"Come along, you two," Verity said. She gave Elise a pointed look as she passed them to follow her husband.

Elise glanced up at Garrett and saw the humor dancing in his eyes. He leaned down to whisper in her ear:

"Something tells me this is going to be a very strange vacation."

Once they were all seated in the van, Aristotle started the engine and pulled out of the small paved parking area onto a dirt road barely wide enough to accommodate the vehicle. Until that moment, Elise hadn't given a thought to where they would be staying. She'd spotted a number of houses during their descent in the plane, but nothing large enough to constitute a hotel. She settled back in her seat, figuring she'd find out soon enough.

Looking out the window, she cataloged the variety of flowers she spotted. Birds of paradise, orchids, gardenias, and others she couldn't name. The pilot hadn't lied: The island was beautiful. They were traveling upward toward the top of the mountain.

Ten minutes later, they pulled into the circular drive of a large home built near the apex of the mountain. A large, lighted fountain decorated with frolicking cherubs stood in the center of the drive. Elise stared up at the two-story structure, built in the Spanish architectural style. The outer walls were the light beige color of the shoreline. The sloping roof was made of Italian tile. Rows of pure white frangipani adorned the front of the house.

"We're home," Verity announced.

Aristotle came around to open the passenger door for Elise. She stepped out into the brilliant afternoon sunshine, savoring the mingled aromas of the flowers and the pervasive scent of the ocean, which hung in the air.

Garrett stepped out beside her and surveyed the property. "Nice."

What an understatement! Between the first-class airline tickets and the impressive house, Elise wondered exactly what sort of radio station Alyssa had won the trip from that it could afford to throw around this kind of money. Especially since they reaped no benefit from it. She'd expected that the station, or at least the travel agency that had arranged the trip, would send some kind of representative to take some publicity photos at the very least. Aside from the car that had picked them up at home to take them to the airport, they hadn't heard one peep from the people who'd sponsored the trip.

"This is the owner's villa," Verity explained as she shepherded them toward the house. "So everything is in beautiful order. I hope you will enjoy your stay here." She opened the door and stepped back. "Come in."

Elise stepped over the threshold into the large foyer, her sandals clicking on the red Spanish-tile floor. The walls were painted the same sandy beige color as the exterior. A large antique chest stood against the wall. A Mayan sun god statue sat atop it. The chest itself, designed in the Spanish style, would go for a fortune at auction. The statue, if authentic, was priceless.

Verity led them on a tour of the villa, through the living room at the left to the solarium to the gardens at the back of the house, then through the kitchen and dining room.

The gardens were perfectly landscaped and the rooms were large and airy. But the dominant feature of the house was the variety of pre- and post-Colombian art-work from all over the Caribbean: paintings, figurines, urns, weapons, furniture. A fortune in collectibles.

When they had circled around to their starting point by the staircase that led to the upper floor, Verity said, "Your rooms are upstairs."

"Rooms?" Garrett questioned, as they started up the stairs.

"Your apartment," Verity clarified. "There are three of them upstairs. The master bedroom, the red suite, and the blue suite, where you will be staying."

Aristotle waited for them on the upper floor. Elise had wondered where he'd disappeared to during their tour. Obviously he'd busied himself bringing their suitcases to their rooms, as all four Louis Vuitton bags now sat inside the door.

"We'll leave you two to get settled. If you need anything, we'll be downstairs fixing supper." Aristotle and Verity went out, closing the door behind them.

The moment had finally come. She and Garrett were completely alone. The plastic smile she'd worn all day faded from her face. She turned to Garrett, who explored the ornate cabinet that stood by the wall.

"So, what do you think?"

"You mean other than feeling like I'm trapped in an art museum?"

"Philistine," Elise accused, not for the first time.

"You knew that before you married me." Garrett pressed a button and the doors to the cabinet slid back, revealing a television with a twenty-five-inch screen. "Eureka!" Garrett turned to her, a little boy's grin on his face.

Elise shook her head in disgust. "Don't tell me you came all this way to watch television."

"Not television. Football. You can't expect me to miss the games this week."

Elise made a disgusted sound in her throat and turned away from him. She glanced around the ornately decorated room. No doubt they called this the blue suite because almost everything in the room was some shade of blue. The walls were a pale sky blue, the curtains were a cobalt blue that matched the fabric of the sofa and love seat. The woven rug that rested under the glass coffee table was a mélange of swirling blue hues. On the wall hung a beautiful seascape. Even from her position in the center of the room, she could make out the broad brush strokes that heralded it as an original oil painting, not a print.

Elise gasped as Garrett's arms closed around her from behind. "You do realize I was kidding—about the football, I mean."

"Were you?"

"You know I was." He gave her waist a squeeze. "You know what this place reminds me of? Remember the hotel we stayed in on Cancun—minus the artwork, of course?"

Elise hadn't thought of that trip in ages. Spring break of her freshman year they'd gone to Mexico, the first trip they'd taken together. They'd made love for the first time on that trip, but only after she'd gone to his room to seduce him.

Years later, when she'd asked him why he'd brought her there and then hadn't touched her, he'd told her that he'd wanted to take her away from the strife at school and at home to find out if she stayed with him because she wanted to, or because she felt beholden to him. He'd wanted to know if she really loved him.

And he'd also sweated bullets the whole time, wondering if she'd come to him and make love to him. He never would have initiated intimacy between them, given all that had happened in the previous months. He'd just about given up hope when she'd come to his room the last night.

And now, so many years later, she needed to know if her husband truly wanted to be with her. She didn't want Garrett staying with her because of their children or because their lives had become hopelessly entwined. She wanted to know that the love between them was still alive and still strong enough to keep him with her, even if all the other factors weren't involved.

She needed to shake up the complacency of their marriage and see what shook out. Maybe she should take a page from his book and find out.

She pulled away and turned to face him. "Which bedroom do you plan to take?"

Garrett's eyebrows lifted. "Excuse me?"

"Which bedroom do you plan to take?" Elise crossed to where the suitcases stood. She picked up her overnight bag and slung it over her shoulder. "I figure the one on the left is the larger one, so I'll leave that one for you."

She picked up her other bag and walked toward the smaller bedroom to the right. She saw Garrett in the periphery of her vision, standing where she'd left him with his arms crossed over his chest. "What do you think you're doing?" he asked.

"I believe it's called unpacking. Then I'm going to take a nap until dinnertime." She closed and locked the door before she lost her nerve.

A second later, Garrett knocked on the door, but she didn't answer him. "Elise, open this door right now."

She didn't suppose she'd get away with locking him out without giving him some sort of explanation. She pulled the door open, but only enough for him to see her face. "Yes?"

"What is this all about?"

She didn't know what to tell him, not without giving it all away. "We've got two beautiful bedrooms. There's no point in letting them go to waste."

She knew he didn't believe that. He sighed, cupping her face in his palm. "I don't understand you."

"That's the point, isn't it?" She took a step away from him. "Please, Garrett, let's not argue about this."

He stalked away from her, and she knew she'd angered him or hurt him, or both. But she had to do this. She closed the door and, just as she said she would, she unpacked her suitcase and lay down on the bed for a nap. But once she heard the outer door slam, signaling that Garrett had left the room, she lay awake a long time, wondering exactly what she'd set in motion.

Garrett loped down the stairs to the first floor. Verity had said that she would be in the kitchen making dinner, so he headed in the opposite direction.

A door of the solarium led straight to the garden. He paused at its edge, surveying the colorful flora, but in reality taking in nothing.

He shoved his hands in his pants pockets, and let out a heavy breath. What on earth had gotten into Elise now?

Elise. He knew she wasn't playing some sort of game with him. Whatever motivated her to claim a separate bedroom mattered to her. But he hadn't come all this way to end up on worse footing with her than when he had started out.

"Damn," he said aloud.

"You and the missus have a fight already?"

Hearing Aristotle's voice, Garrett looked down and to the right. The old man knelt in the dark earth, a spade in his hand and a huge grin on his face.

"Most of our guests wait until the second day, at least."

Garrett couldn't help returning the infectious smile. "Then I guess we're ahead of schedule."

"You New Yorkers have to do everything so fast. So, what's the problem with your missus?"

Garrett sighed and shoved his hands in the pockets of his trousers. "Elise is very—"

"Bossy? Opinionated? Hoity-toity?"

Garrett smiled. He supposed Elise was all those things at times. "Very upset with me, and I have no idea why."

Aristotle lifted one shoulder. "So, what's new about that? Seems women are born knowing how to get mad over nothing."

"What do you do when Verity gets mad at you?"

Aristotle lifted his hands and spread them in a way that encompassed the area before him. "You see me out here in the garden, don't you?"

Garrett chuckled.

"It's funny, though, sooner or later she gets around to telling me what's bothering her. Usually, it's something so simple, I wonder why I couldn't figure it out for myself."

Aristotle gazed over his shoulder at him. *Wily old man,* Garrett thought. He didn't miss Aristotle's implication that he should know what was on Elise's mind. Verity might be that easy to figure out, but in this instance with Elise, Garrett hadn't a clue.

"What's on your agenda for this afternoon?"

Garrett shrugged. "What is there to do around here?"

Aristotle tilted his head to one side. "Not much. Unless you go down into the city and mix with the tourists. Even then, the answer is not much. Most people come here for day trips from Jamaica or Puerto Rico to look at the fish and gawk at the natives. There are a couple of restaurants and a dance hall for the young folks. That's about it. If you follow the path right there, it'll take you down to the beach. It's pretty secluded there.

The only other way to get down there is to cross through the underbrush."

"If we wanted to go into town, is there a car we can use?"

"You'd get lost in two minutes. And being a man, you wouldn't ask for directions. If you want to go, I'll drive you. Or better yet, Verity's granddaughter can take you."

"Thanks. I'll let you know what our plans are. In the meantime, what time should we be ready for dinner?"

"Six o'clock should be fine."

Garrett checked his watch. That gave him about an hour to unpack, shower, and catch a small nap himself. "I'll see you later, then."

Aristotle nodded and turned his attention to the soil. Garrett went back to his room to unpack.

Elise woke from her nap at five o'clock, just as she'd planned. She lay in bed a moment, listening. She didn't hear a sound from Garrett, and as light as she usually slept, she'd assumed she would have heard him if he'd come back. She wouldn't bother to speculate. She'd get dressed and find out for herself.

Each bedroom had its own bathroom. Elise padded to hers and turned on the water. Now that she'd launched her half-baked plan to save her marriage, she didn't know what to do. And she had to come up with something other than simply isolating herself from her husband. Garrett wouldn't put up with that for too long anyway.

Elise pulled her salmon-colored sundress over her head and smoothed it down over her hips. Its square neckline dipped low over her breasts and the dress rode low on her hips. It drove Garrett crazy every time she wore it. She told herself she wore the dress because it alone had survived the trip relatively unwrinkled. In truth, she wanted Garrett to want her; she wanted to see desire flare in his eyes when he saw her.

She added a pair of high-heeled sandals, fixed her hair and makeup, and stepped out of her room. She crossed to the door to his room, but when it came to knocking, she chickened out. She could hear the shower running. If he came to the door in a towel, or less, what little resolve she had would melt away like the Sweet'n Low in her morning coffee. She backed away from the door, turned, and headed downstairs instead.

She found Verity in the kitchen, stirring a pot of aromatic soup. "That smells delicious."

Verity smiled, exposing two deep dimples in her dark cheeks. "Tastes just as good, too."

Elise glanced around the spotless kitchen. "How long have you and Aristotle been the caretakers here?"

"Near thirty years now. Of course, we can't do as much as we used to. We hire a landscaper now instead of Aristotle doing all the work himself. And our granddaughter, Selena, has been helping out with most of the housework. But we get on all right."

"Everything is lovely."

"Thank you, miss. But where is that handsome husband of yours? Dinner is almost ready."

"I'm right here."

Elise looked up to see Garrett standing in the archway to the kitchen. The expression in his eyes didn't disappoint her. His hot gaze roved over her, from the top of her head to her sandal-clad feet and back to her face. Her eyes drank him in, too. He wore black linen pants topped off by a matching silk T-shirt that delineated his powerful chest and arms. Elise's breath caught in her throat, until Verity elbowed her and one word tumbled out of her mouth: "Hi."

Garrett smiled, obviously amused. "Hi yourself." He strode to her, placed a hand on her waist, and leaned down to kiss her cheek. "You look fabulous, sweetheart."

"Thank you." Elise glanced over at Verity to gauge her reaction to Garrett's demonstrativeness in her presence. Verity winked at her and went back to stirring her pot.

"And Miss Verity, if what you're cooking in that pot tastes half as good as it smells, I think I'm in love."

Verity waved him away with a flick of her hand. "You men will say anything to keep a woman slaving away in the kitchen for you. Isn't that right, miss?"

Elise shrugged. Garrett had never tried any inducement whatsoever to keep her in the kitchen. She could make a decent meal, but no one actually salivated to eat anything that came out of her kitchen. She saw it as a deficiency in herself, but Garrett didn't care one way or the other. "We have a housekeeper at home. I'll have to ask her."

"You do that." Verity patted her arm. "Everything is arranged out on the lanai. Why don't you two have a seat and I'll get the dinner served."

Again, she felt the sting of Verity's disapproval, but she ignored it. Garrett took her hand and led her through the door onto a stone patio sheltered by a stone overhang. A small square table and two chairs stood at the edge of the lanai. The waning sun cast a rosy glow on the setting.

Soft West Indian music drifted to them, from where Elise couldn't tell. Two drinks sat atop the colorful tablecloth.

"I guess these are for us," Garrett said, handing one to her.

"I guess," she echoed. She took a sip of the frothy, pink liquid. It tasted like a piña colada, with the pineapple juice replaced by a strong cherry flavor. She took a deeper sip, then licked the foam from her upper lip. "What do you suppose is in this?"

"Franjelico, probably." Garrett set his drink on the table. "Too sweet."

Elise took another sip. "Maybe, but delicious."

Garrett took the glass from her and set it beside his. "And probably made with some one-hundred-fifty-proof alcohol, which neither of us is used to. I don't want you passing out at the dinner table."

Something about the way he said that made her question him. "Why not?"

He cupped her nape in his hand and stroked his thumb over her cheek. "I want you wide awake and with all your faculties intact for what comes after dinner." He lowered his head and kissed her lips, a light sipping caress that left her wanting more.

Elise swallowed, her throat suddenly dry. How was she supposed to tell him that she would not be sharing his bed tonight, when her own body heated and her brain flooded with images of doing just that?

Aristotle's sudden appearance saved her from having to say anything. He carried a tray laden with two earthenware soup bowls. He set the tray down on the edge of the table, then placed a bowl in the center of each of their place settings. Picking up the tray, he stepped back.

"You don't care for the drink?"

"It's a little sweet," Garrett said.

"How about a nice dry white wine?"

"That would be lovely," Elise said.

Nodding, Aristotle went back inside.

Elise allowed Garrett to seat her, then unfolded her napkin on her lap. She looked down at the thick soup in her bowl, then stirred its greenish-brown contents with her spoon. "Maybe we should have asked what's in this."

"Just try it." Garrett followed his own suggestion, dipping his spoon into his bowl. He tasted a spoonful. "It's good. A little spicy, maybe."

Elise sampled a spoonful. "Mmm," she agreed.

Verity came out again, carrying a glass of wine in each hand. She set a glass down in front of each of them and put her hands on her hips. "So, how do you like it?"

"It's delicious. What is it?"

"Here we call it pepperpot. It's made with spinach, okra, chicken, beef, and spices."

"If you ever get tired of working here, you could come live with us. The pay is lousy, but we've got two great kids."

"Speaking of the children," Elise cut in, "is there a phone we can use to call them? We didn't even let them know we got here safely."

"I can bring a phone out here, if you like."

"Yes, please."

Elise dialed Daphne's number first. She picked up on the third ring.

"So, how is paradise treating you?" Daphne asked, after the sisters had exchanged hellos.

"Very well. The place is gorgeous and the island is lovely, though so far we only saw it out of the van window coming here. How's Andrew?"

"Fine. Nathan popped some popcorn and has all the kids in front of the big-screen TV downstairs watching a Disney movie. Do you want me to get him?"

Elise didn't want to pull Andrew away from what was obviously a fun time. "No, just take care of my baby."

"You know I will."

Elise called Jenny and Michael next. After a few rings, Michael came on to tell her that Jenny and Alyssa had gone to the theater. Elise clicked off the phone and set it on the table.

"It appears both of our children are too busy to talk to us."

Garrett leaned back in his chair and watched his wife. She didn't say anything more, continuing to eat her soup with her eyes downcast. He covered her hand with his own. "Sweetheart, would you prefer they were both miserable?"

She gazed up at him with a rueful smile on her face. "No, but I wouldn't mind if they missed us a little."

Garrett chuckled. "Give them time. We haven't been gone a day."

"I know, but I miss them already."

Truth be told, so did he. But he refused to let that ruin the first time alone he'd had with his wife in years. When he'd walked into the kitchen and seen her standing there in that dress and a pair of sandals that would have done Joan Crawford proud, he'd immediately forgotten his annoyance at her for barricading herself in a separate room.

Elise knew what that dress did to him, and he assumed she'd worn it, in part, as a gesture of conciliation. He still wondered what had caused her to seek refuge in a separate room. But he'd worry about that later.

A West Indian ballad played over the stereo. "Come dance with me." He took her hand and pulled her to her feet. He sensed a hesitancy in her, but she came to him, wrapping her arms around his neck. He pulled her closer with his hands at her waist. She snuggled against him, laying her cheek against his chest. His fingers splayed over her bare back, savoring the smoothness of her skin as they swayed together to the beat of the music.

She lifted her head and looked up at him, her eyes searching his face. The sun had set fully while they'd eaten their soup. The only illumination came from the moon on the horizon, the candles on their table, and the wall sconces in the shape of torches at the side of the house. The orange light cast a warm glow on Elise's skin and lent her eyes a vibrant sherry color. He'd never seen her look lovelier.

He couldn't help himself. He lowered his head and claimed her mouth. He half expected her to pull away from him, but she melted against him, kissing him back sweetly.

Hearing Aristotle cough, Garrett pulled away from Elise. The older man approached, bearing a large tray. He laid a plate for each of them on the table.

"I see you two are enjoying our island moonlight," Aristotle said, a wicked grin on his face.

"We're doing our best." Garrett led Elise back to the table and seated her. Taking his own seat, he looked down at his plate. Peas and rice, a salad of cabbage and carrots, and a whole red snapper, stewed with onions and peppers. As Aristotle retreated to the house, Garrett focused on Elise's face.

"Is something wrong, sweetheart?"

She glanced from her plate to him and back again. "There's a face on my food."

"There's a whole head."

Elise laid her napkin on the table. "I can't eat something that's staring at me."

"The fish is dead. It can't stare at anybody. And what makes you think it's a he?"

"A female fish would have more sense than to get caught."

Garrett sighed. He knew Elise would never eat the fish with the head attached. "Give me your plate."

She passed it to him. He cut off the head and put it on his own plate. He passed it back to her. "Is that better?"

"Thank you."

Garrett shook his head. "I knew that surgical rotation would come in handy one day."

"Very funny."

Unable to resist teasing her, he said, "You know, they say the eyes are the best part."

Elise's jaw dropped but she recovered herself. "Garrett Taylor, don't you dare."

"Spoilsport." Laughing, he turned his attention to his plate.

When they finished the meal, Aristotle came out to clear the dishes away. "Would either of you care for dessert or coffee?" he asked.

Garrett glanced at Elise. "No, thank you. I think we'll turn in for the night." He stood and held his hand out to Elise. The reluctant expression returned to her eyes. What had happened in the last few minutes to make her reticent about being alone with him? Yet she placed her hand in his and rose from the table.

Elise followed Garrett inside the house and up to their room. They'd barely made it into the room with the door closed, when Garrett pulled her into his arms. He simply held her, running one hand over her back, while the other squeezed the back of her neck. She leaned into him, even though she knew she shouldn't. The warmth of his big body, the tenderness of his hands on her skin, intoxicated her. Garrett wasn't the only one who needed touch to feel whole.

For a moment she indulged her desire simply to be held by him. Then, steeling herself, she pulled away from him, enough to look up at his face. "I guess it's time to say good night." She leaned up and kissed his cheek, then took a step away from him.

He grabbed her arm. "Where are you going?"

"To my room."

"Why? If you are punishing me for something, I'd like to at least know what crime I've committed."

"I'm not punishing you for anything."

"Then what? Damn it, Elise, will you please tell me what this is all about?"

Elise shook her head. If she had to tell him, that defeated the whole purpose. Couldn't he see for himself that their marriage was in trouble? Making love would only mask the problem, not solve it.

It took all her resolve to slowly step back, out of his grasp. "Good night, Garrett," she whispered. She walked away from him, stepped inside her room, and closed the door.

Nine

The next morning, Garrett awoke to the sound of Elise knocking on his door. Last night, he'd lain awake wondering when she would give up this foolishness and come to him, but she never did. Either out of spite or to be perverse, he'd locked his own door. If she'd changed her mind and wanted to be with him, she couldn't have merely slipped into his bed. She'd have had to knock on his door. Eventually, he'd fallen into a deep dreamless sleep.

"Are you decent in there?" Elise called.

"Sure." He padded to the door, unlocked it, and opened it.

A self-satisfied smile turned up his lips as her eyes widened and scanned downward over his body before returning to his face. She swallowed a couple of times before speaking. "I thought you said you were decent."

"I am decent. I'm also naked." He noticed she looked everywhere but at him. He'd awoken aroused, just as he had almost every morning of his married life. She was trying her damnedest not to notice. The only question he had was why. "What can I do for you, Elise?"

Her head snapped up and he knew she remembered

the last time he'd asked her that question when they were in a similar position. And she remembered what followed.

"I-I made arrangements to go into town. I wanted to know if you wanted to go with me."

"Sure. Do we have anything for breakfast?"

"Verity sent up some eggs, fresh fruit, coffee, and some scones. If you like, I'll fix you a plate."

"That would be great. Give me ten minutes."

He shut the door and went into the shower. The cold blast of the water pelting his body did nothing to cool his ardor for his wife. Garrett submerged his face under the water. Something told him it was going to be a long week.

Elise had arranged breakfast out on the balcony. Garrett claimed the wrought-iron chair across from her and reached for the coffee she'd poured for him. His gaze traveled over her as he sipped from his cup. She wore a beige sundress with a tight-fitting bodice that hugged her small breasts. On her wrist dangled the bracelet Alyssa had given her. As usual, her hair and makeup were flawless.

He glanced at his plate, but his normally strong appetite had disappeared completely. He forked down some of the breakfast anyway, then pushed his plate away. "Are you ready to go?"

He rose from his chair and started to clear the table, but Elise stopped him.

"That pair downstairs seems very proprietary about their jobs, and I don't want to offend them."

She minded offending a couple of strangers, but offending her own husband by refusing to share his bed, that she didn't mind at all. Garrett shrugged and walked back inside. Once Elise grabbed her purse, they left the room.

A young woman with shoulder-length black hair
waited for them in front of the van. She extended her
hand toward Elise. "I'm Selena, Verity's granddaughter."

"Pleased to meet you," Elise said. Elise gestured toward him. "This is my husband, Garrett."

Selena extended her hand. "Yes, I know. Pleased to
meet you."

Garrett helped Elise into the van, then climbed aboard
himself. Selena started the engine and pulled out onto
the dirt road. "How are you folks enjoying your stay
so far?" she asked, after they'd been driving a few minutes.

"Everything is wonderful," Elise said, "but I was curious how the island got its name."

"Legend has it," Selena began, "that a Spanish trading boat making its return trip from the New World to
Spain got lost in a storm and crashed here sometime in
the early seventeen hundreds. The captain had lost most
of his crew and all their provisions and was so grateful
to be alive, he dubbed it *Isla de los Milagros*.

"Despite being smack-dab in the middle of the Caribbean, Milagro had yet to be explored. At first the
sailors believed it to be uninhabited. But strange things
began to happen. They found homes that appeared to
be lived in, some with fires still blazing in the grate,
but no people. What few possessions had survived the
shipwreck disappeared. And at night, they could hear
the cries of island birds, most of all the one they named
la bruja, a type of parrot whose caw sounds like a
witch's cackle. Being a superstitious lot, they were terrified.

"Then one night they were rousted from their makeshift beds in the forest to find themselves surrounded
by the men of the tribe. They were lined up in a clearing

in the village. Sure they were about to be executed, they pleaded for their lives. Until they saw the young women of the village entering the clearing.

"The villagers had hidden in underground caves fed by a hot spring, waiting for the visitors to leave. When it became apparent they weren't going anywhere, the elders decided that they would be given the opportunity to marry into the tribe. You see, in our culture, a man would rather die himself than allow harm to come to his wife or family. The elders felt this was the best way to ensure the men's loyalty."

"So the sailors were given their choice of the tribe's women?" Garrett ventured.

Selena made a horrified face. "Absolutely not. The women were invited to see if they could suffer one of the foreigners as her husband. They must have been able to, because all the men were married off two days later. Today we celebrate *Dia de las Promesas,* that coincides with the night of those betrothals. Everyone brings a dish to share and there is dancing. You should come."

Garrett glanced at Elise, who regarded him expectantly. "We can go if you like."

She smiled and turned away. "Do people still visit the underground caves?"

"Not anymore. An earthquake over a hundred and fifty years ago sealed them off and devastated most of the island. Some say the caves served their purpose and disappeared. Some say the caves are magical, that to spend the night in them is to find your heart's desire. Every now and again some tourist hears of the legend and goes looking for them. They never find anything."

* * *

The marketplace was like nothing Elise would have imagined—a madhouse, with people everywhere; young, old, babies strapped to their mothers' backs, women carrying enormous baskets on their heads or hawking their wares in loud voices. Vendors lined the square, selling everything from fresh fish on beds of ice to shell necklaces to live animals to be slaughtered. Most of the food lay out on the bare ground, or on a thin blanket. The sound could deafen a person, but the mélange of smells would make an anorexic's mouth water.

Unused to the bright morning sunshine, Elise pulled her sunglasses from the straw bag she carried and put them on. As they strolled through the market, she noticed a variety of accents and languages. The Milagrans varied a great deal in physical features, as well—every shade from blond and blue-eyed, to those with African features and blue-black skin.

Selena leaned closer to her and said, "Unlike your America that considers itself a melting pot, we think of ourselves as a rich stew. Everyone is welcome here, just as it has always been. During the times when slavery was a standard practice all over the Caribbean, Milagro became a haven for those lucky enough to escape. That is why we have so many cultures here, so many different people."

Elise nodded. Selena was a prime example of the island's diversity. Her complexion was a few shades darker than Elise's, but her long jet-black hair was naturally straight and her eyes were blue.

"Where do you want to stop first?"

Elise looked around. She simply enjoyed being in the midst of all those people. She hadn't seen such madness since the last sample sale at Calvin Klein. "We'll follow your lead."

"Granny Verity needs some peas for tonight's dinner," Selena explained. By the time they finished, Selena had purchased peas, string beans, plantains, okra, and at Elise's insistence, a strange triangular-shaped fruit called akee. Selena led her to another vendor, picked up a mango, and handed it to her. "We grow the best fruit in the Caribbean."

"Mmm," Elise agreed. Even the produce market on Broadway Street didn't carry fruit this plump and soft. She handed the fruit back to Selena, her attention diverted by a woman selling T-shirts nearby. She picked up a white one that had I STILL MISS MY EX printed on the front. The back read, BUT MY AIM IS GETTING BETTER.

"That's a bloodthirsty sentiment." Elise glanced up at Garrett, relieved to see a smile on his face. She'd thought she'd pushed him too far last night, especially after the way he'd greeted her this morning. She didn't want him angry with her, she wanted him to see for himself that their relationship was no longer what it should be.

"Dena will love it. Her divorce became final last month."

Garrett shook his head. "Too bad. I thought Roger was a nice guy."

"Apparently, so did his secretary." She held the shirt out to the vendor. "How much is this?"

The woman quoted her an amount. She noticed the surprised look in Garrett's eyes when she paid it. She turned to face him. "Why are you looking at me like that?"

"You could haggle Neiman Marcus himself into giving you that shirt for cost, yet not one word of protest at that outrageous price. Don't tell me you're becoming a spendthrift in your old age."

"I am not a spendthrift, nor am I old." Elise shrugged. "These are simple people, and we have so much."

He squeezed her shoulder. "So you're just going soft?"

"A little. Do you mind?"

"Not at all." He drew her toward him with an arm around her waist. "I saw a necklace at another table that Alyssa would love. I'll let you overpay for that, too."

She rolled her eyes. "Such utter generosity."

They spent the rest of the morning shopping for souvenirs at one stall or another. She bought matching T-shirts for her and Garrett that read, NO HURRIES, NO WORRIES, which seemed to be the unofficial Milagran motto. By noon, Elise's stomach started to rumble.

After stowing their purchases in the van, Selena led them to a small restaurant at the edge of town. "You haven't been to Milagro if you haven't eaten at Mamie's cafe," she informed them.

Mamie's was housed in a small one-story building. The structure, made of the same pale stones as the house, sported a vibrant mural depicting men and women in island costume on the outside. Like every other building they'd passed, it appeared clean and well kept.

Elise stepped inside the dimly lit restaurant and looked around. Another mural decorated the walls, this one of islanders frolicking on the beach. Two dozen small square tables covered in pale blue linen occupied the front of the restaurant. A long wooden bar dominated the back of the restaurant. Several oscars and some smaller fish swam around in the blue-tinted water of an enormous tank built into the back wall.

"Let's sit here," Selena said, pointing to two tables that had been pushed together.

Elise sat with Garrett next to her and Selena across from her. Her gaze slid to Garrett to find him watching her. "What do you want to eat?" he asked.

Elise picked up her menu and opened it. It listed a variety of seafood, as well as some other wholly unappetizing choices. She knew oxtails were actual slices of an ox's tail made into a stew, but was cow's-foot soup made with an actual hoof? Elise shuddered and closed the menu. "Why don't you order for both of us."

She saw the amusement dancing in Garrett's eyes. "Nothing with a head still attached, I promise."

An ancient jukebox sat in one corner of the restaurant. Elise glanced at Selena. "Does it work?"

Selena shrugged. "I think so."

Elise fished some quarters out of her change purse. "Let's see."

The jukebox's playlist consisted of a variety of American songs from the seventies and eighties, as well as a smattering of older songs by Caribbean artists. As she scanned the titles, she felt someone come up behind her. She didn't have to turn to look to know it was Garrett. "What should I play?"

"I don't know. What are you in the mood for?"

"Nothing after 1983, obviously." She tried to insert a quarter in the coin slot, but it didn't budge.

"Try these." Garrett placed two hexagonal coins in her palm. "Compliments of Selena. They don't use American coins here."

"Thank you." She inserted the coins and selected an old Bob Marley song and "Jamaica Farewell," a ballad she'd heard and loved.

A few moments later, the waitress brought out their food. Garrett had ordered several dishes, allowing her to pick what she wanted. She filled her plate with fried plantains, shrimp, a dumpling filled with eggplant and spices called a bake, and, to be daring, a conch fritter.

When they finished eating, they headed back to the van for the trip home. On the way back, Elise sat next to Garrett in the back seat. She leaned her head against his shoulder, content that he slipped his arm around her waist to hold her closer.

When they pulled up in back of the house, Garrett stayed behind to help Selena with the packages while Elise went inside to let Verity know they'd arrived. Verity awaited her in the kitchen. "How did you enjoy your day in town?" she asked.

Elise pulled off her sunglasses and tucked them into her handbag. "The market is a phenomenon. We had lunch at Mamie's. I had conch for the first time."

"You're a regular adventuress, miss."

Elise smiled, finding Verity's humor infectious. "What should I try next?"

"You haven't seen our little stretch of beach yet. Aristotle can bring down a couple of chairs and some towels for you to use."

"Thank you. When Garrett comes in, would you tell him I went upstairs to get ready?"

"Will do, miss."

Smiling, Elise went up to her room to change.

Garrett emerged from the ocean and walked to where Elise sat in one of the chairs Aristotle had brought down for them. He plucked the towel from the chair next to her and began to dry himself. "Why didn't you come in? The water's great."

Elise lifted one shoulder. "The salt water is murder on my skin, you know that."

"Nonsense. You didn't want to get your hair wet."

"If your hair dried looking like something that came off a porcupine's back, you wouldn't want to get it wet either."

Chuckling, Garrett laid the towel on the lawn chair and arranged himself as best he could on the too-small seat. Elise's hair never looked anything but perfect. He'd teased her once that if the house were burning down, she'd ask the fireman to wait a minute so she could comb her hair before he carried her out.

Leaning back, he scanned the horizon. Clear blue water extended as far as the eye could see. Above, only a few puffy clouds marred the azure sky. "I'll say one thing for this place. It is beautiful."

"Mmm," Elise agreed.

A little farther down the beach, Selena walked along the water's edge. She wore a red-and-white striped bikini. He'd seen a similar suit when he'd gone shopping with Alyssa and had considered buying it for Elise. She still had the figure for it.

Alyssa had looked at him as if he were insane. "Mom would *never* wear that," she'd informed him, as if he should know better. Alyssa had picked out a more modest suit for her mother in burnt orange.

"She's young enough to be your daughter. Or maybe you're considering her for one of the 'twenties' you're going to replace me with in a couple of years. I guess I shouldn't complain. You know my motto: It never hurts to shop early."

Garrett sighed. Although a faint smile lingered on Elise's lips, the expression in her eyes was dead serious.

"For God's sake, Elise. You know very well that was only a joke. I've been teasing you about that since you were thirty."

"Well, maybe it's gotten a little stale." She stood and slipped on her sandals. "I'm going back to the house."

For a moment, he watched her rear view as she headed up the path. On the store rack, the suit had seemed more modest, but it molded to Elise's frame in a way that made him want to hang the consequences and follow her. But he knew in her present frame of mind, she'd never let him anywhere near her. He picked up Elise's magazine, the current issue of *Architectural Digest,* opened it midway, and used it to cover his face. It was going to be a very long week.

Elise stalked up the path and let herself in the house through the door that led into the kitchen. She closed the door behind her, then leaned her forehead against the cool glass panel set in the wood.

"So, miss, what did you do to that husband of yours now?"

Elise spun around and stared at Verity, openmouthed. "I beg your pardon?"

Verity stood at the counter shelling the peas they'd bought at the market into a big plastic bowl. "You heard me. What did you do to him?"

"I didn't do anything to Garrett." Just what she needed, more of Verity's disapproval. She didn't know why this virtual stranger's opinion mattered to her, she only knew it did.

Verity shook her head. "If things were well between you, I wouldn't have to make two beds instead of one."

"You don't make any beds," Elise countered. "Your granddaughter does."

Verity grinned. "That's true enough, miss. But why would you let that man of yours sleep by himself? That's too fine a man to be left on his own. Some woman would snap him up like this." Verity snapped her fingers.

"If it's a new woman he wants, he's welcome to her."

Verity shook her head gravely. "Now, you know you don't mean that."

No, she didn't mean it. And she shouldn't have snapped at Verity, either. She only had to look into Verity's concerned brown eyes to know that caring, not nosiness, motivated her comments.

And she'd snapped at Garrett for no earthly reason. She'd seen him staring off in Selena's direction and lit into him like the wicked witch her staff accused her of being. She didn't know why, but suddenly a flash of anger had possessed her, and she'd taken it out on him.

"I'm sorry, Verity. I'm not feeling well. My heart is pounding and my head is swimming and I feel warm all over. Maybe I stayed out in the sun too long."

"Sounds more like a hot flash than a heat stroke. You wouldn't be starting the change, would you?"

The change. Elise had always hated that expression. It made it sound like she'd be howling at the moon by midnight. It was on the tip of Elise's tongue to tell Verity it was none of her business, but she huffed out an exasperated breath instead. Like it or not, "the change" was exactly what she was going through. Alone.

With what other woman could she discuss such a delicate topic? All the women she knew who might be able to offer her counsel on the subject were too busy convincing the world that they never aged at all.

A hint of a smile lifted her lips as she imagined broaching the subject with Judith McDonald over blintzes at the Russian Tea Room. After she recovered from her swoon, Judith would demand her retainer back—in cash. Frankly, she didn't have anyone else to talk to.

Besides, something maternal and comforting about Verity struck a chord in Elise, which was probably the reason Verity's disapproval of her stung so much. Elise bit her lip. She'd read somewhere that women who lost their mothers at a young age constantly looked for substitutes in older women. Until now, she'd always thought that was a lot of baloney.

Elise inhaled, letting her breath out slowly. "According to my doctor, I am perimenopausal."

"Congratulations, dearie." Verity clapped her on the shoulder.

"Menopause is something to celebrate?"

"If you ask me it is. Sex gets better after forty as it is. And then with no worries about the monthly curse, no fear of babies. You can't get much closer to heaven than that."

"Or my sex drive could dry up like the Sahara."

"With that husband of yours? I don't think so."

"I could grow a thicker mustache than Groucho Marx."

"That you could. Then you just wax it off like everyone else." Verity fastened a penetrating look on her. "What are you really worried about?"

It sounded silly, even in her own head, but she felt old. Although Garrett had never said so, she knew he enjoyed showing her off to his friends and colleagues—his always gracious, never-a-hair-out-of-place, perfectly proper wife. Unlike some of the other doctor's wives, she never embarrassed him, never tried to upstage him or make him look bad. She maintained her figure through twice-weekly trips to her karate dojo and thrice-weekly trips to the gym, and had started dyeing away the sprinkling of gray hair that had started to crop up a couple of years ago. She worked hard at being the woman Garrett wanted.

And more than that she didn't want to lose her ability to bear children. When she'd given birth to Andrew, she'd intended to have her tubes tied. Both of them had decided they didn't want any more children. But in the aftermath of Andrew's birth, she'd forgotten about it. Later, when she'd wanted to have the surgery, Garrett had talked her out of it. He'd said he didn't want her to mutilate her body unnecessarily, but she realized he wanted to keep that option open to them, in case they changed their minds. But now life was taking that choice away from her, and she resented it. It was too soon.

"How did Aristotle react when you went through this?"

Verity chuckled. "At first, he thought I'd lost my mind. I did, too, as it didn't occur to me at first what was happening. But my Aristotle is a sweet man. He was very patient with me when my hormones got the better of me. I would think your husband, being a doctor, would be just as understanding."

"He doesn't know. I just found out myself."

"Oh, miss, you must tell him." Verity patted her shoulder. "And don't you worry. I've got a potion that will fix you up right quick. I'll brew you a cup and send it up to your room. In the meantime, you take a nice long bath."

"Thank you." A firm believer in Western medicine, she had no intention of drinking any island potion. But she didn't see any point in arguing about it, either.

Verity ushered her out of the kitchen, and Elise went to her room. Verity's suggestion of a bath didn't sound half bad, though. Elise ran a lukewarm bath and tossed in some of the bath salts that sat on a rack in the bathroom.

The cool water immediately soothed her heated skin. She sank back against the bath pillow and closed her eyes. She had almost started to doze when she heard the outer door to their apartments open, and Garrett calling her name. She glanced toward the bathroom door, realizing she'd forgotten to close it and that she'd neglected to lock her room door, as well. Two seconds later, Garrett appeared in her doorway.

The bath salts provided a lovely jasmine scent, but no bubbles. She might as well have been standing in front of Garrett stark naked. The heated look in his eyes as he strode toward her told her he'd noticed.

He sat on the commode and set the cup and saucer he carried on the side of the tub. "Verity asked me to give you this."

Elise sat up a little and picked up the spoon. The dark green contents swirled when she stirred it. If she weren't mistaken, bits of leaves floated on its surface. "Thank you."

"Why is Verity making you tea? You don't drink tea."

She fastened her gaze on Garrett, remembering what Verity had said about talking to him. "I wasn't feeling well."

Garrett touched his palm to her forehead, then her cheek, then touched the back of his hand underneath her chin. He laid his hand over her heart, then circled lower to cover one breast, then the other. He lingered there, stroking his thumb over her nipple. "You feel fine to me."

His hand dipped under the water, moving over her

rib cage and lower, over her belly. This wasn't how she'd planned to tell him, but she wanted to do it now before she lost her nerve. She would never get out one coherent word with Garrett's hands on her. She grabbed his hand in both of hers. "Don't, Garrett, I—"

"Don't what, Elise? Don't touch you?" He withdrew his hand and dried it on a towel. "Is that what we've come to?"

"I didn't mean it that way."

"Save it, Elise. I don't have time to go into it now, anyway." He stood and walked to the bathroom door. "I just came up to let you know that I'm going into town with Aristotle. One of the kids is sick and he wants me to take a look at him."

"Do you want me to go with you?" For a moment she thought he'd say yes. Before Alyssa had been born, Elise had often accompanied him to the hospital when he'd been called in on an emergency. She hadn't done much but wait for him, or bring him coffee. But they would talk on the long drive from the city to their home in Westchester, and when they got home they would make love and she would hold him, especially if a case had gone bad. It was their way of staying close, of sharing everything. Right now it seemed a lifetime ago.

Garrett shook his head. "If you're not feeling well, you should stay here. I don't think we'll be back before dinner."

He strode out of the room. Elise put her face in her open palms. Obviously, Garrett had finally gotten her message. But this time, he was the one to withdraw, to walk away. After a lifetime of Garrett complaining about her doing the same thing, she finally understood how demoralizing it felt to be the one shut out and left behind.

Well, she'd gotten her wish. She'd shaken up her marriage, but good. And now that she'd driven Garrett not only to understanding, but away from her, how was she going to get him back?

Ten

Garrett loped down the stairs, almost bumping into Selena, who was on her way up. She held a cordless phone in her hands. "I was just coming to find you," she said. "You have a phone call."

Feeling a sense of dread, he lifted the phone to his ear. He and Elise had left their cell phones, beepers, and other means of being contacted back in the States by mutual consent. If someone was calling them here, it probably meant trouble. "Hello?"

Jasmine Halliday's throaty voice came to him over the phone lines. "Cutting it close to your deadline, aren't you, Dr. Taylor?"

Relief flooded through him, realizing nothing pressing at home had prompted the call. Then, irritated at the unnecessary intrusion, he said, "A little."

"I don't mean to be a nuisance, Dr. Taylor, but if you are interested in doing the book, we really do need to get the contract signed."

"I understand your position." A few days ago, he'd been completely jazzed by the prospect of coauthoring the book. But he couldn't contemplate signing a contract for it without at least speaking to Elise about it. And considering that the only people who knew they'd come to the island were Elise's family, he wondered how Jasmine Halliday knew where they were. "How did you get this number?"

"I'm afraid I led your sister-in-law to believe this call was an emergency."

Blast Daphne's soft heart. If she'd ever heard a sob story she didn't fall for, he didn't know about it. "It's all right."

"Do you have the contract with you?"

"Yes."

"There's still time to send it to Peter overnight."

There might be, if the island boasted anything remotely as modern as Federal Express. "I'm sorry, Ms. Halliday, I haven't made up my mind yet. I'll let you know when I do."

Garrett left the phone on the kitchen counter and headed outside to where Aristotle waited for him.

Garrett leaned back in the wicker chair he occupied and downed a gulp of the bottle of Red Stripe he'd been nursing for the past half hour. He glanced over at Aristotle, who lounged in his own chair, looking the epitome of the laid-back Caribbean male.

They'd just come from the house of the boy whom Aristotle had wanted him to see. After five minutes of being in the house, Garrett knew why Aristotle had asked him to come. Most Milagrans, it seemed, relied on the healing powers of a local herb woman rather than on any sort of doctor at all. In the absence of any tests, Garrett couldn't be certain what was wrong with the boy, who hadn't been able to tolerate solid food for a week, yet showed no sign of fever or infection. Whatever the problem, it was beyond the scope of herbs and potions, but the boy's mother had refused to get him medical treatment off-island.

The Milagrans themselves fascinated him. As word spread that he, an off-islander, had come to see the boy, neighbors began popping in, probably to make sure he wasn't torturing the boy with Western medicine.

From what he'd seen, the Milagrans were a remarkably healthy and long-lived group. He thought someone ought to do a longevity study on this bunch to see what made them tick.

The boy's mother had insisted on feeding him dinner as payment for his services, a simple meal of rice, beans, and some sort of stewed meat.

When they left the house, Aristotle thanked him for making the trip, but in truth, Garrett hadn't minded. It gave both him and Elise a chance to cool off apart from each other. He'd spent the afternoon turning his situation with Elise over in his mind. The only conclusion he'd come to was that he shouldn't have left her the way he had—and it didn't take a genius to figure that one out.

Garrett sighed. Elise had never denied him this long before; she'd never denied him, period. They were blessed with compatible sex drives and a firm policy that only one of them had to be fully awake to make love. There were times during his residency when Alyssa was a baby that they would never have touched each other if they'd waited for both of them to be awake, unhurried, and conscious. Even in the last couple of weeks when she was pregnant with Andrew and she couldn't stand for him to touch her, she'd found other ways to satisfy him. He had to admit the sudden bout of celibacy was making him a little crazy.

He'd allowed Aristotle to talk him into stopping at the one bar on the island. The men, Aristotle's cronies, enjoyed an easy camaraderie Garrett found appealing. No one asked him about his golf swing, which was remarkably bad since he rarely played. No one complained about how much their malpractice insurance had skyrocketed. No one played can-you-top-this when it came to listing their children's accomplishments.

The men seemed preoccupied with shooting pool, drinking beer, and the local women, in that order. The men's deference to and consideration of Aristotle made Garrett wonder what position in Milagran society the older man held.

"What has you so stressed, young man?"

Garrett blinked. He hadn't realized he'd zoned out until Aristotle spoke. "I'm sorry?"

"You can't still be having problems with your missus."

Garrett snorted, letting that be his only response to Aristotle's comment.

"I thought I told you to take care of that." Aristotle called to a man behind the bar, speaking to him in a language Garrett didn't understand. "I've got just what you need." The man behind the bar stepped around and handed Aristotle a pamphlet. Aristotle tossed the booklet on the table in front of Garrett. "Take a look at that."

Garrett noted the devilish smile on Aristotle's face, then looked down at the pamphlet. The cover read, THE MILAGRAN GUIDE TO GREAT SEX. Aristotle tapped the table. "Go on. Read it."

Garrett opened the cover, certain he knew what lay inside. He'd seen a similar gag way back when he was in college. The first page was blank, save for one word. "In," Garrett read aloud. "Out," read the second page. Garrett turned to the third page and read, "Repeat if necessary."

The other men in the bar, Aristotle included, erupted in guffaws at Garrett's deadpan delivery. When Aristotle recovered himself, he said, "Some rascal printed up a bunch of these and made a mint selling them to tourists."

Garrett tossed the pamphlet on the table. "Not only the tourists, apparently."

"We Milagrans enjoy a good joke."

"Well, that was nothing like a good joke." Garrett folded his arms across his chest, scrutinizing Aristotle. He didn't mind providing the men with a source of humor, but he doubted off-color jokes were uppermost in Aristotle's mind. "If you have something to say, why don't you just say it so we can go home."

Aristotle sighed, sobering. "I'm an old man not too far from meeting his Maker, which I figure allows me to say pretty much whatever I want. And I'll tell you something. It's a known fact that no woman is going to make love to you if she's mad at you. They're just not made that way."

Aristotle leaned back in his chair. "When's the last time you told her you loved her or that you appreciate all she does for you?"

Garrett lifted his shoulders and let them drop as he exhaled a breath. Honestly, he couldn't remember. But words had never meant much to him. His parents had told him they loved him, but that didn't prevent them from abandoning him whenever the mood struck. His aunt had told him she loved him, probably because it was the Christian thing to do, but he'd always known she attached no sentiment to the words. Her actions declared much more loudly that she considered him a burden, one of which she couldn't wait to be relieved.

In his mind, words didn't matter; actions did. To his knowledge, he'd never done anything to make Elise doubt his feelings for her.

"Elise knows how I feel," he said finally.

"Does she, now?" Aristotle tapped the tabletop with

the fingers of his left hand. "Take it from an old man who's been married to the same stubborn woman for more years than he cares to admit. Go home, take your lovely wife in your arms, and tell her you love her. Mark my words. You'll be surprised at the results."

Elise would probably call the men in the white coats, assuming he'd lost his mind. Although completely comfortable demonstrating his feelings physically, verbal effusiveness had never been his style.

Aristotle stood, a grin on his face. "We ought to get ourselves home. Maybe you can make things up with your missus tonight."

Garrett downed the rest of his beer and set the bottle on the table. Maybe, but he wasn't going to hold his breath.

A short while later, Garrett let himself into their rooms and went to find Elise. She lay on her side in bed, facing away from him. In all the years they'd been married, he'd never mastered the art of coming into a room without waking her. He knew she had to be awake, but she didn't stir, didn't give any indication of her awareness of his presence.

He wanted nothing more than to slip into bed beside her, to simply hold her, to feel her soft, warm body next to his. But he lacked the energy to wrangle with her or the wherewithal to withstand another rejection from her. With a sigh, he pushed off the door frame, went to his room, and got ready for bed.

The next morning, Elise awoke with a start. Her eyes focused on her husband leaning against the door frame of her room. If it weren't for the change of clothes and the smell of freshly applied aftershave that wafted to her, she would have sworn he'd been standing there all night.

But that was impossible. She'd lain in bed last night waiting for Garrett to come home. She'd known the instant he'd entered the door, and moments later, she'd sensed him standing by the door to her room. She'd squeezed her eyes shut and willed him to come to her. She knew that if she'd turned to him or called him, he would have joined her, but it wouldn't have been the same thing as if he'd come to her on his own. Eventually, she'd turned anyway, willing to admit defeat because she wanted her husband with her. But Garrett had already gone.

Now she leaned up on her elbows and managed a weak smile. "Hi."

"How are you feeling?"

It took her a moment to remember that when he'd left she'd told him that she was feeling poorly. "Better. How was the child you went to see last night?"

"Not good. His mother was hoping the local herb woman would cure him. He is the product of a liaison with an off-islander who'd lived here for a while. Once he abandoned her, she distrusted foreigners. I convinced her to have him looked at by a colleague of mine in Florida."

Elise nodded. "And that took you hours last night?"

"No." She sat up, leaning her back against the pillows as he came to sit beside her on the bed. "While I spoke to the mother, her great-grandmother fixed dinner. The woman was one hundred and seventeen, and her mother died less than a year ago. These people are amazing. Would you believe Aristotle is pushing ninety?"

"Get out! And you let him carry those suitcases to

our room. We're lucky the poor man didn't have a heart attack." She relaxed, realizing he hadn't stayed away out of anger at her, but because, as a doctor, he'd been intrigued by the Milagrans.

He ran his hand up and down her arm, his expression sobering. "Baby, we need to talk. I . . . we can't go on like this."

She nodded. She'd known this moment would come, and honestly she felt relieved more than anything. She should have been up front with him about how she felt from the beginning. "I know, Garrett, and I'm sorry. I should have been more forthcoming in the first place. I've been trying to show you that our marriage is in trouble."

"Don't you think I know that? Why do you think I agreed to come here in the first place? I could see us heading down a path I didn't want to take, but I didn't know what to do about it. I figured some time alone might be the remedy we needed. Until you slammed your bedroom door in my face."

"I didn't know you knew. I felt like I was alone and drowning, with no one to throw me a life preserver. I never would have done that if I'd known you felt the same way I did."

He leaned down, kissed her temple, then rested his forehead on her shoulder. "So, what do we do now?"

She wrapped her hands around his waist, holding him closer. "I honestly don't know."

"Then let's play it by ear, okay? Just enjoy spending time together. Like the T-shirt says, no hurries, no worries. Think you can do that?"

She nodded. "On one condition."

He lifted his head to smile down at her. "What's that?"

"We keep our hands off each other, at least for a little while."

His brow furrowed. "Why?"

"Don't you see? That's part of our problem. We spend so little time together, and most of it making love, when we should be connecting on another level."

She held her breath, watching him as his eyes probed hers. Part of her wanted him to tell her she was crazy, and refuse. Part of her wanted him to refuse, flat out, and tell her he wanted her too much to put up with such nonsense. So when he sighed and said, "If that's what you want," that part of her flooded with disappointment. She lowered her head to hide that emotion from him.

He stroked a lock of hair behind her ear. "So, what do you want to do today?"

She shrugged. "We're tourists. Why don't we take a boat back to Puerto Rico? I'd love to see more than just the airport."

"Sounds like a plan. I'll see if Aristotle can arrange it."

He rose from the bed and left the room. Elise wrapped her arms around herself, content that they'd made a good start.

Aristotle arranged for a boat and a driver to take them to Puerto Rico. He dropped them off at the dock in the capital city of San Juan, promising to be back for them that afternoon.

"What do you want to do first?" Garrett asked Elise as they walked the footpath of the bridge that led into the city.

"First stop is a drugstore so I can buy a disposable

camera. We haven't taken one picture while we've been here. Then I would love to see Old San Juan."

Once they bought the camera, they joined a tour going to the historic city. Most of the passengers on the tour bus were from a group visiting from Florida. The only other solo travelers were a young couple, both blond and blue-eyed, who spoke with a Midwest twang. As the bus bounced over the cobblestone streets on the way to the city and over the constant, monotone voice of the bus tour guide, they introduced themselves as John and Barbara O'Connell from Illinois.

"This is our first trip out of the United States," Barbara said.

"Honey, Puerto Rico is part of the United States," John said, in an indulgent voice.

"You know what I mean. Actually, it's our first trip anywhere. We got married two days ago."

Barbara held out her hand to show off a modest ring set as if she were displaying the crown jewels of England. "They're lovely," Elise said, and Barbara beamed at her.

"Honey, I'm sure the Taylors don't want to hear every bit of our personal business." John gave Elise a look of sympathy. "My Barbara would start a conversation with a stone if there was no one else around to listen."

"I'm not that bad," Barbara protested, smacking her husband on the arm.

Enjoying Barbara's enthusiasm, Elise said, "I don't mind, really. This is our first time on the island, too." She glanced up at Garrett, who'd been mostly silent since the introductions had been made, wondering if he minded her striking up a conversation with the other couple. He winked at her and put his arm around her shoulders.

"Don't you just love this place?" Barbara asked,

drawing Elise's attention. "Everything is so beautiful, and the weather. When we left home it was fourteen degrees and snowing."

"We weren't much better off in New York when we left."

The tour bus lurched to a stop, cutting off whatever response Barbara would have given. After everyone got off the bus, the driver introduced them to the guide who would take them through the city. They stopped first at a sixteenth-century house that had been converted into a museum. The antique furnishings on display included everything from a child's four-poster bed to pots and pans and the weapons of the day. Elise would have loved to get a closer look at everything, but the rooms were cordoned off from visitors with thick red rope.

The O'Connells walked in front of them the whole time, holding hands or whispering to each other or sneaking kisses when they thought no one noticed.

Elise turned to Garrett, who stood beside her. "Do you think we were ever like them?"

"Good Lord, I hope not. If you see a shop that sells earplugs, we're stopping."

"You know what I mean. Young and hopeful and so in love we couldn't control ourselves in public."

His expression sobered. "Is that how you want us to be?"

"Not now, no. But I'd like to think we started out with the same zeal they have."

He pulled her closer with an arm around her waist. "Do you remember the night we closed on the house? We made love in every bedroom, including the maid's room, with nothing to cover the floor but an old blanket. I always considered that the night Alyssa was conceived. We were so caught up in each other we didn't bother to use any protection. So, yes, I'd say we had our share of youthful zeal."

Elise smiled, remembering. Her father had lent them the money for the down payment on the house. Garrett had wanted something smaller, in a neighborhood they could afford themselves, but her father had been insistent. Why start out and entrench themselves in a place the family would eventually outgrow? Besides, the surrounding school district was one of the best in the country. Her father must have known something they didn't, because less than a year later, Alyssa had been born.

In those days, she wouldn't have dreamed of asking Garrett *not* to make love to her. They'd shared that kind of tear-off-your-clothes-and-throw-you-on-the-bed sort of passion women read about in romance novels.

Garrett had never actually torn off her clothes or thrown her on the bed, per se, but the keen desire to be with each other had burned in them. When had that faded to the comfortable, companionable lovemaking they now shared? They'd become so . . . civilized.

She'd always heard that passion faded in a marriage, but love endured. A little predictability was bound to set in. How many different ways could you make love without swinging from the chandelier or breaking the furniture?

But did that mean the feelings had to dim, too? When was the last time either of them had burned to be with the other? She glanced up at Garrett, wondering what he would say if she asked him that question. Remembering his easy acquiescence to her request that they remain apart physically, she looked away, doubting she really wanted to hear his answer.

* * *

After leaving the museum, they strolled through *El Morro,* a vast Spanish fort built in the 1600s to protect the island from intruders. Garrett stood by while Elise insisted on photographing everything, from the walls, which crumbled in places, to the sign that instructed in both English and Spanish how to fire a cannon, to the impressive view of the Caribbean Sea that rolled onto the beaches below them. She even got Barbara to take a picture of them, him standing on the ground, her standing on a pile of ancient cannonballs on display, joking that she was finally taller than he.

As he lifted her down from the pile, their bodies brushed together, stirring to life his desire for her that he'd kept in abeyance all day. His eyes locked with hers, and he wanted nothing more than to lower his lips to her sweet mouth. He kissed the tip of her nose instead and set her away from him. She lowered her head and her shoulders dipped. Had she wanted more from him, too?

He didn't know why that knowledge surprised him, but it did. He'd only agreed to the ridiculous condition because he hadn't been offered much of a choice. He'd assumed she'd made that request because her passion for him had cooled due to the strain between them. While he would never try to force her into something she didn't want, he wasn't above a little gentle persuasion to get at the truth of her feelings.

He tilted her chin up with the knuckle of his index finger and whispered one word, "Later." She pulled away from him almost immediately, but for a second there, he would have sworn he saw her smile.

Once they left the fort, the tour guide informed them they had an hour for lunch before the bus would return home. They ate a late lunch of *arroz con pollo*—chicken and rice—red beans in a savory sauce, and *tostones*—sweet plantains cut width-wise instead of lengthwise—and some home-brewed beer at a tiny open-air café.

After the bus dropped them off in front of the El San Juan Hotel, they said good-bye to the other couple, who stayed at another, less expensive hotel nearby. "What do you want to do now?" Garrett asked.

"Let's go inside and have a drink."

Garrett ordered a beer for himself and a glass of chardonnay for Elise. But the bar was crowded and noisy. After they finished their drinks, they decided to go for a walk on the beach behind the hotel.

The setting sun cast a rosy glow on the water out on the horizon. Elise and Garrett strolled hand in hand along the coastline, deserted except for a few children playing at the shore. Garrett broke the comfortable silence that had settled between them. "What are you thinking?"

She slanted a glance up at him, a faint smile turning up her lips. "I was wondering when was the last time we shared a day like this, just the two of us?"

Garrett squeezed her hand, pulling her closer so that he could put his arm around her waist. "I'm ashamed to admit it, but I don't know."

The sound of a distant motorboat reminded Elise that the driver who had brought them there probably awaited them at the dock. "We probably should start heading back."

Garrett stopped walking and pulled her into his arms. "Not quite yet."

She looked up into Garrett's intense gaze. "I thought you promised to behave yourself."

"I did." He touched his thumb to her cheek. "But I didn't think behaving myself meant I couldn't kiss you."

"It doesn't."

"Then kiss me, sweetheart."

She rose on her tiptoes and he met her halfway. But his mouth had barely settled on hers when they heard the sounds of nearby children headed their way. She pulled away from him, burying her face against his chest.

Resting his chin on the top of her head, he dragged in an uneven breath. What internal nuisance alarm did children possess that alerted them when adults, even total strangers, didn't want to be bothered? He squeezed the sensitive skin at the back of her neck. "I guess we'd better go."

Elise nodded, as he laced his fingers with hers and led her back to where the boat waited for them.

It was late afternoon by the time the driver pulled up to the dock at Milagro Island. Selena waited for them with the van to bring them up to the house.

"Are you hungry?" she asked, once they were all seated in the van. "Aristotle and Granny Verity went out, but I'm sure I can scrounge you up something when we get back to the house."

Garrett looked over at Elise, who shook her head. Thanks to the late, heavy lunch, he hadn't much of an appetite, either. "I think we'll head up to our rooms when we get home."

Once they got to their apartment, Garrett closed and locked the door behind them. He joined Elise on the sofa, pulling her into his lap for a long hug. He buried his face against her neck, inhaling the remnants of her perfume and her own natural scent.

Whether by accident or on purpose, her soft, moist lips grazed his neck. A rush of desire flooded through him, one he didn't bother to resist. He lifted his head, only to lower it again to cover her lips with his own. His tongue slid into her mouth, rubbing gently against hers in invitation.

He sensed the hesitation in her, but after a moment, she kissed him back, sliding her arms around his neck. He scrubbed his hands up her sides, his thumbs grazing the undersides of her breasts. When she didn't protest, he grew bolder, cupping his hand over her right breast. He rubbed his thumb against her distended nipple. She moaned and arched against him, making him wonder how far she'd let him go before she stopped him. Or if she would.

Satisfied he'd gotten the answer he'd wanted as to whether her passion had dimmed, he pulled away from her. Stroking her hair back from her face, he asked, "So, what do you want to do this afternoon?"

"I'm feeling lazy today. Let's go back to the beach. I might be adventurous and go in the water."

He feigned a shocked look. "Wonders never cease."

She smacked him on the shoulder. "I'm not that bad."

He kissed her forehead. "Let's go get changed."

A short while later, Elise walked into the sea, stopping when the water reached her waist. She watched Garrett swim toward her. Having made the mistake of saying she'd join him in the water, she knew he'd come out and get her if she didn't make some token attempt at going in.

He emerged from the water in front of her like some bronze Poseidon rising from the ocean. Her breath stalled in her throat as he walked toward her. Lord, he was beautiful. Although he'd begun to gray at his temples and laugh lines had begun to settle around his eyes and mouth, she still found him one of the handsomest men she'd ever met. And though his body wasn't as rock-solid as it had once been, he could still put men half his age to shame.

His gaze settled on her, sending a pulsing warmth rushing through her. He wanted her. She saw it in his eyes and the way his hands flexed at his sides, as if they itched to touch her. She longed to touch him, too. She ached for him and wished it had never occurred to her that continued abstinence might be a good thing for their relationship.

Garrett's hands settled on her waist. "What's the matter?"

She shook her head. "Nothing. The water's a little cold."

"I've noticed."

She followed his gaze down her body to her breasts. Her nipples had peaked and were clearly visible through the thin fabric of her bathing suit. She splashed a handful of water at him.

He caught both her hands and put them around his neck. Then grasping her waist, he leaned back in the water, taking her with him into the deeper water.

"Hold on to me," he said, "the water here is over your head."

"How convenient." He knew she wasn't a strong swimmer. She could float and tread water, but that was about it.

"What do you mean? I was hoping to give you one of those swimming lessons we've been talking about for years."

He looked down at her, the picture of innocence. But she knew he knew what she'd assumed: that he intended to take advantage of her vulnerability in the water. And he probably sensed her disappointment that he didn't.

"This is completely unnecessary. The only time I ever go into the water is with you."

"So if you're drowning, you intend to drag me down with you?"

The incongruity of that scenario made her laugh. "No."

"Seriously, sweetheart, it isn't safe. Everyone should know how to swim."

She gave in, because she knew he wouldn't. She spent the afternoon learning how to kick properly while Garrett held her hands, how to put her face under the water without getting any up her nose, and the rudiments of a basic stroke. Overall, she enjoyed herself, but she wondered if her skin would ever unpucker.

"That's enough for you for today," Garrett announced, as the sun began to set on the horizon. "Your lips are starting to turn blue."

Her teeth chattered. "You noticed."

"Why didn't you say something?"

Because she'd enjoyed the teasing camaraderie they'd shared that afternoon. She'd relished having Garrett's hands on her, even in a nonsexual way, as he'd shown her what to do. And she enjoyed the feeling of competency she gained knowing she could actually swim a few decent strokes without managing to drown herself.

Elise shrugged. "I was having a good time."

He took her hand and began to lead her from the water. "The next thing you'll have is pneumonia," he said, carrying her from the water. Once they reached the beach chairs, he grabbed one of the towels and wrapped it around her.

"So, how'd I do, coach?"

"Not bad for a first attempt. Hit the showers." He swatted her backside for emphasis.

By the time they'd showered and dressed for dinner, it had started to rain, a rarity for Milagran weather. Elise had asked Verity to bring supper for them into the solarium as the rain lashed the lanai, making it impossible to eat there. Garrett had relished his meal, while Elise had barely touched a thing, not even the ubiquitous cup of tea Verity included with every meal.

He sat on the sofa, ostensibly reading a copy of the *Times* imported from New York; in reality, watching Elise pace in front of the large window kept him more enthralled. After all her talk about a lack of communication between them, he wondered when she would get around to telling him what was on her mind.

"I thought rain in New York depressed me," she said finally. "In the city, at least, there's nothing but skyscrapers to feel the brunt of a storm. Those poor trees out there are taking a beating."

"Those poor trees are designed to take a heck of a lot more buffeting than what little they're getting from that storm." And he doubted the fate of some island trees really concerned her.

He folded the paper and laid it on the coffee table. "Come here, sweetheart."

She glanced over her shoulder at him, then did as he asked, coming to sit on her knees on the sofa, but as far away as possible.

He leaned over and took her hand. "What's really bothering you?"

She sighed. "I want a night."

"A knight? Does he have to have shining armor or will this tarnished one over here do?"

She pulled her hand out of his grasp and placed it in her lap. "Not that kind of knight. I want a night of the week, inviolable, just for us."

"What would we do with this night?"

"Whatever we wanted. We could ask Mrs. Allen to stay late, we could meet in the city for dinner or a show. It wouldn't really matter. Maybe we could simply . . . talk. But we would guarantee some time alone together."

"Did you come up with that just now?"

"No. While I was in the shower I started thinking that if we went back to the same old routine, nothing would change."

"What else did you come up with?"

"That's the extent of my brilliance for today. What do you think?"

"What night do you want?"

"How about Thursday?"

His late night, but it wouldn't take much to rearrange his schedule. "It's yours."

She launched herself at him, throwing her arms around his neck. "Thank you, Garrett," she whispered against his ear.

He cupped her face in his palms and tilted it so that he could look at her. "Did you honestly think I'd say no to spending time with you?"

She averted her eyes. "I don't know."

They had deeper problems than he thought if she didn't know that the rift between them affected him as much as it did her. He remembered what Aristotle had said about Elise needing to hear in words how much he cared for her. He might have been right, but Garrett couldn't seem to form a sentence in his mind that made a lick of sense.

Instead, he lowered his mouth to hers, while his hands

roamed over her back, telling her with his body what he could not express with words.

She melted against him, her fingers gripping his shoulders as he loved her with his mouth. When she finally pulled away from him, they both breathed heavily.

He set her away from him and stood. "Speaking of nights, I think we should call an end to this one."

She looked at him with eyes that were at first dazed, then resigned. She rose from the sofa. "Good night, Garrett."

He shoved his hands in his pants pockets as he watched her walk from the room, her reluctance almost a palpable thing.

For the first time since he'd known her, it appeared Elise didn't know what she wanted. Otherwise she wouldn't have hesitated to hold him to their bargain. But rather than push her, he'd give her the time to come to her own conclusion.

If it killed him, he would not make the next move. If she wanted him, she knew where he lived. Sooner or later, when she realized that denying themselves did nothing but make each of them miserable, she'd come knocking. And he wasn't going anywhere.

Eleven

"Wake up, sweetheart."

Elise opened her eyes to find Garrett sitting on her bed, a hand braced on each side of her. The yellow sunlight streaming in the window suggested the sun had just begun to rise.

She surveyed his appearance, realizing he was dressed to go out. "Where are you going?"

"Do you still want to go to this thing tonight?"

"Sure. Why?"

"Among other strange and bizarre island customs, the men and women are not supposed to see each other on this day until the event begins."

"How do they manage that?"

"Here, if you want to play, you have to work. The men meet down at the clearing to get the area ready. The women cook."

"How pre—Gloria Steinem. The men do the work that takes fifteen minutes while the women slave over a hot stove all day."

"Hey, I don't make the rules."

"No, you just benefit from them." She touched her fingertips to Garrett's cheek. "You don't have to do this, you know. We are not Milagrans."

"For today we are." He took her hand and kissed her

palm. "You're the one who wanted to go native. I wouldn't dream of depriving you of the full island experience."

She didn't know what to say to that. She'd rather spend the day alone with her husband than attend any public celebration she could think of. But Garrett seemed determined to go.

He leaned forward, bracing his hands on the mattress on the other side of her. "Will you miss me?" he asked.

She lifted one shoulder and let it fall. "Maybe."

"Just maybe?" He leaned closer and touched his lips to hers. He pulled away almost immediately, then tilted his head the other way and kissed her again, just as briefly, just as unsatisfactorily.

When his lips touched hers again, she slid her arms around his neck to hold him where she wanted him. She opened her mouth for him and his tongue plunged inside, mating sweetly with her own. His hand stroked up her side, until his thumb rested just beneath her breast. She gasped and clung to him, as his thumb roved upward, grazing her nipple.

This time when he pulled away, she let him go. He sat back, a self-satisfied smile on his face. "Still say you're not going to miss me?"

She hit his shoulder with the side of her fist. "You big tease," she accused.

"Yup." He leaned toward her again, this time kissing her forehead. "It's all I'm allowed to do since you put me on a leash." He ran a finger down her nose. "I'll see you in a few hours."

He rose from the bed and left. She sank back against her pillows, frustration radiating from every pore. He'd done that on purpose—roused her senses, then left her wanting. Perhaps that's what she deserved for not putting an end to this charade sooner.

She'd wondered when last either of them had burned for the other, and she had her answer: now. She couldn't speak for Garrett, but she knew she wanted him with an intensity she hadn't known in a long time. Considering Garrett's reaction to her overture this morning, she knew he wouldn't go back on his promise to behave himself. That left her in the position of having to seduce her own husband.

Elise smiled. A tough job. But she was just the woman to do it.

"No, no, no," Verity said in a voice full of exasperation. "You are supposed to roll it into a ball and flatten it, not squish it to death."

Elise glanced down at her hands. The mixture of fish, eggs, onions, and green peppers that was supposed to be a codfish cake was a sticky mess squeezed between her fingers. How anyone could be expected to shape this slimy mass into a presentable "cake" was beyond her.

"Now I know why you need a housekeeper at home," Verity groused. In a softer voice, she continued, "Please, go sit in that chair so we can finish."

Elise walked to the sink and turned on the water to wash her hands. Selena's soft laughter drew her attention.

"Granny, I think Elise is preoccupied."

"Yes," Verity agreed. "Elise, come sit on the chair and talk to me."

Sighing, Elise shut off the water and did as Verity asked, bringing the chair close to the counter where Selena stood, deftly forming codfish cakes for Verity to fry. She hadn't realized her anxiousness to see Garrett had shown on her face.

"Why haven't you been drinking the tea I gave you?"

"How did you know I didn't drink the tea?" Every time but the last, she'd been careful to dispose of it before Verity had come to collect the tray. She figured Verity thought she was being helpful by providing it, and she hadn't wanted to throw the woman's generosity back in her face.

Selena and Verity exchanged a glance. Selena looked away, smiling. Verity said, "Because if you had, you'd be grinning like a cheshire cat, not frowning like a sour-puss."

"Why? What did you put in it? Some strange island aphrodisiac?"

"Now, miss, your husband is a doctor. You know there is no such thing."

Elise said nothing to that, deciding instead to change the subject. "I'm sure we can find something to discuss other than my sex life."

"What would be the fun in that?" Verity asked. "Besides, that is what this whole day is about."

Elise's eyebrows lifted. "Sex?"

Verity heaved out a comic sigh. "Foreigners! Not sex, love. You Americans have your Valentine's Day, we have ours."

"So, this is just an excuse to gorge ourselves on chocolate and send each other overpriced floral arrangements?"

"Not at all," Selena cut in. "I told you that we celebrate the first island betrothals. Today we are not selecting marriage partners, but for the first dance, you are supposed to pick your true love. The first man you touch is yours."

"Ah. A Sadie Hawkins dance."

"Sadie who?"

"A Sadie Hawkins dance is one where the women

pick their dance partners rather than the other way around."

"Sounds like a smart woman, this Sadie," Verity said. She dipped a spatula into the pan and pulled out a cod-fish cake, sizzling hot and fried to a golden brown. She placed it on a plate and offered it to Elise. "Try that."

Elise accepted the plate, broke off a small piece of the cake, and brought it to her mouth. The savory fish melted on her tongue. "This is heaven."

Verity beamed. "Thank you, miss."

Elise smiled back, but Verity's sobriquet for her dulled her pleasure a little, for it held a measure of censure in it. Would Verity ever stop calling her that?

"Now, the two of you get out of my kitchen," Verity continued. "I have to finish up and you have to get ready."

Selena flashed an impish grin at Elise. "What are you planning to wear?"

Elise shrugged. "I haven't the faintest idea."

"Come on then." Selena waved her forward with a flick of her hand. "We'll look through your clothing, and if there's nothing suitable, we'll go through mine."

Remembering what Garrett had said about going native, Elise said, "On second thought, let's start with yours."

An hour later, Elise presented herself to Verity, bathed, perfumed, and coiffed. She wore one of Selena's outfits—a multicolored halter top that tied around her neck and at her midsection and a sarong skirt that tied low on her waist. On Selena the skirt came to midcalf; on Elise it grazed her ankles, drawing attention to her sandals, the same ones she'd worn their first night on the island.

"How do I look?" she asked.

"Just like an islander," Verity answered, looking her

up and down. "Only one thing missing." Two white orchids lay on the kitchen counter. Verity pinned one of them over Elise's left ear. Elise noted Verity wore a flower in her hair, too. "It is customary," Verity explained with a shrug.

Elise didn't believe that any more than she believed the Brooklyn Bridge was for sale. Especially when Verity pinned the other flower in Selena's hair. Verity gave her granddaughter an assessing look that made Selena blush and look down at the floor. Now what was that about?

Verity clapped her hands together. "I think we're ready." As it turned out, Verity had made not only the fish but fried plantains and a jug of fruit punch, undoubtedly laced with the overproof rum Garrett had warned her about. Once each woman had something to carry, they set off down a path out in back of the house.

After a few minutes, they came to a large clearing where a fake hardwood floor had been set up. At one end, a band composed mostly of steel drums and other exotic instruments played island rhythms. Dozens of men and fewer women milled about the area or sat in the assortment of chairs scattered at either side of the floor. Children played around the perimeter, laughing, chasing one another, or merely staring at the adults to see what they would do. It was a festive atmosphere, and Elise found herself immediately caught up in it.

Verity led her to a table where some women were laying out the food. Elise had wondered how the Milagran women managed not to touch the men until the first dance, but she knew now. All the men stayed on one side, all the women on the other, as if an invisible line down the middle separated the two.

Her eyes focused on Garrett, who sat on one of the

wicker chairs surrounded by a group of laughing, jovial men. As she helped Verity and the other women, she noticed how the men hung on his words, handed him their children to inspect, and otherwise treated him as if he were the long lost heir to the Milagran throne. Yet the women around her treated her with cordial civility, nothing more.

She smiled, bitterly. She'd never seen Garrett go anywhere where people didn't automatically welcome him. Part of it, she knew, was that Garrett genuinely liked people. He didn't expect them to conform to his expectations of them; he accepted them as they were—something she'd never learned how to do. He was so easygoing that, in comparison, she appeared the perennial shrew, always the one to put on the brakes or ruin everyone else's fun. Just once, she would like to be the carefree one and let Garrett worry about the consequences.

Elise sighed. Just how ridiculous was it to be envious of her own husband?

Verity elbowed her, drawing her attention. "What's the matter now? I thought I'd finally see a smile on your face once you got a look at that fine man of yours."

Elise trained her eyes on Garrett, letting her gaze roam over him. Verity had certainly picked the right adjective to describe him. He wore a white shirt tucked into a pair of white linen pants. The starkness of his attire accentuated the bronze of his skin, deepened by the days they'd spent in the Caribbean sun.

Elise exhaled, realizing she'd been holding her breath while she watched her husband. She'd been waiting for him to look her way, to notice her, and perhaps show her silently that he wanted her at that moment, as much as she wanted him.

As if sensing her watching him, he turned his head and fastened his eyes on her. Heat rose in her cheeks and pooled in her belly as his hot gaze panned over her, downward from her face and back again. He raised one eyebrow in a questioning gesture, undoubtedly wondering about her barely-there ensemble.

She lifted one shoulder in a sort of shrug. If someone had told her a week ago she'd be wearing such a skimpy outfit, she'd have told them they were crazy. But the look in Garrett's eyes made it worthwhile.

Verity grabbed her elbow. "Come along, you. There will be time enough for that later."

"I beg your pardon," Elise said, as Verity led her away. "I thought you said this wasn't about sex."

"It isn't. But it is a promise of shared intimacy. And since being in love tends to lead to making love . . ." Verity trailed off, shrugging. "In an hour, there won't be anyone here but kids and old people. Everyone with children has already made arrangements for them to be cared for during the next couple of days. It's our way of kindling new love and reaffirming old love."

A socially sanctioned two-day honeymoon every year. Elise could get used to that. A pediatrician's wife, she said, "I'd love to see the birthrate here nine months from now."

"Would it surprise you to know half the people on the island are born on the last day of September?"

Verity grinned, helping Elise load her plate with savory island dishes and a cupful of the punch Verity had made. After the women filled their plates, the men and children took their turn. Elise picked at her food, unable to concentrate on eating.

Soon, the participants had finished eating and an excited hum energized the crowd. Suddenly the music stopped. Elise turned to Verity, who sat beside her at one of the small tables around the perimeter of the clearing. "What's going on?"

"It's time for the first dance." The music resumed, a slow, seductive Latin rhythm that reverberated through Elise like a heartbeat.

"What happens now?"

"Shh," Verity said, her eyes on Selena.

Selena got to her feet, a seductive smile on her face. She crossed the invisible line that separated the sexes and made her way through the men until she reached a handsome brown-skinned man, nearly as tall as Garrett. She placed her right hand on his heart. He took her hand in his and led her to the center of the dance floor.

"My granddaughter chose well," Verity said.

"You were worried?"

"Selena is nearly twenty-two. She has never before deigned to participate. I was beginning to wonder about her."

The other women came forward to pick their men and join Selena on the dance floor.

Curious, Elise turned to Verity. "What happens if the person you ask to dance refuses?"

"He can't, not without breaching island customs. The men are a captive audience for the women. That policy has led to some very interesting scandals over the years."

"I can imagine."

Verity elbowed Elise. "How long are you going to keep your husband waiting?"

Elise scanned the shifting crowd to find Garrett. He stood now, his arms crossed over his chest, his gaze dark and intense. She'd thought the whole division of the sexes business silly beyond words when Garrett had told her about it. That's what this whole ceremony revolved around—creating a feeling of anticipation and uncertainty in the participants. She'd had as much anticipation and uncertainty as she could stand at the moment. Elise stood, smoothed her skirt over her hips, and walked toward her husband.

Garrett watched Elise advance toward him, threading her way through the crowd. From the moment he'd seen her enter the clearing with Selena and Verity, wearing the orchid he'd sent to her in her hair and that incredible outfit molded to her body, he'd wanted to drag her off— any promise he'd made to her be damned.

Aristotle had poked him in the ribs and told him to cool his jets. He'd behaved himself for the most part, making an effort not to look at her and torture himself with what he couldn't have. But seeing her walking toward him heated him right back up again.

Elise stopped in front of him, her hands clasped behind her back, a siren's smile on her lips. She squared her shoulders and tossed her head back. "Will you dance with me?"

A hint of a smile curved his lips. He'd do a lot more than that before the night ended, if she didn't watch herself. Still, he couldn't resist making her squirm a little. "Maybe if you ask me nicely."

Her eyes narrowed. "What does that mean?"

"You're supposed to touch me."

She stepped closer to him, and her scent wafted to him on the ocean breeze. She placed her hand on his heart, then trailed her fingers down his arm to clasp his hand in hers. "Dance with me, Garrett?"

He lifted her hand and kissed the back of it. "I thought you'd never ask."

He led her to the dance floor. Ignoring the slow,

insistent beat of the song and the animated dancing of
the others, he pulled her into his arms to sway gently
to the music. Elise laid her cheek against his chest and
her fingertips clutched his shoulders. For a long while
he contented himself with simply holding her.

Then her fingers threaded through the hair at his
nape and she moved against him in a way designed to
arouse.

He lifted his head and looked down at her. She regarded him with an intensity in her amber eyes that did
something wicked to his insides.

She tilted her head to one side and, affecting a Mae
West come-hither look, she said, "Is that an ophthal-
moscope in your pocket, or are you just happy to see
me?"

He laughed, but his breathing hitched as she rubbed
up against him. "Right now," he said, "I'm practically
ecstatic."

With the same sexy smile on her lips, she leaned
toward him. "Do you mind if I make a confession?"

"What's that?"

Her warm breath fanned his hear. "I'm not wearing
any underwear."

He froze as a current of white-hot desire snaked
through him. She'd spoken those words as if daring him
to discover the truth of them himself. He took her hand
and began to lead her away from the others.

"Where are we going?"

"Back to the house." She looked as if she might protest, but it was too late for that. He leaned down to
whisper in her ear, "You can go either on your own
two legs, or over my shoulder, or—if you really want
to do it barbarian-style—I can drag you off by your
hair. But we are leaving—*now.*"

He didn't wait for an answer from her, merely pulled

her along with him toward the path that led to the house. Once he got her into their room, he leaned his back on the door to close it. She had already stepped farther into the room.

"Come here," he said, his voice a deep growl in his throat.

She walked toward him, her hands clasped behind her back. She stopped a hairbreadth away from him. "Do you want something, Garrett?"

Didn't she know she was playing with fire? His eyes burned and her scent singed his nostrils. His body pulsed with the sort of need he hadn't experienced since the first time she'd made love to him. But even then, he'd felt in control of his own libido. In the past few days, she'd heated him up, pushed him away, taunted him with her nearness, and nearly crossed his eyes when she'd made that "confession" down at the clearing. He'd had about all from her he could stand. Like a shotgun with a hair trigger, it wouldn't take much for him to go off.

"You know what I want."

"Do I?" She closed the gap between them by sliding her arms around his neck and pressing her body to his. "Maybe you'd better show me."

Desire sizzled through him as his arms closed around her and his mouth found hers. His tongue invaded her mouth, hot, hungry, greedily taking what she'd denied him for so long. His hands gripped her hips, pulling her against his erection. She moaned into his mouth, inflaming him more, turning the kiss even wilder than it had been before.

Her fingers tugged at his shirt, pulling it free of his waistband. His breathing ragged, his heart pounding, he allowed her to pull it over his head. Leaning back against the door, his hands settled over her breasts, kneading, squeezing, molding her soft flesh to fit the palms of his hands. But he wanted more. He undid the ties that held her top in place and let it fall to the floor. His eyes drank in the sight of her small, perfectly rounded breasts. Then he lowered his head, taking one nipple and then the other into his mouth and suckling her. Her back arched, and her head lolled back on her shoulders. His name was a breathless sigh on her lips.

But he had to know if she had been telling him the truth or simply baiting him. He undid the knot at her hip and the skirt fell away. He slid his hands around to cover her buttocks. His fingers tensed, squeezing her soft flesh, finding nothing but her smooth, bare skin.

"Oh, God," he groaned against her throat. He picked her up with his arms around her hips and carried her to his bedroom. Her hands were on him, caressing him with featherlight touches, and her mouth rained moist, sensual kisses on his heated flesh.

He dropped her onto the bed. She landed on her back, her legs sprawled provocatively. She leaned up on her elbows, her avid eyes on him as he shed the rest of his clothing. All he could think about was being cradled between those thighs and burying himself inside her.

An instant later, he covered her body with his and thrust into her. She arched into him, locking her legs around his waist. Her fingers tangled in his chest hair, her thumbs stroking his nipples. It was too much. It would be over before it started if he let her have her way. He grasped her wrists and pressed her arms back against the mattress, over her head.

He thrust into her again as she rocked her hips against his, taking him deeper inside her. She gripped him, both with her legs and more intimately with vaginal muscles. He squeezed his eyes shut, struggling in vain for a control he did not possess. She squeezed him again and he succumbed, thrusting into her like a madman, his body perspiring, his heart beating like a jackhammer.

She called his name, a breathless, broken cry that was his undoing. He threw his head back, and with a series of harsh groans, poured himself inside her.

Spent, he collapsed on top of her, burying his face against the side of her throat. He dragged in air, wondering what she must think of him. He'd never done anything like that before, never allowed himself to be so out of control that all he thought about was fulfillment. He prided himself on showing her only gentleness, always seeing to her needs before he worried about his own, always showing her without words how much he cared for her.

He'd just made love to her with all the finesse of a bull elephant in must. But he'd been positive he hadn't gone on that ride solo until he looked down at her face and saw the tears on her cheeks.

He brushed the moisture from her cheeks with the pad of his thumb. "I did not hurt you, Elise. Tell me I didn't hurt you."

She shook her head and her eyes drifted open halfway. "What are you talking about?"

"You were crying."

She lifted a hand and swiped at her eyes. "You'd cry, too, if I made you feel anything near what you just did to me." She ran one of her feet up the outside of his leg. "Do you think you could do that again sometime when I'm not expecting it?"

"You mean surprise you?"

She nodded and he laughed, rolling onto his back and pulling her on top of him. "As long as I live, I don't think I'll ever understand you."

Right then, she didn't need understanding; she needed him. She cupped his face in her hands and brought her mouth down to his.

Twelve

Elise woke the next morning to the sound of island birds singing outside her window. She and Garrett had fallen asleep spoon fashion, her back to his front. She looked over her shoulder at him. It didn't surprise her that he still slept. Neither of them had gotten much sleep last night. Although tired herself, she knew she'd never fall back to sleep. Carefully, so as not to wake him, she slid from the bed.

She went to her own room, showered and dressed in her red caftan, and went downstairs to find Verity. As she'd expected, Verity stood at the kitchen counter, but Elise hadn't expected to find several youngsters seated at the small kitchen table.

Then she remembered that Verity had said the couples with children had made arrangements for them to be kept elsewhere. Apparently, for some of them, that elsewhere was here.

"Good morning, miss," Verity said cheerily. "I hope you don't mind. Your husband said it would be all right, and it's only for this morning."

"It's fine." She understood her husband well enough to know that if told a child, any child, needed something, he'd do all in his power to provide it. Which is why it hadn't surprised her when Garrett had gone off with Aristotle to see the child the other night. Her husband couldn't be content spoiling their own children; he had to take on the rest of the world's as well.

"Is there anything I can do to help?"

"You can pour the young ones some juice."

Elise reached for the pitcher of orange juice at the center of the table and filled the children's cups. They munched on a breakfast of bacon, fried plantains, and corn bread.

As she set the pitcher down, Elise felt a hand tug on her clothes. She looked down to find the culprit—a little girl who couldn't be more than five years old.

The girl smiled up at her, holding out a cloth doll. "Do you like my dolly?"

Like the girl, the doll had dark skin and black hair plaited into two braids. "She's very pretty," Elise said. "Just like you."

"I'm smart, too. What's your name?"

"Mrs. Taylor. What's yours?"

"Anna."

"That's a very pretty name, Anna."

"Anna, you eat your breakfast and leave Mrs. Taylor alone."

Elise opened her mouth to say she didn't mind, then closed it. She didn't want to undermine Verity's authority with the children.

"Can I get you something, miss?"

"Some coffee would be nice. And some of those plantains, if you have any left. I think I'm becoming addicted to them." Elise faced Verity, who scrutinized her with a narrow-eyed stare. Then a knowing smile broke out across her face.

"You are sounding chipper this morning."

"I'm feeling pretty chipper." Elise didn't see any point in trying to hide from Verity what she must already know. Anyone who'd seen Garrett rush her off the dance floor the previous evening could have guessed what they'd spent the night doing.

Grinning, Verity placed a cup of coffee and a plate of plantains in front of her. "If you don't mind, I'm going to take this into the garden. I'd love to see the flowers in full bloom."

"Please do. Aristotle prides himself on his garden. He'll be happy to know that you are enjoying it."

Elise let herself out the back door and headed along the path that led around the side of the house. It led to an alcove shrouded by a latticed bower from which heavy bougainvillea vines thick with blossoms grew. Underneath the bower sat a small wrought-iron bench and matching round table. Undoubtedly, it was a place for lovers. She settled on the bench, holding her cup and placing her plate on the table. She closed her eyes, breathing in the heady scent of the flowers.

She leaned back and let out a sigh, more contented than she'd felt in a long while. Last night had been a magical one, full of making love and reconnecting, one she couldn't have imagined sharing with her husband only a few days ago. They'd made love, but they had also talked, laughed, shared memories that they thought they had forgotten. They'd fallen asleep in each other's arms, exhausted yet happy. The island had given them their own little miracle, and she would give anything if she could just manage not to mess it up. She rose from the bench and walked back to the house to find Garrett.

Verity and the kids had left the kitchen by the time she let herself back into the house. Verity had already done the breakfast dishes and stacked them to dry on a drainboard beside the sink. Elise quickly scraped and washed her dishes, not wanting Verity to catch her. She could understand the older woman's pride in her job, but she questioned the wisdom of whoever charged two octogenarians to maintain a place this size. Elise dried her hands on a dishtowel, then followed the sound of children's laughter into the solarium.

Elise stopped in the doorway, laughter bubbling up inside her. Garrett, dressed in the T-shirt she'd bought him at the market and a pair of shorts, sat on the sofa, three of the youngsters snuggled up beside him, giggling as he treated Anna to a game of "Bucking Bronco." Garrett bounced her on one leg, simulating the dips and turns of a wild horse. Anna shrieked and clung to his hands, obviously enjoying herself.

If she'd needed a reminder of why she loved her husband, she had a powerful one right in front of her. He'd had a choice between a career of self-aggrandizement and one in which he could help others, and he'd chosen the latter long before life made the choice for him. She admired that more than she would ever be able to express to him.

When little Anna had tired of the bronco game, Garrett lifted her from his lap and set her on the sofa.

"I'm next," the lone boy in the group shouted. "I'm next."

"Ladies first," Elise said from her spot at the door.

Garrett turned to look at her. The smile on his face eased away to become a heavy-lidded gaze of masculine appraisal. She supposed she passed muster, as Garrett held out his hand to her and said, "Come here."

She walked over to the sofa and Garrett scooted one of the kids out of the way so that she could sit beside him. He kissed her cheek, then whispered in her ear, "Want a ride on my lap, little girl?"

"I'll wait my turn—perhaps in a more private setting."

"I think I can arrange that. What would you say to a hike and having a picnic up on the mountain?"

"I'd say hello, Hike, how are you?"

It was the kind of dry, silly humor he used on kids to put them at ease. He rolled his eyes back and let his head loll to one side, as if her joke had rendered him comatose. The children climbed all over him, trying to "revive" him.

Elise giggled and extracted herself from the fracas. "I'm going to get dressed. I'll meet you back here in ten minutes."

Up in her room, Elise quickly pulled on a pair of beige, elastic-waisted shorts and matching T-shirt and laced up the tennis shoes she was grateful to have had the foresight to pack. She ran a comb through her hair and declared herself ready.

Garrett waited for her at the bottom of the stairs, facing away from her. He carried a knapsack on his back, which she assumed contained the ingredients for their picnic. As she approached, he turned to face her. "Are you ready to go?"

She nodded. "Where are we going?"

"A little spot Aristotle told me about."

He led her out the back door and onto the path that led to the beach, but rather than curving left down to the sand, they headed right, toward higher ground. Unlike the path down to the beach, which was smooth from use, this path was rocky and uneven. Several times, they had to climb over boulders or squeeze themselves through lanes made narrow by the overgrowth of flora.

After twenty minutes of walking, Elise started to perspire and her face and neck burned with an internal fire. Her heart sped as if she'd run a five-mile race rather than walked less than a mile. She stopped, tugging on Garrett's hand to get his attention.

"Do you mind if we stop for a few minutes?"

"Not at all." He cupped his palm over her shoulder. "Are you all right, sweetheart?"

"I'm a little tired, I guess." She fanned herself with her hand. "It's awfully hot out today."

"I doubt it's eighty degrees." He laid his palm on her forehead. "If you're not feeling well, we should go back."

"No." She wanted this time alone with him, and going back wouldn't have any effect on what ailed her. "I'm okay now." She straightened and preceded him along the path.

Eventually they came to a broad meadow, ringed with azaleas. A lone palm tree stood sentinel over the area.

"This must be the place," Garrett said. He walked to the center of the meadow and dropped the knapsack to the ground. He beckoned to her. "Help me spread the blanket."

Garrett pulled a red-and-white checkered blanket from one of the knapsack's pouches and tossed one end of it to her. Though thin in texture, the blanket was large enough to accommodate both of them easily. They took off their sneakers and socks and left them on the side of the blanket.

"Are you hungry?" Garrett asked.

Honestly, she didn't have much of an appetite. She tried to nibble on the seafood salad, fresh vegetables, and some leftover codfish cakes Verity had packed for them, knowing Garrett would be suspicious if she didn't eat something.

The food had been packed in a large Tupperware container tucked inside another that had once been full of ice. A plastic bag of fruit salad was the only thing that remained in the ice water. Garrett had eaten everything else.

With her usual neatness, she collected the debris from their lunch in a plastic bag and tucked it inside the knapsack. When she sat back facing Garrett, he gazed at her with such a hungry, intense look that her cheeks flooded with heat and she found it impossible to hold his gaze.

It hadn't occurred to her that he'd brought her up here to seduce her, but something about the way he looked at her told her he'd planned this long before they'd taken their first step out of the house. His hand slid beneath her shirt to cup her right breast.

She pushed his hand away. "Garrett," she protested, "have you lost your mind? We are not a couple of teenagers rolling around in the grass."

"No, we are grown adults who can do as we please."

"Someone might see us."

"Who? A mountain goat? We nearly killed ourselves getting up here. Besides, from what Aristotle told me, all this is the owner's land. No one else would come up here."

As he spoke, he'd relieved her of her T-shirt and now made short work of removing her bra. He dropped it onto the blanket beside her. She immediately crossed her arms in front of her. In truth, with the amount of foliage surrounding them, she didn't fear anyone spying on them. But she was afraid. She sensed an aggressiveness she'd never felt in him before. Last night, she'd given him permission to look at her differently, to treat her differently. She wondered if this heralded the demise of the gentle, sensitive lover she'd known for almost twenty years.

He touched his fingers to her cheek. "Relax, baby, and let me look at you."

She scanned his face for signs of the Garrett she knew. In his eyes, she saw the same hunger, but also the love she knew he felt for her. Slowly she moved her arms away.

Garrett cupped his hand over one breast and then the other. "Are you still warm?"

She nodded.

She stared at him, puzzled, as he turned away from her, toward the container of food. "What are you doing?"

He didn't answer her, which let her know he was up to something. When he turned back, he offered her a piece of melon. She nibbled it from his fingers. The ice-cold fruit, ripe and juicy, melted in her mouth. He popped a piece of fruit into his own mouth and chewed. Then he leaned forward, braced one hand on the blanket beside her and covered her mouth with his.

His tongue, cool and tasting of the sweet fruit, plunged into her mouth. She captured it and sucked on it, as his other hand cupped her nape and squeezed. Her neck arched, as a pleasure-filled shiver traveled down her spine and up to her scalp simultaneously. But he broke the kiss, and suddenly a chasm of distance separated them. At first she thought he'd pulled back from her. Instead, he'd lowered her to lie on the blanket beside him.

He cupped her right breast in his palm, rolling her nipple between his thumb and index finger. "Did that feel good?" he asked her, his voice as rough as coarse gravel.

With his hand on her like that, she could only manage a weak nod. She didn't see him put a piece of fruit in his mouth, but when he lowered his head to take her left nipple into his mouth, she felt it, deliciously cool and wet, and oddly soothing. She shivered and her hips arched off the blanket. Before she could settle back down again, Garrett slid his hand over her hips and pulled her shorts and panties from her body.

She stiffened, for the first time since she'd known him feeling vulnerable and naked in more than a physical sense—not because he frightened her, but because she had no idea what he would do.

He lifted his head and stroked his fingertips over her cheek. His eyes, dark, concerned, but ringed in fire, bored into her. "I would never hurt you, Elise."

"I know."

"Then let me love you."

His lips touched down on her belly, moving lower. She squeezed her eyes and let the sensations wash over her. His mouth and his hands moved over her, cooling her skin, but igniting an inferno within her. She whimpered, and her cries echoed through the meadow, reverberating back to her.

He pushed her legs wide and settled between them. She felt his cool breath on her heated skin before the tip of his tongue touched the most sensitive core of her. He slid two fingers, ice-cold from handling the fruit, inside her. She screamed his name, but her heated flesh gripped his fingers and her body arched toward him.

He teased her with exquisitely slow movements of his lips and tongue, designed to arouse, not satisfy. She writhed beneath his tender onslaught, her breath coming in harsh gasps and sighs, her body perspiring and aching. She rocked her hips against him, demanding more.

"Garrett, please," she moaned.

"Please what, baby?"

"I want you inside me."

It took him all of two seconds to divest himself of his clothing. He positioned himself between her thighs and rubbed himself against her. "Is this what you want?"

He didn't wait for her answer. He thrust into her, and her body shivered as she enveloped him. "Oh, God," she whispered against his chest.

He kissed her mouth, her cheeks, her eyelids, the soft column of her arched throat, all the while moving gently within her. She wrapped her legs around his waist, silently urging him to hurry.

He brushed her damp hair back from her face. "Not yet, baby. Not yet."

She closed her eyes as he buried his face against her throat, continuing the same deliberate pace that drove her mad. His lips caressed her throat with featherlight touches that made her tremble. Deep in her belly, an exquisite tension coiled, making her writhe beneath him, making her ache for the ecstasy she knew would follow.

His hands slid beneath her, cradling her in his arms. "Now, Lesi," he whispered in her ear. "Come for me now."

Surrounded by the warmth of his big body, his provocative words ringing in her ears, she let go, releasing the modicum of control she still held. Pleasure exploded in her brain and rippled through her body, making her buck against him wildly and cry out his name. Hearing Garrett's own harsh groan, she held him to her, kissing his shoulders, his chest, the side of his neck. For a long while, they lay together, recovering. He squeezed her more tightly to him, and her eyes flickered open.

He gazed at her with heavy-lidded eyes. "How are you doing?" he asked her.

"I'll let you know when I can talk again."

He chuckled and pressed his lips to her mouth for a brief kiss. She closed her eyes and replayed the last few minutes in her mind. If Garrett had rocked her world off its axis last night, he'd sent it crashing into the sun this afternoon. She'd never felt anything like what she'd just experienced with him. He'd said he wanted to love her, and he'd kept his word. She'd never felt more cherished by him than she did right now.

"What's the matter?"

She met his gaze, but she didn't want to tell him. She didn't want to dissect how she felt, only wanted to bask in the glow of the warm island day and being with him. "You're smushing me."

"Sorry." He rolled onto his back and pulled her on top of him. His hands rested low on her back. "Is that better?"

"Much."

She snuggled against him, leaning her head on his chest. The warm afternoon sun beat down on her, and a gentle ocean breeze stirred her hair. For the moment, she was completely content to lie in her husband's arms. Then she heard him snore.

She lifted her head and looked down at him. His eyes were closed and his breathing was deep and even. "Garrett?"

He mumbled something, but didn't stir. "Not too typical," she muttered, but she didn't really mind. Slowly, gently, so as not to wake him, she slipped from his arms and stood.

Awakened by the call of an island bird flying overhead, Garrett stretched and reached for Elise. Alarmed, he lifted his head and scanned the glade. He almost laughed finding Elise, nude as the day she was born, wandering through the wildflowers. Every now and then, she stooped to smell a blossom or to pick one for the bouquet she collected in one arm.

He couldn't remember seeing her this carefree. He was glad he was able to give her a day like this, with no commitments, no worries, only the two of them enjoying a balmy island day.

Finally, she straightened and walked toward him. He closed his eyes slowly, so as not to attract her attention. He didn't want her to feel self-conscious that he'd watched her. She stood over him and dumped the armload of flowers on his stomach. He jerked in surprise.

"I know you are not asleep anymore."

He brushed the flowers from his body. "How did you know?"

She lay down beside him. "You stopped snoring."

He turned on his side to face her. He picked up one of the flowers and grazed her breasts with its petals. "Elise Taylor, nature girl. I kinda like that."

"Do you?" She stretched, more as an enticement than a means of relieving tension. He hugged her to him, hearing her soft laughter.

"What's so funny?"

"I just noticed our shoes. They look like two tugboats leading two great big steamships out to sea."

He turned his head to have a look for himself. Their shoes were lined up with hers in front and his behind. "Are you trying to say I have big feet?"

"Yes, but they're not the biggest thing about you." She ran her hand down his body to cup him.

Garrett groaned as her fingers encircled his shaft and squeezed. Her soft hands stroked him, bringing him almost painfully erect. "Don't play with that too much. It might go off."

"Really? Let's see." She rose to a kneeling position, straddled his waist, and took him inside her.

He gazed up at her through half-closed lids, marveling at her boldness when two days ago she wouldn't even let him touch her.

She lifted one shoulder and let it drop. "You promised me a ride on your lap, didn't you?"

His fingers grasped her hips, lifting her and setting her down again. "I'm not complaining."

"Y-you'd better not."

He smiled, hearing the breathless catch in her voice. He cupped her face in his hands and brought her mouth down to his. He thrust into her as his tongue invaded her mouth, drinking in her sweetness, absorbing the ragged moan that made it past her lips.

He ran his hands down her back, to cup her buttocks in his palms. She broke the kiss and drew back, her amber eyes dark and hypnotic. He inhaled, and the heady aroma of their lovemaking, mingled with the fragrance of the island flowers and the tang of the ocean, filled his nostrils. He closed his eyes, wanting to prolong this moment between them forever.

Then she leaned down and whispered four words he'd never heard from her lips before: "Come for me, Garrett." And he lost it. His arms closed around her, crushing her to him, as wave after wave of pure ecstasy flooded through him. He felt her contract around him, her fingers digging into the flesh of his shoulders. He brought her mouth down to his, taking her cries into his mouth until they finally subsided.

They lay there together a long while, locked in each other's embrace. Completely relaxed, completely sated, he ran his hands over her lax body. After a while, she shifted to lie on her side next to him, facing toward the horizon where the sun set in brilliant hues of red, orange, and gold. Garrett turned on his side, facing her. He stroked his hand over her belly. "What's wrong?"

"Nothing. But I wish I had a sketch pad with me. That sunset is glorious."

It occurred to him that it had been years since he'd seen her draw anything except plans for somebody else's house. He circled his hand down to her hip and gave it a squeeze. "Why don't you draw anymore?"

She lifted her shoulders and, sighing, let them drop. "Between work and the kids and the house, who has time? With so much to do it seems, I don't know, frivolous."

In that moment he vowed to buy her the biggest sketch pad and the largest box of charcoals he could find, as soon as he got back to the States—and allow her enough leisure to enjoy them.

As the sun set, it took with it the heat of the day. Elise shivered. "It's getting cold."

The temperature hadn't dipped that much in the last few minutes. Yet Elise's skin had broken out in goose bumps. He scrubbed his hand over her arm to warm her. First hot, now cold, she'd been irritable, to put it mildly, hadn't had much of an appetite. He cataloged her symptoms and came to a stunning prognosis. Could Elise be pregnant?

He could understand her reticence to tell him if she were. They'd both decided they didn't want any more children, though neither of them had sought to prevent them in a permanent way.

He coaxed her onto her back and splayed his hand over her abdomen, just above her pubic bone. He found no evidence of a pregnancy, but it might be too soon to tell.

For now, he wouldn't press her about it. Maybe she didn't know yet herself. But he ought to get her back to the house, before darkness fell. He kissed her forehead again. "As much as I've enjoyed our day, I think we'd better go."

A short while later, Elise and Garrett let themselves in the back door. Verity stood at her usual place at the sink. But instead of her characteristic dimpled grin, Verity's face bore a troubled expression that worried Elise. Elise silently signaled to Garrett that she would join him upstairs later and came to stand beside her at the counter.

"Verity, what's the matter?"

The older woman let out a long breath, a sigh as old and heavy as the ages. "Selena and Winston came to see us today."

Elise assumed Winston was the young man Selena had selected at the festival. "Why does that make you sad?"

"Although Winston was born here, he left for the States as soon as he reached majority. Milagro is not a place for the ambitious. Here we farm, we fish, we conduct our lives much as we have for centuries. The young people who want more must find it elsewhere, and they do. Selena and Winston want to get married."

Elise bit her lip. That meant Selena would leave the island with him.

"When I saw Winston at the festival," Verity continued, "I felt such pride to see one of our young men return home, but I didn't know he'd come back for Selena. They were close when they were younger, but I had no idea they'd remained such fast friends. I don't begrudge Selena her happiness, but I wish I'd had more time to prepare."

Verity turned away, going to the sink to rinse the vegetables. Elise noted her slow, sluggish movements, not those of the brusque, energetic Verity she'd come to know. And she suspected more existed to this story than Verity let on. She knew she'd be prying to ask the question that circled around in her head. But if Verity didn't want Elise snooping in her affairs, all she'd have to do is say so.

"What happened to Selena's parents?"

"My daughter married an off-islander, some reputed big shot that blew in here like a hurricane and swept her off her feet. He promised her the moon and the stars, and, naively, she believed him. We fought terribly, and in the end I told her if she wanted to marry him, she could do so without my blessing."

Verity pressed her lips together, obviously fighting tears. Elise covered Verity's hand with her own, hoping to offer her comfort.

"We each said some things that we later regretted," Verity continued. "I forgave my daughter, but she never forgave me. I never saw her again until she lay in her coffin at the burial service. She and her husband died in a car crash. He'd been drinking."

Elise squeezed Verity's hand. "You can't possibly blame yourself for that."

"No, but I had always been very protective of my Sarah, guarding her from any of life's heartaches. I even refused to let her keep company with boys, though the people here tend to date and marry very young."

Verity wiped away a single tear that had made its way down her cheek. "Aristotle was not my first husband. I had married young and to a man who I grew to despise. I sought to keep her from making the same mistake I did."

"Isn't that what every parent tries to do?"

"Yes, but perhaps if I had shown her the world instead of offering her blinders, she would have seen through a man like Reginald for herself."

Elise didn't know what to say to that. She recognized in herself the same overprotectiveness, the same desire to shield her children from harm. "What has that got to do with Selena?"

"History repeating itself, I suppose. Except that I know Winston is a good man, and Selena has a good head on her shoulders. I vowed to myself when she came to us after her parents' deaths that I would not do to her what I had done to her mother."

"Then all you can do is give her your blessing and let her go. But unlike your daughter, Selena will be back. I can see in the way the two of you interact how much she loves and respects you."

Verity brightened, the characteristic sparkle coming back into her eyes. "Or we can go visit her. But I will miss her. She has been the light of this old woman's life."

"Don't let Aristotle hear you say that," Elise chided. "He thinks he's the light of your life."

Verity laughed heartily. "That old man thinks the sun doesn't shine except to warm his back." Verity switched on the tap and let the water run over her vegetables. "Now, it's time you got out of my kitchen. I have supper to prepare."

Elise smiled and patted Verity's hand. "And I need a shower. I'll see you at dinner."

She started toward the kitchen door when Verity called to her. "Thank you, Elise."

Elise beamed, hearing Verity use her given name and the unspoken compliment the word contained. "Anytime, Verity."

Thirteen

Garrett noticed the frown on Elise's face the moment she came through the door. "What's the matter with Verity?" he asked.

Elise bent one leg and sat facing him, resting the other leg on the floor. "It seems Selena and Winston want to get married."

"What's so bad about that? I met Winston. He seems like a nice kid."

"He is, but he lives in Florida and wants to take Selena back with him."

"Verity doesn't want her to leave?"

"It's not just that. Verity made some mistakes with her own daughter, which caused them to be estranged. She didn't approve of the man her daughter married and the two of them never spoke again."

She huffed out a breath. "Sometimes I think that's the fate awaiting Alyssa and me—she'll bring home some do-nothing who thinks gluing bits of junk together is making art and I'll hit the ceiling."

He covered her hand with his. "If you do, I'll be right up there next to you." He sighed, as his attempt at humor bombed miserably. He squeezed her hand. "Why don't you call her?"

Elise shook her head. "She'll think I'm checking up on her. The concert was last night."

"Let her think whatever she wants." Although Alyssa chafed against the boundaries Elise had set for her, he knew she appreciated them nonetheless. Unlike the parents of most of the kids Alyssa knew, Elise didn't hand her kids a credit card and send them shopping when they really wanted their mother's attention. The kids knew they had her ear and her concern. Despite her demanding, time-consuming job, no one would consider her an absentee mother.

"If it will make you feel better, you should call her," he reiterated.

She got up and walked to the cabinet that housed the TV, resting her hands on one of the shelves. "You know what would make me happy? To have some indication that what I'm doing is the right thing. Half the time I feel like I'm wandering around blind, searching for the answers. And oddly enough, I miss my mother. I wish I could turn to her and ask her advice. She *always* knew what to do."

Elise sighed, lowering her head. "Having a paragon for a mother is a double-edged sword. While she was alive, she was always, always there for us, but in comparison, I feel completely inadequate."

He got up from the sofa and wrapped his arms around her waist from behind. "Sweetheart, your mother was a nice lady, but she was no paragon."

Elise stiffened in his arms. He squeezed her waist. "No, listen to me. I may have only met her once, but as an outsider, I think I saw some things you were too close to the situation to see. I can't tell you how many times I saw your mother look to your father for advice or support or guidance. Your mother may have been the vocal one, but, baby, your parents were a team."

She said nothing for a moment, seeming to digest what he said. "And we're not?"

"Not like they were, no."

"I see."

The hurt in her voice tore at him. He rested his chin on the top of her head. He didn't blame her for that. If anything, the fault lay more with him than with her. Though he complained about his schedule and lack of time with the kids, he knew on a deeper level that he'd hung back from being more involved in his kids' lives, fearing that his intervention would more likely screw them up than benefit them.

But before he got a chance to say anything, Elise pulled away from him. "I guess we'd better find out if Verity bothered to make us anything for dinner."

As they sat at the table out on the lanai, Elise pushed her food around on her plate. Verity had outdone herself with the shrimp scampi, but Elise couldn't bring herself to eat it.

Garrett motioned toward her plate with his fork, drawing her attention. "You know, if you don't eat, you'll be the only woman in recorded history to come back from vacation skinnier than she started out."

"I guess the salt air has taken away my appetite."

Garrett shook his head. "It works the other way around."

"You know me. I enjoy being contrary."

She lifted her wineglass to her lips and took a deep sip. She could sense Garrett's frustration with her melancholy, but she couldn't seem to shake it. She brought a forkful of savory rice to her mouth just to please Garrett, tasting nothing.

Verity came out onto the lanai. "Excuse me for disturbing you two, but there's a phone call for you, Elise."

"Thank you." Elise took the phone from Verity, wondering who could be on the other end. "Hello?"

"Hi, Mom. It's me."

Her gaze slid to Garrett, guessing immediately that he'd gotten Alyssa to call. He winked at her, confirming her suspicions. "How's everything going, sweetheart?"

"Everything's cool. Aunt Jenny and Uncle Mike have been so great."

Which probably meant they'd let her get away with murder. "How was the concert?"

"The absolute bomb! Uncle Mike hired this humongous limousine to take us, so when we got out everybody kept staring at us like we had to be somebody special. And we had seats in the front row. Lance Archer came offstage and sang right to me." Alyssa sighed dreamily.

Elise could imagine that. The singer and sixteen of his favorite bodyguards. "That's wonderful, sweetie," Elise said, even though she had no idea who Lance Archer was.

"How are you and Dad enjoying your vacation?"

"It's the absolute bomb."

"Mom, *please*, do *not* try to sound cool. It just does *not* work."

Laughing, Elise said, "Okay. Everything is wonderful." Elise paused, her gaze meeting Garrett's across the table, wondering what his reaction would be to what she said next. "What would you say to watching your brother one night a week so your father and I could go out?"

"You mean baby-sit? How much are you going to pay me?"

"What's the going rate for baby-sitters?"

"Twenty dollars an hour."

"You've got to be kidding. We'll give you ten and we'll pay for the tennis camp you want to go to this summer."

"It's a deal."

"Do you want to talk to Dad?"

"Sure."

Elise handed Garrett the phone. While he spoke to Alyssa, she speared one of her shrimp on her fork and brought it to her mouth. That had gone much, much better than she'd expected. Garrett had been right and she'd worried about absolutely nothing. When she caught his gaze, she mouthed the words *thank you*. He winked at her again in response.

"Yes, sweetheart, you did fine," Garrett continued. "I'll tell her." Garrett turned off the phone and placed it on the table. "She says to tell you that she promises to take good care of her brother—even if he is a tremendous pain in the neck."

"You don't mind that I asked her, do you?"

"Not at all. I was going to suggest the same thing myself." He leaned back in his chair, dropping his napkin onto his plate. "Correct me if I'm wrong, but didn't we already decide to send her to that camp?"

"You've got a lot to learn about haggling, Dr. Taylor," she retorted, and popped her last shrimp into her mouth.

The next morning, Elise awoke to something tickling her nose. She swiped at it, only to meet with something rock-hard and unyielding. She opened her eyes to stare at Garrett's chest.

"Good morning to you, too." Garrett's sleepy voice rumbled in his chest as his hands moved lazily over her body. "What's on the agenda for today?"

She snuggled closer to him. "First, I'd like to make love to my husband . . ."

"Lucky man. Who is he?"

She hit him on the shoulder with the side of her fist. "You, silly."

"Oh, that's right." He scrubbed his hand up her side to cup her breast. "Then what?"

"I don't know. Maybe we could go down to the resort and see what the real tourists do around here for fun."

"Maybe later," he said, shifting so that she lay beneath him. "Much, much later."

They borrowed the motorboat and took a leisurely tour around the island, stopping for lunch at a quayside vendor for a lunch of jerk chicken and Elise's favorite fried plantains. Afterward, they anchored the boat and swam in the clear blue waters, amid a school of colorful sailfish.

It was late afternoon by the time they came back to the house. Garrett remained out back, talking to Aristotle, who'd gotten news of the young boy Garrett had seen. Elise continued on into the house. As she passed the front hallway, the doorbell chimed.

"I'll get it," Elise called to anyone who might be within earshot. She pulled open the door. A young woman wearing a beige printed sundress stood on the threshold. The dress ended at midthigh and molded to the woman's slender figure, accentuating cleavage and leaving little to the imagination concerning her other attributes. Her hair, jet-black and bone-straight, hung past her shoulders. She lifted her sunglasses to reveal striking deep brown eyes fringed with lush mascara-coated lashes.

Elise's eyebrows lifted as one word formed in her mind: trouble. "Can I help you?"

The woman smiled, revealing a single dimple in her left cheek. "Is Garrett Taylor staying here?"

Elise scanned the woman's face, really looked at her. She couldn't be more than twenty-five years old. Who was she? And what did she want with Garrett so urgently that she tracked him down on vacation?

The woman licked her lips, drawing Elise's attention to her mouth, colored a dark berry shade that seemed somehow familiar. In her mind's eye, she saw Garrett's shirt, the one with the stain on the collar, the same shade of lipstick this woman wore.

Nausea roiled in Elise's belly and soured the taste in her mouth. If there were some easily explainable reason for this woman to show up on their door, wouldn't Garrett have told her about it already?

Elise tilted her head to one side and fastened a piercing look on the young woman. "What exactly do you want with Garrett Taylor?"

Before the young woman could answer, she heard Garrett call her name.

"You have a visitor," she called back.

"Who is it?"

By then he'd reached the small entrance hallway. He stopped short, his eyes on the young woman, his expression a mix of surprise, recognition, and enough guilt to give credence to Elise's worst suspicions.

With as much dignity as she could muster, she said, "It seems your other 'twenty' just showed up." Then she brushed past him, went to her room, and started to pack.

"I hope I didn't come at a bad time," Jasmine Halliday said, drawing Garrett's attention from his wife's retreating back.

Garrett snorted. Was there a good time for her to show up? But she wasn't responsible for the conclusion Elise had obviously drawn. Remembering his manners, he said, "Not at all." He led her to the solarium and gestured toward the sofa. "Why don't you sit down."

She did so, while he claimed a spot on the love seat across from her. "What brings you all the way out here?"

"Actually, I wasn't that far away. Jeanie talked me into going on vacation with her and her family on Aruba. Vicente, her husband, has family there. Perhaps I shouldn't admit this, but all the kids were driving me crazy."

She sighed, folding her hands in front of her. "So, I hopped on a boat coming over here, hoping we could resolve this matter today."

Garrett leaned back and folded his arms. If the matter were so pressing, why didn't the editor call him himself? Why did his acquiescence seem to matter to her on more than a professional level? He didn't see any point in speculating. He asked her point-blank. "Why?"

Her shoulders sagged as she sank back in her seat. "I suppose I should have been honest with you in the first place. Paul has this doctor buddy who he wanted to work on the book. The man doesn't know a tongue depressor from a fountain pen. I figured if I could get you to sign on quickly, I wouldn't get saddled working with him."

"And—" Garrett said, sensing more existed to this story than she'd told him.

"And, it's kind of silly, but the first time I saw you I was drawn to you immediately. Did Jeanie tell you our father died last year?"

Garrett's brows knitted together, wondering what one had to do with the other. "Yes, she mentioned it."

"You remind me of him. The same gentle aura, even graying the same way around the temples." She pursed her lips and tears sprang to her eyes. "I'm sorry. I didn't mean to get maudlin."

"It's all right." Half of him wanted to laugh. He'd known that some sort of personal feelings factored into her desire for him to coauthor her book. Knowing he reminded her of her dead father might have given him a kick in the ego if he cared one way or the other. "And as far as the book goes, I'll let you know as soon as I get back to the States."

He saw her to the front door and watched her climb into a waiting car and leave.

Elise knew the moment Garrett entered their apartments. The door swung open with uncharacteristic force and slammed shut a second later. In another moment, Garrett stood in the doorway of her bedroom, his gaze swinging from her to the open suitcase on her bed and back.

He folded his arms over his chest and leaned against the door frame. "Going somewhere?"

His eyes bored into hers and she knew that she had never really seen him angry before. Here was the full-blown emotion staring her in the face. A kind of quiet fury radiated from him, which frightened her all the more since the whole of it was directed at her.

But she would not back down. If he had cause to be angry, she had even more.

"I don't know. You tell me." She tossed the article of clothing she held in her hand into her suitcase and stood with her hands braced on her hips. "Who was that woman, Garrett? How do you know her?"

"I thought you knew. She's my lover. I invited her here when you went into your nun-in-a-cloister routine."

"If you are going to be ridiculous about this—"

"You didn't think it was so ridiculous a little while ago. I saw your face before you came tearing up here. I saw the accusation in your eyes."

"And I saw the guilt in yours. What could you possibly have to feel guilty about?"

"Tell me something, Elise. What the hell have these last few days been about? All the plans of how we would change things when we got back to New York? When I made love to you, did I give you the impression I was thinking of someone else?"

He fell silent, shaking his head. All the anger in him seemed to recede, replaced by a bone-deep sorrow. "We've been married for seventeen years. Don't you know anything about me? I could never, ever betray you that way. The only woman I've so much as looked at in the past twenty years has been you. Don't you know that?"

"Garrett, I—"

"That's right, it's you. It's always been you. What you wanted. What you needed. I've never said no to you about a damn thing. And now, when I need something from you . . ."

He trailed off, turning his back to her. Although he stood motionless, she could see the tension in him. "What do you need, Garrett?"

She sensed the war inside him, whether to stand fast or break down and confide in her. Keeping his back to her, he said, "It doesn't matter, Elise."

Then he turned his head toward her. She saw such sadness in his eyes, it stunned her. She knew in that instant that, whatever the relationship between Garrett and that woman, she'd misjudged him.

"Garrett——" she began, not knowing what else to say.

"Excuse me," he said. "I have some packing of my own to do."

Elise followed him to the door, her eyes glued to him as he silently walked to his room and quietly closed the door behind him. She pressed her lips together, not knowing what to do. She had never seen her husband like that, filled with such raw emotions, both anger and pain.

She didn't know what to do about either emotion, but she knew they could not end their time here like this. If they went home now, it surely would be the end of their marriage, because she doubted he'd forgive her in his present frame of mind. And she couldn't stay here, in the same room, with him only a door away.

She stepped back into her room, changed into a pair of jeans, a casual shirt, and her sneakers. She didn't bother to tell Garrett she was going out, but as she passed Verity on the first floor, she told her she was going out for a walk.

Honestly, she had no idea where she wanted to go. She took the path that led up the mountain, simply because it was less likely anyone would follow her there. She needed to think, and she could only do that alone. After a while, she came to the boulder she'd rested on the other day. She hadn't realized it the first time, but hieroglyphs had been carved into the stone.

She squatted in front of it and ran her hand over its face, dislodging dirt that had been caked into the design by the elements. She had no idea what the carving meant, but she appreciated its beauty.

Disheartened, she sat on the stone, drawing her feet up under her so as not to harm the design. Instead of sitting there, she should have been going back to the house to talk to Garrett. He'd never done anything to make her believe he'd been unfaithful. He didn't even stay late at work without informing her first. Yet she'd condemned him without ever giving him a chance to offer an explanation. She also recognized that her knee-jerk response had more to do with her own insecurities than anything Garrett had done.

Sighing, she leaned her back against the face of the mountain, but the wall behind her moved. Suddenly she was falling backward, tumbling over and over, as her fingers clawed for purchase. Then, abruptly, she hit bottom and blackness came.

Fourteen

Standing on the balcony to their rooms, Garrett checked his watch for the fourth time in fifteen minutes. Elise had been gone nearly two hours. In that time, night had started to descend. Elise was out there somewhere. According to Verity, she'd simply walked out the back door and hadn't been back.

When she'd first left their rooms, he'd been too angry and hurt to care where she went. Besides, he'd mistakenly thought she'd confine herself to the house and its grounds, not go traipsing off to God-knows-where without telling anyone.

And now that he'd had time to cool down, he couldn't blame her for jumping to the wrong conclusion finding Jasmine Halliday on their doorstep. He'd had the wrong impression of her himself. He wondered if he would have been any more forgiving if a strange man had showed up at the door looking for Elise.

If he'd told her about the book contract in the first place, they wouldn't have had anything to fight about. He hadn't meant to light into her the way he had, but anger had bubbled up from a deep well he hadn't known he possessed. He couldn't imagine how hurt she must have been by some of the things he'd said.

He checked his watch again. Only two minutes had

ticked by since the last time he'd looked at it. They'd had arguments before, though none as damaging as this one. Invariably, Elise retreated somewhere afterward, but never for this long. He didn't know why he didn't think of it before, but maybe she couldn't come back. Maybe she'd fallen or injured herself in some way that made it impossible for her to get back. He'd gone looking for her a couple of times on the path they'd taken to the glade and hadn't found her. Maybe she'd gone a different route and simply gotten lost.

"I'm going to go look for her again," he told Aristotle and Verity, whom he found in the solarium, huddled together on the sofa.

"Can we do anything?" Verity asked.

This time he didn't intend to go out unprepared. He asked Verity to pack food, water, a blanket, a flashlight, and anything else she thought he might find useful. If she were hurt, he had no idea what shape he'd find her in. He added a few supplies from his medical bag, slung the knapsack over his shoulder, and headed out the door.

"I hope you find her," he heard Verity call after him.

Dear God, he'd better.

Awakened by the ringing of the alarm clock, Elise groped for the button that would silence the damn thing. Her fingers encountered only rocks and dirt where her bedstand should be. Slowly, it permeated her fuzzy brain that this couldn't be her bedroom, and that though her eyes were open, all around her was pitch-black.

She sat up with a start, and the ringing intensified. She cradled her face in her hands. No alarm sounded anywhere; the ringing came from her own head. A dull pain throbbed just behind her left ear. She touched her fingertips to it and they came back moist. She'd cracked her head on something, but good.

Sensing the cave wall behind her, she leaned her back against it. Now she remembered sitting on the rock and falling, she didn't know how far, to land here. How long had she lain there? And where exactly was she? Unwittingly, she must have discovered an entrance to the caves. Just her luck to land herself in a ditch with no food, no water, and no way to get out.

She closed her eyes and dreamed of the symbols on the stone, a cross and a heart and three wavy lines all run together, one on top of the other.

There was that boulder again, the one Elise had rested on the other day. Which meant he'd gone full circle around the island without finding her. Full dark had fallen during the time he'd been out looking for her, but he hadn't found one trace of her.

A high-pitched cackle pierced the night quiet, making him jump. *La bruja,* the bird Selena had told them about, he presumed. That sound could scare the bejesus out of anybody.

In complete frustration, he bellowed her name. "Where the hell are you?" he muttered in a quieter tone.

He didn't expect an answer, and he suspected the ethereal, answering call that echoed back to him was either a figment of his imagination or pure wish fulfillment on his part. Just the same, he called her name again. "Elise?"

"Garrett, Garrett, help me."

He shined the high-powered flashlight he carried in the direction of her voice. The face of the mountain greeted him. "Where are you?"

"Down here."

"Down where?" He leaned his hand against the mountain wall, and it gave way. He caught himself before he fell through the opening in the mountain concealed by hanging foliage. He felt around the edges, checking for the size of the hole. Barely big enough for a normal-size adult to fit through, which meant Elise would have had more than enough room.

He shouldered his way through the entrance, dislodging dirt and plants and causing loose rocks and gravel to rain down on him. He shined the flashlight through the hole, relief flooding him as he saw Elise standing about ten feet below him, shading her eyes from the glare of the flashlight. Until that moment, he'd fully expected to look through that hole to find it empty.

"Baby, are you all right?"

"I will be when you get me out of here."

He extended his arm into the hole as far as he could. "Grab my hand." Even on tiptoe, she couldn't reach him. After a few moments of trying, she whimpered and withdrew her hand, resting her forehead on the rock wall.

"What's wrong?"

"I hit my head. It hurts too much to stay in that position."

Why hadn't she told him that when he'd asked her if she were all right? If he were with her, he could boost her out and climb back out himself. "Stand back. I'm coming down."

She did as he asked, plastering her body against the wall, but out of the way enough for him to have somewhere to stand. He had to back into the hole, which dislodged more dirt and rocks that rained down on both of them. By the time he dropped down beside her, dirt covered her and her shoulders jerked from coughing up dust.

He pulled her into his arms, holding her as if his life depended on it. He cupped her face in his hands and kissed her mouth, just a brief pressing of his lips to hers. Just enough to assure him that she was alive and whole and still his.

He drew her closer, pressing her cheek to his chest. "What happened? How did you end up down here?"

"I was sitting on that boulder up there, minding my own business. But when I leaned back, the mountainside gave way and I fell down here. I think I blacked out for a while."

"Where did you hit your head?"

She turned and touched a spot behind her left ear. "It hurts like the devil."

He lifted the flashlight and examined the wound as best he could. She must have bled a lot, judging from the amount of blood caked in her hair, but the cut measured only about a quarter of an inch long and didn't appear to be too deep. The area had swollen considerably, however. He needed to get her out of there, somewhere where he could keep a better eye on her.

"How bad is it?"

"I've seen worse." He lowered the flashlight. "I've had enough of this adventure down the rabbit hole. Let's get out of here. If I give you a boost, do you think you can make it to the top?"

She nodded, smiling gamely. "Who knew rock climbing at the gym would ever come in handy?"

Chuckling, he set the flashlight on its end on the ground so that its beam traveled upward. "Come here." He offered her his cupped hands to step on, but before she could move, the dirt and debris that had been trickling down on them intensified. A rumbling sound echoed within the cavern, but its source came from above. Garrett pulled Elise to the ground and covered her body with his own, as the earth above them trembled and showered them with debris.

When the earth seemed to have settled, he lifted his head and looked down at Elise. She lay motionless beneath him. And for an instant icy fingers gripped his chest, taunting him that he hadn't done enough to protect her. Then she opened her eyes and began to cough.

When she subsided, she looked up at him with a grin on her face. "Is this what's called a full-body press?"

Despite himself, he laughed. He shook his head, marveling at her ability to joke with him when she'd probably spent hours alone and injured and probably hadn't eaten anything since lunch. Not for the first time, he thanked God for her inner resilience and strength. "That's a full-*court* press, Elise, and that's basketball."

She shrugged and lifted a hand to wipe the dirt from her face. "Somebody should have warned us they'd booby-trapped this island. What was that, anyway? An earthquake?"

"No, a landslide, probably." And if he'd managed to get Elise topside as he'd planned, she would have been caught in the middle of that. He could have lost her tonight, more than once. That prospect chilled him to his marrow, as he honestly had no idea what he would do without her. His grief would make Jasper's mourning look like an afternoon in the park.

He retrieved the flashlight and shined it on the spot that a few minutes ago had been a narrow hole. A large rock had wedged itself into the opening, which was probably the only thing that had kept them from being buried alive.

And finally, he knew what he wanted to say to her.

But this wasn't the time or place. He needed to get her off this ledge before the hole above them caved in. If they were going to get out of there, they'd have to find another exit.

He got to his feet and pulled her up next to him. For a moment, they each occupied themselves with dusting off as much dirt as they could. "The minute I get home, I am burning everything I have on," she said.

"I'll help you. But for now we need to get down from here." He shined the flashlight on a narrow outcropping along the wall. It wound around the cave wall and eventually downward. "Think you can handle it?"

"Do I have a choice?"

He shook his head. "Not much."

He turned to start down the path when she grabbed his arm, pulling him back. "About what happened back at the house, I—"

"Don't, Elise, not now. Let's worry about first things first." He cupped her cheek in his palm. "And the first thing we need to do is find a way out of here." He couldn't see her face clearly in the darkness, but he felt her nod against his hand. "Stick close to me, okay?"

She nodded again, but for good measure, he laced his hand with hers and held it against his body. Slowly they began to make their way downward.

When they reached the cave floor, he shined the flashlight in a circle, looking for some indication of which way they should go. A strategically placed exit sign would have been nice. Barring that, he had no idea which direction to head.

Elise, who had remained silent by his side, squeezed his fingers as he illuminated a section of the cavern that resembled an enormous pipe organ. "It's beautiful, don't you think? Mother Nature's concept of interior design."

"Mmm," he agreed. "The old girl has her moments."

Garrett inhaled. Given the apparent age of the caves, he would have expected a musty smell to pervade them, making it difficult to breathe. But a slight breeze stirred the air, suggesting a source of ventilation. If air could get in, perhaps they could get out.

Elise walked beside Garrett, trying to hold herself together. The ringing in her ears had stopped, but her head felt like an oversize cotton candy and several spots on her body were scraped and sore. Her stomach had gone so long without food that she no longer registered hunger. And if someone didn't find her a bathroom soon, her bladder would probably burst.

But she wouldn't tell Garrett any of those things—not unless she had to. He needed her strong and he needed her moving. In all likelihood, if she really stopped to think about all that had happened to them in the last day, she'd faint dead away.

She remembered the one brief kiss he'd given her, so full of tenderness that thinking about it now made her ache. She clung to that memory and let it give her hope.

They crossed a section where stalagmites jutted from the cave floor, some of them as tall as Garrett and others so small that she stubbed her toes on them as they walked. Stalactites hung from the ceiling as well, but she tried not even to think about them. Bats—pale, almost albino-looking creatures—clustered among the natural structures. So far they'd adopted a live-and-let-live policy, and she intended to do everything she could to keep things that way.

A short while later, Garrett halted, setting the knapsack on the floor.

"Why are we stopping?"

"Because you are about to drop, and this is the first clear patch we've found in the last ten minutes." The beam of the flashlight flickered as he stooped and unzipped the small front pouch of the knapsack. He pulled out the blanket they'd taken on their picnic and spread it on the ground. "Sit," he said.

Nobody had to ask her twice. She sank to her knees, stretched out, and closed her eyes.

"Are you hungry?"

Her mouth immediately began to water. "You have to ask?"

"Not really."

She opened her eyes, focusing in Garrett's direction. He'd stood the flashlight on end so that it illuminated their little stretch of blanket. "What have you got?"

"Cold chicken, corn bread, and some water to wash it down."

"I'll take one of each."

They ate in silence, Elise too consumed with getting food into her mouth to worry about conversation. But once her belly was full, another pressing need came to the fore. "You don't suppose there's a bathroom around here, do you?"

Garrett chuckled. "Sorry, but these are strictly primitive accommodations. I don't think cave people worried too much about indoor plumbing."

She took the flashlight, grasped it, and stood.

"Where are you going?" Garrett asked.

"If I have to suffer the indignity of relieving myself in a cave, I'm going to do it alone."

"Don't go too far."

"Believe me, I won't."

* * *

Shaking his head, Garrett rummaged through the knapsack until he found the spare flashlight and turned it on. He repacked their leftovers, hoping their scent wouldn't attract whatever animals lived in the caves. They'd gone as far as they dared tonight. They both needed rest, and he needed to keep an eye on her. This spot would have to do for the night.

He pressed the button on his watch that illuminated the dial. Elise had been gone long enough. He'd give her another two minutes; then, whether she liked it or not, he intended to go find her.

Before he'd finished lowering his arm to his side, a bloodcurdling scream that could only have come from Elise rent the air.

"Elise, where are you?"

"Over here."

He followed the sound of her voice, but she didn't sound hurt or frightened. Actually, he thought he detected a note of excitement in her voice. He didn't know what he expected to find when he reached her, but finding her crouched over the long-dead human remains of ancient Milagrans was not it. A half-dozen decomposed bodies lay on the floor of the small chamber as if they had been tossed in, one on top of the other. A network of cobwebs and dust covered the bodies. In the glow of the flashlight, the scene appeared particularly grotesque.

She turned her head to look back at him over her shoulder. "Look what I found."

He knew a cadaver wouldn't have frightened her. Her father had kept a facsimile of one in his study since Elise was a child. "What were you screaming about?"

She shuddered. "A snake. I think I scared it off."

"No kidding." He crouched down beside her. Around the neck of one of the bodies hung an elaborate neck-lace on a heavy chain—a cross with a giant ruby in the shape of a heart suspended from it. He touched his fingers to the stone, causing dust to rise in the air. "This must have been beautiful once."

"But in all likelihood, not Milagran."

He withdrew his hand. "Why do you say that?"

"The cross is a Christian symbol, not a pagan one. Aside from that, I noticed that the boulder by the opening to the cave had been carved with three symbols—a cross, a heart, and three wavy lines. It didn't make sense until now. The lines could represent the ocean."

"So you think our friends here are the Spanish sailors Selena told us about?"

She nodded. "Something tells me the history of this island doesn't have as rosy a glow as they would like everyone to believe."

"Maybe not." He stood, extending his hand to her. "Whoever these poor souls are, it doesn't concern us. Leave them to their secrets, whatever they are."

"All right."

She took his hand and he pulled her to her feet. He squeezed her to his side with an arm around her waist. He led her back to where they'd laid the blanket. "Aside from that, you had a serious blow to your head today. You should be lying down."

"Yes, Doctor."

"A patient who actually listens and doesn't drool. A pediatrician's dream come true."

"And you didn't even have to give me a lollipop."

They reached the blanket. Elise immediately sat down on its edge. "I guess this is it for tonight?"

"I'm afraid so." He set the flashlight he carried on the ground. "I'll try to make us as comfortable as possible."

She nodded, and he saw the bone-deep fatigue in her. He positioned the knapsack on the blanket to use as a pillow. He knelt in front of her and took off her sneakers. Then he picked her up, settled her on the makeshift bed, and lay down beside her. "Better?"

"Much."

"Then go to sleep." He touched his lips to her temple.

She nodded and shifted slightly. She remained silent for so long that he would have sworn she'd fallen asleep. "Garrett?"

"Yes, baby?"

"What if we don't make it out of here? What if we can't find a way out and end up entombed like those poor men?"

She'd finally voiced the one fear that neither of them had addressed. "That won't happen."

Garrett huffed out a heavy breath. "I have something to say to you, and not because I don't think we'll get out of here, but because I do."

She eyed him through half-closed lids. "What is it?"

He cupped the side of her face in his palm. "I love you, Elise. I know I don't say it often, but that doesn't mean I don't feel it. You are my whole life. You have been ever since that first day I saw you walking across the football field carrying that hockey stick that was almost as big as you were.

"And I know that sometimes I overindulge the kids, but I remember what it was like to live in a house where no was the answer to even the simplest request. I remember what it was like to be unwanted and have nowhere else to turn. I never want our kids to feel like that."

He buried his face against her neck, emotion clogging his throat. Her arms closed around him, cradling him, comforting him. He'd never told her much about his childhood, except that it was a place he didn't want to revisit. But suddenly, with her soft, gentle hands caressing him, words spilled from him, telling her of a life of deprivation and loneliness, of a young boy who was fed, clothed, housed, but given nothing else. He told her of things he hadn't known he had locked inside him until they poured out of him for her to hear.

"When I was twelve, I finally understood what I was dealing with. I had always wanted a dog, and that year it was like a taste in my mouth I wanted one so badly. My aunt, of course, said no. She said God had given her enough burdens in the form of me, and she had no intention of taking on another.

"As luck would have it, a pregnant German shepherd had been hit by a car on our block, crawled under the front of the house to have her puppies, and died. That morning when I left for school, I heard the puppies crying. I begged my aunt to let me keep one of them, if I promised to find homes for the others. She never answered me, and I spent all day at school with the hope that she'd finally reconsidered.

"But when I got home that night, all the dogs were gone. My aunt told me animal control had taken away the mother, and I assumed they had taken the puppies as well. But that night, when I went to take out the trash, I discovered what had happened to them. Four little bodies lying at the bottom of the outside garbage can. She'd drowned them and left them for me to find.

"According to her, without a mother, they probably would have died anyway, and being dumb animals they had no immortal souls to concern anyone. She simply put the poor things out of their misery. But what she did had nothing to do with God or faith. It had to do with power. She had it and I didn't. After she went to bed that night, I buried them in the backyard. I never asked her for a damn thing after that."

When he finally fell silent, he realized that she was crying. He lifted his head and looked down into his wife's tear-streaked face. He kissed away the tears on her cheeks. "I'm sorry, sweetheart. I didn't tell you to make you cry."

"I know." She touched her fingertips to his cheek. "If I'm upset about anything, it's that you didn't feel comfortable telling me this before. After seventeen years of marriage, you would think I should know everything there was to know about you."

"I didn't want you to know. I didn't want you to think less of me."

"How could I possibly think less of you because of the actions of adults that should have looked out for you and didn't?" She offered him a tremulous smile. "If anything, it makes me love you more. With a childhood like you had, it would have been easy for you to become hard or cynical or hateful. But you are the most gentle, loving man I have ever known. If you ask me, that's pretty remarkable."

Elise smoothed her palm over Garrett's chest, her gaze following the movement of her hand. Searching her own soul, she knew she, too, had done Garrett a disservice all those years. She'd always regarded him as an easygoing, undemanding man. Most times she'd been grateful he never questioned her decisions, but sometimes she'd resented always being the one on whom responsibility fell.

As far as she could remember, he'd never challenged her on anything that wasn't for their children's benefit. She understood now, that if he'd asked for nothing, it wasn't because he didn't care, but because he didn't expect his needs to be met by anyone, not even her.

"What do you need, Garrett? And what has that woman got to do with it?"

He snorted. "Believe it or not, she is a writer who asked me to coauthor a child-care book with her."

"That's wonderful. Why didn't you tell me about it?"

"I haven't known about it all that long, and if you'll remember, you weren't speaking to me for a while. And then I was more concerned with what happened with our relationship to worry about it. Besides that, I thought she had more than a professional interest in having me work on the book."

"And did she?" Elise held her breath, waiting for his response.

"Yes, but not the one I suspected. Turns out, I remind her of her father, who happens to be dead, by the way."

"Oh, Garrett." Elise pressed her lips together as mirth bubbled up in her. No man, not even one as lacking in ego as Garrett, wanted to be thought of as a dried-up old man by a woman like Jasmine Halliday. But she couldn't quite contain the laughter that welled up in her, born partly out of humor and partly out of the realization that everything between them would be all right.

She pressed the back of one hand against her lips. "I'm sorry."

"No, you're not." Smiling, he tickled her side, making her giggle. "So, you wouldn't mind if I accepted the book offer?"

"Not as long as that black-haired hussy keeps her hands to herself."

"I'm serious, Elise."

She sobered, seeing the somber look that came into Garrett's eyes. She ran her fingertips over his cheek. "Sweetie, I love you. I want you to do whatever you want. You have always supported me in whatever I've done. What kind of wife would I be if I didn't do the same for you?"

He said nothing to that, but his smile in the darkness

was enough for her. He leaned to one side, his hand splaying on her abdomen. "Is there something else you want to tell me?"

She wondered if Garrett had guessed the reason for her changeability these past few days. But she didn't want to tell him now, not in this place so far from normalcy.

"Yes, but not now. I'm not trying to keep anything from you, Garrett. I promise. I want to tell you in our own home, in our own room. This place doesn't have anything to do with our lives. I want to go home."

"It's too bad you didn't pack your ruby slippers, Dorothy. Since we're stuck here for the night, maybe you ought to try to get some sleep."

"How am I supposed to do that with six bodies lying nearby, and God-knows-what crawling around in the dark?"

"Shh," Garrett said, stroking his hands over her back in a soothing motion.

Elise closed her eyes, sighed, and drifted into a restless sleep, dozing and waking every couple of hours. And every time she opened her eyes, Garrett was there, holding her, his concerned face hovering over hers. He probably wondered why she couldn't just lie down and sleep. She couldn't understand it, either. Fatigue pulled at her as if she should have been able to sleep a thousand years.

And finally, she opened her eyes to find herself alone. "Garrett," she called, sitting up.

"I'm here." She saw the beam of the smaller flashlight then. He knelt beside her. "Are you ready to go?"

She scanned his handsome smiling face. "You found a way out?"

"That I did."

She threw her arms around his neck and hugged him, nearly knocking him off balance. "Thank God."

He kissed her temple. "You can congratulate me on my brilliance later. For now, let's get out of here."

She nodded and rose to her feet to help him refold the blanket. Once Garrett replaced it in its pouch in the knapsack, she took his hand. "I don't mean to question your brilliance, but how did you find a way out?"

He led her in the same direction they had been going last night. "I followed the sound."

She almost asked *what sound?* but she heard it now, too. It reminded her of a relaxation tape she had, of water running into a stream.

The sound intensified in the few minutes they spent walking, until it seemed to surround them. Garrett stopped, leaning his hand against the cave wall. A narrow stream of water trickled down beside his hand. She followed its path upward with her eyes. About fifteen feet up, a large hole opened up, letting in blessed morning sunshine.

She turned to Garrett. "A waterfall?"

He nodded. "If we can get up there and don't manage to drown ourselves, we should be able to get out of here."

She narrowed her eyes, planting her hands on her hips. "Do you mean to tell me that I spent the night in a dirty, smelly cave, populated with bats and corpses and God knows what else, when I was *this* close to fresh air and clean water?"

"I'm afraid so." He pulled her closer to him with an arm around her waist. "Are you sorry we didn't keep going last night?"

"No." If they hadn't spent the night there, Garrett probably wouldn't have told her about his past. He'd have continued to keep it locked inside him, and she would have gone on resenting him out of a lack of understanding. She refused to put up with his laissez-faire attitude anymore, however, but she'd save that discussion for another time.

Garrett winked at her. "Me, either."

The path up was slippery, but not steep. Elise scrambled up to reach a tunnel large enough to allow them to stand. A few feet in front of her, water rushed past the open mouth of the tunnel. Garrett joined her a moment later, and together they walked toward the opening. An overhang jutted out above them, preventing them from getting completely drenched as they made their way out of the side of the waterfall and down onto the green grass that ringed the falls.

"Civilization, such as it is," Garrett said, looking out over the pond where the water collected in a deep pool.

Elise shook her head. "A bath."

Fifteen

Without hesitation, Elise stripped off her clothes and waded into the water until it reached her waist. The water was surprisingly warm, at least as warm as her own body temperature. The abrasions on her palms and knees smarted, but she didn't care.

Garrett came up behind her, scooped her up, and carried her to the center of the pond. "Feel better?"

"Much. The water is heavenly, but why is it so warm?"

"Didn't Selena say that there used to be an underground hot spring? Maybe it started to flow upward after the earthquake. I heard about that happening on another island, except that one was due to a volcano, I think."

Elise shrugged. Only she would try to dissect paradise. They were both safe and whole and unharmed by the night's experience. That's all that mattered.

She nodded toward the shore. "You didn't happen to pack any shampoo in that knapsack of yours, did you? I think my hair is permanently plastered to my head."

"No such luck. But I'll do what I can."

"You just want to poke at my cut."

"That, too."

He eased her onto her back in the water, so that she

floated beside him. Tenderly, he rinsed away the remnants of the blood in her hair. The cut stung, but his fingers moved over her scalp gently. She closed her eyes as a small moan of pleasure escaped her lips.

"Enjoying yourself?"

"Mmm," she agreed. "I think I'm going to recommend this treatment to Elizabeth Arden. Full body shampoos given by gorgeous, nude serving boys. She'll make a mint."

He lifted her from the water into his arms. He stroked the water back from her face with one hand and held onto her waist with the other. "So, you think I'm gorgeous, huh?"

She tilted her head to one side and considered him. Why had he chosen to focus on that particular word? Could her egoless husband be developing a swelled head? If so, she didn't mind indulging him.

"That's what I thought the first time I saw you—what a gorgeous set of buns on that guy." She ran her fingers down his back to cup said buns in her hands.

"You have never used the word *buns* in your life, except to describe something that came out of the oven." He lowered his mouth to hers for a kiss that started gentle, but quickly intensified. She wriggled against him, wrapping her legs around his waist. She broke the kiss to look up at him with half-closed eyes. "I want you, Garrett," she whispered.

Then she kissed him again, sliding her tongue into his mouth. He sucked on it, and she moaned. An answering, satisfied groan rumbled up through his chest. Grasping her hips, he thrust into her. Her back arched and her fingers dug into his shoulders.

"That's it, sweetheart," he murmured against her throat. She moved against him frantically, but he had little more control than she. A few moments later, when her body contracted around his, he covered her mouth, absorbing her cries into his mouth to mingle with his own.

Afterward, he held her to him, as the two of them waited for their bodies to recover. Surprised he could still stand, he carried her to the side of the pool, where they'd left their belongings.

They dressed in their soggy, filthy clothes, and Garrett slung the knapsack on his back. "I don't suppose you have any idea where we are? I went around this island three times last night, and not once did I see this waterfall."

Before Elise could answer, another sound echoed through the clearing. The sound of underbrush being trampled under someone's feet. Garrett tensed, pushing her behind him, wondering who or what might step out to greet them.

A moment later, Aristotle and some of his cronies from the bar appeared through the underbrush. Aristotle stopped when he saw them, heaving an audible, relieved sigh. "There you two are."

Then his gaze slid from them to the pool and back. A broad grin broke out across Aristotle's face. "I guess I don't have to ask if you two are all right."

He dispatched the other men to call off the search. Once the men had gone he looked them over again, shaking his head. "Young people," he muttered, then motioned for them to follow him.

When they got back to the house, Verity yanked open the door before any of them had reached the threshold. "Come in here, you two," she admonished, waving them in the door. "You look like the Wreck of the Hesperus. We were all worried sick about you."

"Turns out these two were frolicking in the waterfall when we found them."

Elise had expected Verity's usual show of disapproval. The older woman surprised her by locking her in a tight embrace. "As long as you're both all right." Verity stepped back, releasing Elise. "Why don't you go up to your room, and I'll fix you some breakfast."

"Thank you."

Once inside Garrett's room, Elise had to agree with Verity's assessment. She looked at Garrett, who stood behind her, in the mirror. "Why didn't you tell me I looked like this?" He honestly didn't look any better.

"What would you have done about it if I had?"

Laughing, she turned to face him. "Nothing, I guess."

"Come on," Garrett said, taking her hand. "Let's get out of these things. If you're nice to me, I'll wash your hair properly this time."

"How can I resist such generosity?" she teased as she followed him to the shower.

Deliciously warm water pelted her skin once Garrett got the temperature right. He lathered her hair and sudsed her body, then rinsed her under the warm spray of the shower. And when he carried her to their bed, he toweled her body, dried her hair, and covered her with one of his own T-shirts.

She molded her body to his side as he stretched out beside her on the bed. "Thank you, Garrett," she whispered.

"For what?"

"Taking care of me. If it weren't for you, I'd still be trying to unbutton my shirt. I don't think I've ever been so tired in my life."

"Me either."

"Didn't Verity say she was bringing us food?"

"Do you want me to go check?" When he got no

answer, he opened his eyes and scanned her face. From one minute to the next, she'd gone from wakefulness to sleep. He rearranged the blankets to cover them. He'd spent the night awake, watching Elise, rousing her every couple of hours to make sure she still could wake up. He didn't know how much damage she'd done to herself with that fall, and he hadn't wanted to take any chances. But right now, his energy gauge registered empty and his eyes refused to stay open any longer. He wrapped his arms around his wife, closed his eyes, and slept.

Elise woke to find herself alone in Garrett's bed. Judging by the bright sunlight that flooded the room, she couldn't have slept very long. She stretched languorously. The short nap had left her remarkably refreshed.

"The dead rises," she heard Verity say from across the room. The woman stood at the doorway to the room, holding a tray of food in her arms. "I was just coming to wake you for lunch."

Elise sat up against her pillows. "Thank goodness. I'm hungry enough to eat a rhinoceros."

"You'll have to settle for some good Milagran callaloo instead." She placed the tray over Elise's lap.

Surveying the tray, Elise picked up her spoon. "What? No tea?" she teased.

"From the grin on your husband's face when you came in the door, I don't think you have need of it anymore."

Elise showed Verity a grin of her own. "No, I guess not."

"I'm glad for you, Elise. You gave your husband quite a scare when you disappeared."

"I didn't intend to. I discovered one of the entrances to the cave by falling into it."

"So Aristotle told me. You must have been terrified."

"Not really. By the time I started to get worried, Garrett found me."

"Still, to be lost in a strange cave with no idea how to get out? If it had been me, I'd have screamed my head off."

"I did scream, but not from that. While we were in the caves we found some bodies. Six of them. One of them had a necklace around his neck." She scrutinized Verity's face, but got no overt reaction from her. "Garrett and I suspected that they were the remains of the six sailors that landed here."

"Then you'd be correct."

Elise shook her head. "How did that happen? I thought they'd married into the tribe and settled down to a nice happy existence."

"That might have happened if the men who'd arrived here had actually been sailors, though most of those men were no better than criminals themselves. In actuality, they were pirates, fleeing from a fleet of ships that pursued them. The leader considered it a miracle that he washed up here alive, *and* that he'd survived with *el deseo del corazon* still around his neck."

Elise searched the limited amount of Spanish she remembered from high school, then snorted. So, Selena had told them the truth. "The heart's desire?"

Verity nodded. "Worth a fortune even then, it had reportedly been stolen from Queen Isabella herself, and named for the size and shape of the stone."

"So the men were never married off to the women?"

"No, they were, but men like those were not content to be ruled by tribal elders or anyone else. They began to take over, to corrupt those around them. I always wondered why the men didn't attempt to build another boat and leave. But being pirates, they'd probably stolen the ship they'd wrecked. Or maybe it is as Milton said, better to rule in hell than to serve in heaven. I don't know."

"What happened to them? How did they end up in the cave?"

"Fortunately or unfortunately, each of those men died under what we would call mysterious circumstances. When the tribal elders had suffered enough of them, the once peaceful natives had them killed. Like some of the other Caribbean islands, we became expert at repelling anyone who didn't come in peace. I suppose if you'd had more time to explore, there is no telling what you might have found in the caves."

Elise shook her head. "So everything you told us about this island was basically the tourist spiel?"

Verity shrugged. "Not exactly. You have to understand, the caves have been sealed since before anyone alive on the island now had been born. Our ancestors relied more on oral or pictographic history than the written word. I hadn't been certain the legend was true until you told me about the bodies."

"A pretty bloodthirsty tale, if you ask me."

"True. But doesn't every country have at least a little barbarism in its past? Why should we be any different? Your America still bears the scars of its own savagery. And we have ours."

"What do you mean?"

"Although we boast of welcoming everyone, it is only at a distance. We rely on tourism for our economy, we take foreigners' money, yet we practically confine them to the resort we have created for them. Most of the people who work there come in from off-island. We are still so wary of outsiders that we isolate ourselves from the rest of the world, just as we have always done."

Elise set down her spoon, having finished her soup while Verity spoke. That was the trouble with things that lay hidden; even without light, they cast a shadow. Her thoughts shifted to Garrett. He'd kept his own secrets from her, and it had colored their relationship without her ever knowing it.

"Where's Garrett?"

"He's making arrangements for your trip home."

Elise nodded. "I'd better finish packing."

"It's already been taken care of."

"Then I'd better get ready to go."

Verity nodded. She took the tray from Elise. "If you don't mind, I'm going to make you a care package for the flight. Those airlines think a bag of peanuts constitutes a meal."

"I don't mind at all."

"I'll see you downstairs when you're ready."

After Verity left, Elise went to her room to dress. Her bags stood by the door, ready to go. Someone, probably Verity, had laid out on the bed a beige pantsuit and accessories for her to wear home. She quickly donned the outfit, curled her hair into some semblance of a hairstyle, and fixed her makeup. Time to get back to the real world.

She found Garrett in the solarium, ending a telephone conversation with someone. His back was to her. She came up behind him and wrapped her arms around his waist. He stiffened momentarily, probably in surprise, then relaxed, rubbing his fingers along her arm.

While they stood there, her gaze settled on a painting of a young girl that hung on the opposite wall. Something about the picture nagged at her, but she couldn't place her finger on why. And then it hit her, where she'd seen it before. She wondered if Garrett knew, but she doubted it. Which meant she'd pulled the wool over both their eyes.

"We'll see you when we get there," Garrett said into the phone. "Bye."

He clicked off the phone, placed it on a nearby table, and turned, pulling her into his arms. "How are you feeling?"

"Ready to go home." Now more than ever.

"I booked us a flight out of Puerto Rico at four o'clock. Not first class this time. With the holidays, we had to take what we could get."

"As long as I don't have to ride outside on the wing, anything is fine with me."

Garrett chuckled. "We can't have that. You might end up with porcupine hair again."

"Don't remind me." She smacked him on the shoulder.

He caught her hand and brought it to his lips. "We'd better get going if we want to catch our plane to New York. Are you sure you want to go?"

"Daphne told me once that how you ring in the New Year is how you'll end up. I want to be with my family."

"In that case, I hate to break it to you, but last night was New Year's Eve. I'll pass on doing the cave thing again, thank you."

Smiling, Elise rested her cheek on Garrett's chest, calculating the days they'd been there. With no need to follow a calendar, she'd lost track of the time. In the end, she'd rung in the New Year exactly how she'd wanted to: feeling loved and cherished in the haven of her husband's arms.

She raised her head and focused her gaze on Garrett's face. "Happy New Year," she whispered. Going up on tiptoe, she pressed her mouth to his.

* * *

Verity and Aristotle brought them to the landing strip where the Cessna waited to take them to Puerto Rico. Elise stepped out of the van first, scanning the cloudless azure sky, then turning to look at the mountain looming behind them. She glanced back at Garrett, who stood behind her. "Believe it or not, I'm going to miss this place."

"Then you must come back and visit us." Verity stepped out of the van, her arms open. Elise stepped into her embrace and hugged her warmly. When she pulled back, she noticed the tears gathering in the older woman's eyes. "I'm going to miss you, too, Elise."

Elise felt tears brew in her own eyes. "Thank you for taking such good care of us."

"Just like a woman, always getting weepy," Aristotle said, coming up to give her a hug of his own. He stepped back and, still holding her hand, he patted the back of it. "You take care of yourself and that tall drink of water you're married to."

"I will," Elise promised. She watched as Garrett and Aristotle shook hands; then she turned to Verity.

"Please tell Selena good-bye for us and thank her for her hospitality." She leaned closer to Verity. "And take care of this short drink of water you're married to."

Aristotle puffed himself up to his full height. "I heard that."

"Shut up, you old fool," Verity groused. Belying her words, she turned her head and kissed her husband's cheek.

The pilot, who'd been waiting silently, shouted at them over the din of the engine, "You folks ready to go?"

After one quick hug each to Verity and Aristotle, Elise and Garrett boarded the plane. Elise stared out the window as the pilot taxied down the runway and took off. She turned to Garrett, who already had his eyes closed. She leaned against his side and he closed his arm around her. Though she would always think of Milagro Island as the place where she got her marriage back, it felt good to be going home.

When they debarked the plane in New York, Daphne was waiting for them at the gate. Elise embraced her sister warmly, then stepped back. "It looks like motherhood is agreeing with you."

"Thanks. And don't think I'm not completely jealous of your winter tans."

"But what are you doing here? I thought you'd be home with the baby."

Daphne exhaled a long-suffering sigh. "Nathan's family is at the house. Don't get me wrong, I love them all dearly, but sometimes they can be a bit . . ."

"Much?"

"Exactly. I figured I'd come pick you up and get a couple of hours' break from the chaos."

"I'm glad you did. How far do we have to go to get to the car?"

Daphne lifted one shoulder and affected an airy voice. "Our driver is waiting outside. Ever since Arianna's birth, Nathan has been spoiling me terribly, and worse yet, I'm starting to enjoy it."

"Worse things could happen to a person."

"I suppose."

After they claimed their luggage from the baggage carousel, they headed out into the frigid December air. An airport bus whizzed past them, trailing exhaust fumes. Elise grinned up at Garrett. "Ah, the familiar smells of home."

Once they'd stowed the luggage in the trunk, Garrett sat in the front seat of the Lincoln Town Car with the driver, leaving the two sisters alone in the backseat.

"How is everyone?" Elise asked, knowing her sister would have seen everyone the night before. "How's Andrew?"

"Now that you're back, I can tell you," Daphne began. "He had a nightmare last night that you wouldn't come home. He tried to be brave about it, but he really missed you."

"And I was afraid the kids would barely notice we were gone. Why didn't you bring him with you?"

"Nathan's grandmother promised to make him *pasteles* if he stayed until tomorrow afternoon. I hate to tell you this, but your son is a glutton."

Elise snorted. Her son was so skinny most people swore she must not feed him—until they saw him eat. "What about Alyssa? Has she driven Michael and Jenny crazy yet?"

"Not at all. But I don't think you have to worry about her wanting to have children anytime soon. Jenny started spotting and her doctor put her on total bed rest for the duration. She's cranky as hell, and Alyssa has been taking care of her. The two of them have Michael sleeping on the couch."

Elise grinned, imagining how well her brother coped with that situation.

"By the way," Daphne continued. "Alyssa tried to convince me you wouldn't mind her having a sip of champagne at midnight."

"Absolutely not," Elise and Garrett said in unison. Elise hadn't thought Garrett had paid any attention to her conversation with her sister, but Garrett looked at her over his shoulder and winked. "You didn't give her any, did you?" Elise continued.

"Hey, I might be a soft touch," Daphne protested, "but I'm not crazy."

Elise focused on her sister. "How's Dad?" Surprisingly, Daphne's cheeks colored and she glanced away. "What happened?"

"Maybe you should be glad you're sitting down for this. I think our father is seeing someone."

"Get out! Who?"

"I don't know."

"Then why do you think so?"

"Because I walked in on them."

Elise covered her open mouth with both of her hands. "Oh, my God, Dee! What did you do?"

"What do you think I did? I got the heck out of there. They were only standing in his bedroom kissing. But what do you say after that? 'Way to go, Dad'?"

Elise giggled. "That's what you get for letting yourself into other people's houses uninvited. Do you think it's serious?"

"I don't know, but before I went upstairs I peeked in Dad's study. The whole room was neat as a pin."

Elise's eyebrows lifted. "That room has been a disaster area since Mom died."

"Exactly," Daphne said.

Elise glanced at Garrett, wondering what he thought of this latest development. He looked back at her over his shoulder and shrugged.

When they pulled up in front of the house a half hour later, Elise asked Daphne, "Can you come inside for a minute? There's something I need to ask you."

"Sure."

Elise led her sister up to the bedroom, and once they were both inside, she shut the door. She motioned for

Daphne to sit on the bed and waited for Daphne to comply. Elise folded her arms across her chest. "Okay, time to 'fess up. There never was any contest on the radio, at least not for the trip, was there?"

"No, but how did you guess?"

"I suspected something fishy from the start, but I couldn't put my finger on it. I mean, what kind of radio station sends people jetting to obscure islands with first-class plane tickets, no less? Not that I'm complaining, mind you."

"I thought you and Garrett would enjoy the ride."

"Then I saw a painting on one of the walls that I know used to hang in Nathan's apartment."

"The one in the solarium? I should have known you of all people would notice that."

"And all this talk about a mysterious owner who nobody ever mentioned by name. Nathan owns the island, doesn't he?"

Daphne shook her head. "Actually, I do."

"You? Ms. Help-the-Struggling-Masses-Yearning-to-Breathe-Free? You own an island?"

Daphne braced one hand on the bed and waved dismissively with the other. "Okay, so it was a wedding present from Nathan."

"The man buys you an island for a present. It boggles the mind. But how could you leave two sweet old people to run that household by themselves?"

"What sweet old people?"

"The Tremaines."

Daphne collapsed in laughter, falling back on the bed. "You're kidding me, right?"

"No, and I fail to see what is so funny."

"Nathan bought the island from Aristotle and Verity. They were the former owners."

Elise sank down on the bed. She remembered all the

times she thought Verity a bit too presumptuous for a servant, and all the sly winks that passed between Verity and Aristotle. It all made sense now. "So what were they doing passing themselves off as the hired help?"

"I don't know. When I realized that you and Garrett were having problems, and you didn't intend to address them right away, I knew I had to do something. You guys have always been so good together. I didn't want to see you drift apart because you'd hit a momentary rough spot. Then I came up with the idea to send you off somewhere together alone, where you'd be forced to work things out."

"And you enlisted my daughter's help to get us to go."

"I knew if I said, 'Here are some plane tickets, go have a good time,' you'd say no. I knew you wouldn't put up too much of a fight if one of your kids was involved."

"So you used our weakness where our kids are concerned to get us to go."

"Yup."

Daphne looked so pleased with herself that all Elise could do was laugh.

"That's when I called Verity. She told me the regular staff, all off-islanders, had gone home for the holidays. I just assumed they'd hire someone from the village to help out. I told them to have some fun with you two, and I guess they did."

"How did Verity and Aristotle afford to buy the island in the first place?"

"Now, that's a story in itself. Have you ever heard of A.J. Tremaine?"

"I'm guessing—a relative of Aristotle's?"

"Close. Aristotle himself. He was an engineer. In the 1950s he invented some doohickey or other that goes in airplanes. Unlike many other black inventors, he managed to hold on to the patent for his work and made a fortune."

"You mean Aristotle is an American?"

"Born and raised in Detroit. He didn't meet Verity until after his first wife died. Some friends of his had talked him into investing in a tiny Caribbean island. He went there to check the place out and met Verity. He went back home, packed up his things, and moved to the island. Eventually, he bought out the other partners, who had only been interested in the novelty of owning an island."

"So, why did they want to sell the island?"

Daphne's eyes misted up. "I don't know if they would want me to tell you this, but Aristotle is dying."

"Oh, no. I didn't know that."

"He's got a daughter, a greedy individual who has never worked a day in her life. First she lived off her father's largesse, then her husband's. Aristotle and Verity are not married by any authority U.S. courts are bound to recognize. On Milagro, the couple ties a cloth around each other's wrists and they're married. That's it. Aristotle was afraid of what his daughter might do to the lives of the Milagrans with the entire island at her disposal."

Elise considered that. "Why didn't he give the island to Selena?"

"She doesn't want it. She says she has enough trouble worrying about her own life without having to deal with four hundred other people's. Besides, Selena isn't hurting for money. Her father's estate left her well-off, and she's making a name for herself as an artist. She had a show in New York a few months ago, and one of her paintings sold in the hundreds of thousands of dollars."

"And to think Garrett asked Verity if she would come and work for us. How did you two get involved?"

"Turns out Verity is a huge fan of Nathan's and they had known each other for years. When we went to Puerto Rico on our honeymoon, she invited us to visit the island. One thing led to another and the next thing I knew my name was on a deed to the island. Believe it or not, Nathan thought it would make a nice family getaway."

When the sisters' laughter subsided, Elise asked, "Hasn't the man ever heard of a time-share on Montauk?"

Daphne shrugged. "You know my husband. He thinks practical is a four-letter word."

Daphne stood. "And on that note, I'm going to get on home. You and Garrett are doing okay?"

Elise nodded. "We will be, but it's time I came clean to him about something."

"I'm glad to hear it. That's our family curse, you know, keeping everything inside, not letting the ones who love us help us. Thank God Michael has Jenny to pester it out of him, and Nathan, well, he has his own way of worming things out of me."

Elise grinned. "I'll bet he does."

"And I hope Dad has finally found someone to do the same for him."

"Me, too."

Daphne embraced her sister. "I love you, sis. Take care of yourself and Garrett."

Elise hugged her back. "I love you, too. Tell Nathan I say thank you, and kiss Andrew for me."

Daphne stepped back. "I'll get Garrett to let me out, and I want a full report when we drop Andrew off tomorrow."

"Will do."

After Daphne left, Elise went to the bathroom, stripped out of her clothes, and turned on the shower. She stepped under the warm spray of the water, and let it wash away the fatigue of the trip home. Afterward, she toweled herself dry, applied a vanilla-scented lotion that she knew Garrett liked, and made herself beautiful for her husband.

But when she stood back to assess her reflection in the mirror, her cheeks had reddened and her skin felt flushed. She covered her cheeks with her hands. "Not now," she told her reflection. She backed away from the mirror, shut off the light, and turned to exit the bathroom.

She stopped short, seeing a beautiful white nightgown laid out on the bed. She walked to it and bent to touch the sheer, filmy material. The gown reminded her of the one she'd worn that long ago night they'd first made love. Her lips tilted upward in a smile. Garrett had obviously left it for her while she'd showered, and she didn't want to disappoint him. She shed the robe she'd put on after her shower and slipped the gown over her head.

She moved to the mirror on the back of the bathroom door to survey her appearance. Almost immediately, Garrett's reflection appeared in the glass behind her. She spun around, her eyes drinking him in. He wore the navy blue silk robe and matching pajama bottoms she'd given him two Christmases ago. Until now, they had been collecting dust in his bottom drawer. When he relaxed, Garrett was a T-shirt and sweatpants kind of guy, regardless of her efforts to civilize him over the years.

"Where have you been and why do you have that on?"

He stepped into the room, and she noticed he carried a bottle of champagne in one hand and a pair of glasses in the other. "I wanted to impress you with how suave and debonair I can be."

Elise giggled, as he'd pronounced suave *swave* and debonair *deboner*. "Is that why you bought me this gown?"

"No, I happened to be passing by Victoria's Secret and saw it in the window." He set the glasses on the dresser and began to unscrew the cage atop the bottle of champagne. "I bought it for you for Christmas, but forgot to give it to you."

"Thank you. It's lovely."

He kissed the tip of her nose. "I have something else for you." He tilted his hip toward her. "It's in my pocket."

She reached into his pocket and pulled out a small velvet box. "What is this?"

"Open it and find out."

She lifted the lid to reveal a gold heart charm with a tiny red stone in its center. She looked up at Garrett, just as he popped the cork on the champagne. "When did you get this?"

"While you were sleeping this morning. I noticed a woman selling these when we went to the market." He filled one of the champagne flutes and handed it to her. "It's just a little token to remind you that you, Elise Monroe Thorne Taylor, are my heart's desire."

He leaned down to kiss her cheek. When he drew back, she looked at him with a narrow-eyed glare. "Who are you?"

"What do you mean?"

"You look like my husband, but the Garrett Taylor I know does not wax poetic."

"Maybe he should. Maybe he should do a better job of expressing what's in his heart with words instead of actions."

Elise shook her head, watching Garrett as he poured a glass of champagne for himself. Words were nice, but he'd always shown her in his own way how he felt, even if sometimes her own insecurities made her blind to it.

"So that's what this is all about?" She gestured in a way that encompassed their attire and the glasses of champagne.

"No, I thought it would be nice to have our own New Year's celebration since we missed the real thing last night. It's almost midnight."

Garrett lifted his arm to show her his watch. In another thirty seconds the first day of the new year would end. "Shall we have our own countdown?"

A frisson of excitement curled within her as Garrett counted down the seconds until midnight. She glanced up at him as the second hand hit twelve. "Happy New Year, Garrett," she said.

"Happy New Year, baby." He leaned down to touch his lips to hers for a kiss filled with tenderness and anticipation. When he lifted his head, he clinked his glass with hers. "And happy anniversary."

She smiled. "Happy anniversary," she echoed. This really was a new time for them, a new beginning, a new life. She sipped from her glass, her eyes on Garrett as he drank from his.

He set his empty glass on the dresser, took her hand, and led her to the bed. He sat at the head of the bed and she sat facing him. "Isn't there something you want to tell me?"

She gulped down a mouthful of champagne. Warmth rushed through her already heated body. She'd already known she wouldn't get through the night without telling Garrett the secret she'd kept from him. She still hadn't figured out what she wanted to say.

"Before we went on vacation I went to see my doctor.

My period was late, which you know never happens. It didn't occur to me that there could be another reason—I mean, my mother died so young I had no family history to go by."

She stopped, knowing by the blank expression on Garrett's face that nothing she'd said had made any sense. "I'm sorry."

She lifted her champagne glass to take another sip, but he took it from her, placing it and his own on the nightstand.

"Sweetheart, listen to me. We made each other a promise once, that whatever happened, we would always face it together. But in the last few years, we've let the kids and your career and my practice and any number of things come between us. We isolated ourselves from each other. I know I always accused you of doing that, but I've been just as guilty."

He cupped his hand over her shoulder and gave it a squeeze. "Whatever you have to say, we'll face it together, okay?"

His gaze locked with hers. All the love, all the concern, all the passion shone in his eyes for her to see. And she knew he was right: what she'd missed in their marriage had been the security that each of them would always be there for the other. She'd missed knowing that no matter what, she could always turn to him.

She sighed, letting the tension ease from her body. "This is going to sound so anticlimactic, but I have officially started down the slippery slope toward menopause. My period never showed up last month."

He simply stared at her a moment; then he leaned toward her to rest his forehead on her shoulder.

"Thank God. I thought you were going to tell me you were pregnant."

"Would that be such a problem if I were?"

"If you ask me, it would. I know other people do it, people have kids in their forties, but as far as I'm concerned, we're too old for that nonsense."

"Isn't that the operative word, Garrett? Old. Until I sat in my doctor's office and heard her talk about hormone replacement and hot flashes, I'd been feeling in the prime of my life. And I have to admit, some small part of me was happy when I thought I was pregnant, because it meant that I was still young and vital and . . . and . . ." She trailed off, not knowing what word to add.

"Desirable?"

"Yes."

"Baby, you could be ninety, half senile, and unable to get around without a walker, and I would still want you. I'd be the old codger chasing behind you in his wheelchair."

Elise pressed her lips together, picturing that scenario. "Does this mean you're not really planning to trade me in for a couple of nubile young things when I'm a doddering, ancient woman of forty?"

Garrett lay back against their pillows and pulled her down on top of him. "My wife," he said, in a voice reminiscent of an old TV commercial, "I think I'll keep her."

He cupped her face in his palms and brought her laughing mouth down to his, for a kiss full of promises of tomorrow.

Epilogue

At almost the same time, Jasper Thorne stood on the small enclosed terrace that led off his bedroom. The terrace hadn't come with the house, but had been added on years ago at his wife's request. He came here often, as it was the one place in the house where he felt her presence most strongly.

He stared up at the night sky to find the North Star. That's what she had been in his life, his guidepost that had always led him back where he belonged. In many ways, he'd been adrift since the day he lost her.

And now he had another quandary to settle, and, as usual, he looked to her for advice. He'd invited Katherine over to spend the evening with him as each of them had spent New Year's Eve with their families. He'd been giving her a tour of the house, when they'd stopped in his bedroom. Some impetuous demon had seized him and he'd kissed her—not for the first time, but the first time with such intensity. Then Daphne had burst in, and chaos had begun.

Despite both of them being well into their sixties, they had sprung apart like two teenagers caught necking on their parents' couch. Daphne had stammered a few words about having to pick up her sister at the airport and bolted as if the ghost of Jacob Marley were on her tail.

Katherine had made a similar hasty exit a few minutes later. She'd assumed he'd told his children about her, the same way she'd told her children about him. He'd dishonored her and their budding relationship by keeping it a secret, and she'd been rightfully disappointed in him for that.

So now he stood here, alone, as the New Year rang in, knowing that his children's reaction to their relationship hadn't prompted him to remain silent. To speak a thing aloud made it real, made it something to reckon with. He hadn't been willing to admit, not even to himself, that he had been falling in love with another woman. And worse, guilt assailed him, as if to feel anything for someone else meant to betray a woman whom he had adored, but who had been dead for almost twenty years.

A twinge of defiance stirred in him, not directed toward either woman, but at his own need to ask the dead if it was okay to go on living. He knew what Camille would say if she were standing there beside him. She'd tell him to seize his opportunities. If he found a woman actually able to tolerate him, he'd be a fool to let her go.

Still, he sought some sign, some omen, from the one person whose opinion mattered to him. Gazing up at the North Star, he spoke to her.

"Camille, I never thought I'd say this to you, but there is another woman in my life. It isn't the same as it was with us, but it is real. I don't know what's going to happen between us, but I do know I either have to move forward or I have to end things. There's no going back. Tell me what I should do."

Suddenly, the air filled with the scent of camellias,

her namesake flower, and an unexplained warmth enveloped him. He might have been losing his mind, but in the stillness of the dark night, he could have sworn he heard her whisper three words to him.

"Go for it."

Dear Readers;

What happens to your average romance novel couple a year after they say "I do"? How about five years? Or ten? That's the question I wanted to answer when I started writing MIDNIGHT MAGIC. We assume that romance endings are happily ever after, but what if they aren't? What if a romance couple hits the same snags and bumps that we regular mortals face every day?

Every relationship requires that both participants work at keeping it fresh and alive. Elise and Garrett made the common mistake of letting career and family obligations overshadow their marriage and weaken the bond between them.

In another kind of story, this might have been the first step on the slippery slide toward divorce. But my goal was to show that even when love is on the wane, it can be revived if the couple involved does whatever it takes to turn their situation around. I hope I have presented a realistic portrayal of a marriage at the cross-roads that is rejuvenated by mutual respect and caring.

I would love to hear from you. You can contact me at: DeeSavoy@aol.com or at P.O. Box 233, Bronx, NY 10469. I have a new Web site at www.deirdresavoy.com; I hope you'll stop by.

All the best,
Dee Savoy

ABOUT THE AUTHOR

Native New Yorker Deirdre Savoy spent her summers on the shores of Martha's Vineyard, soaking up the sun and scribbling in one of her many notebooks. It was there that she first started writing romances as a teenager. The island proved to be the perfect setting for her first novel, SPELLBOUND, published by BET/Arabesque Books in 1999, which received rave reviews and earned her the distinction of the first Rising Star author of Romance in Color and Best New Author of 1999. Deirdre's second book, ALWAYS, published by BET/Arabesque in October 2000, was a February 2001 Selection for the Black Expressions Book Club. ONCE AND AGAIN, the sequel to ALWAYS, was published in May 2001. MIDNIGHT MAGIC is the third book in the series. Deirdre also won the first annual Emma award for Favorite New Author, presented at the 2001 Romance Slam Jam in Orlando, Florida.

A graduate of Bernard M. Baruch College of the City University of New York, with a Bachelor's of Business Administration in Marketing/Advertising, Deirdre teaches elementary science/literacy. She also facilitates the Writer's Co-op, a writers group that meets at the Barnes and Noble near her home.

Deirdre is a member of The Black Writer's Alliance and African-American Authors Helping Authors (AA-AHA). She lectures on such topics as Marketing Your Masterpiece, Getting Your Writing Career Started, and other topics related to the craft of writing.

Deirdre lives in Bronx, New York, with her husband of ten-plus years and their two children. In her spare time she enjoys reading, dancing, calligraphy, and "wicked" crossword puzzles.

COMING IN NOVEMBER 2001 FROM
ARABESQUE ROMANCES

__MIDSUMMER MOON
by Doris Johnson   1-58314-213-4 $5.99US/$7.99CAN

June Saxon is determined to rebuild her life after a business partner cheated her out of her inheritance. She certainly doesn't need Matt Gardiner offering help to make up for his ex-wife's deceit. And June surely doesn't want the unexpected attraction between them to endanger her future—even as it fires her deepest passions.

__THE LAST DANCE
by Candice Poarch   1-58314-221-5 $5.99US/$7.99CAN

Shari Jarrod is accustomed to challenging projects, but winning over Emmanuel Jones's heart may be the toughest one yet. The perpetual playboy is used to dating the hottest women, not some shy "computer geek" like her. But Shari plans to give Emmanuel the surprise of his life—by transforming herself into a beautiful, sexy woman!

__SWEET TEMPTATION
by Niqui Stanhope   1-58314-240-1 $5.99US/$7.99CAN

Nicholas Champagne believes the bachelor's life is the only life for him—until he meets artist Amanda Drake. Gorgeous and talented, Amanda's the first woman who isn't impressed by his charms . . . and the one woman he can't stop thinking about.

__FIRE BENEATH THE ICE
by Linda Hudson-Smith   1-58314-246-0 $5.99US/$7.99CAN

Champion figure skater Omunique Philyaw has finally won the most precious gold of all: a wedding band. But when an unexpected tragedy hits close to home, Omunique's fairytale future is suddenly on dangerously thin ice.

Call toll free **1-888-345-BOOK** to order by phone or use this coupon to order by mail. ALL BOOKS AVAILABLE NOVEMBER 1, 2001.

Name_____

Address_____

City_____ State_____ Zip_____

Please send me the books that I have checked above.

I am enclosing	$_____
Plus postage and handling*	$_____
Sales tax (in NY, TN, and DC)	$_____
Total amount enclosed	$_____

*Add $2.50 for the first book and $.50 for each additional book.

Send check or money order (no cash or CODs) to: **Arabesque Romances, Dept. C.O., 850 Third Avenue 16th Floor, New York, NY 10022**

Prices and numbers subject to change without notice. Valid only in the U.S. All orders subject to availability. **NO ADVANCE ORDERS.**

Visit our website at **www.arabesquebooks.com.**

More Sizzling Romance From

Marcia King-Gamble

__Reason to Love   1-58314-133-2   **$5.99**US/**$7.99**CAN

__Illusions of Love   1-58314-104-9   **$5.99**US/**$7.99**CAN

__Under Your Spell   1-58314-027-1   **$4.99**US/**$6.50**CAN

__Eden's Dream   0-7860-0572-6   **$5.99**US/**$7.99**CAN

__Remembrance   0-7860-0504-1   **$4.99**US/**$6.50**CAN

Do You Have the Entire
SHIRLEY HAILSTOCK
Collection?

__Legacy

                    0-7860-0415-0 $4.99US/$6.50CAN

__Mirror Image

                    1-58314-178-2 $5.99US/$7.50CAN

__More Than Gold

                    1-58314-120-0 $5.99US/$7.50CAN

__Whispers of Love

                    0-7860-0055-4 $4.99US/$6.50CAN

Call toll free **1-888-345-BOOK** to order by phone or use this coupon to order by mail.
Name_____
Address_____
City_____ State _____ Zip _____
Please send me the books I have checked above.
I am enclosing $_____
Plus postage and handling* $_____
Sales tax (in NY, TN, and DC) $_____
Total amount enclosed $_____
*Add $2.50 for the first book and $.50 for each additional book.
Send check or money order (no cash or CODs) to: **Arabesque Romances, Dept. C.O., 850 Third Avenue, 16th Floor, New York, NY 10022**
Prices and numbers subject to change without notice. Valid only in the U.S.
All orders subject to availability. **NO ADVANCE ORDERS.**
Visit our website at **www.arabesquebooks.com.**